the
wedding
date
disaster

the
wedding
date
disaster

AVERY FLYNN

USA TODAY **BESTSELLING AUTHOR**

Preview of *Her Aussie Holiday* Copyright © 2020 by Stefanie London

Entangled Publishing, LLC
10940 S Parker Road
Suite 327
Parker, CO 80134
Visit our website at www.entangledpublishing.com.

Amara is an imprint of Entangled Publishing, LLC.

Edited by Liz Pelletier
Cover design by Elizabeth Turner Stokes
Cover art by
Elvira Gilyazova/Shutterstock
Mike Flippo/Shutterstock
Zhur_Sa/Shutterstock
Interior design by Toni Kerr

Print ISBN 978-1-64063-912-6
ebook ISBN 978-1-64063-913-3

Manufactured in the United States of America
First Edition September 2020

ALSO BY AVERY FLYNN

THE HARBOR CITY SERIES

The Negotiator
The Charmer
The Schemer

THE HARTIGANS SERIES

Butterface
Muffin Top
Tomboy

THE ICE KNIGHTS SERIES

Parental Guidance
Awk-weird
Loud Mouth

To all the oldest siblings out there. Thank you for always watching out for us younger ones.

CHAPTER ONE

Hadley Donavan was going to murder her best friend's evil twin brother.

Okay, not *really* murder, but there wasn't a jury who would convict her if she did. The man was just that awful. Too full of himself. Too obviously hot. Too rich. Too everything that gave the city's most eligible billionaire bachelor Will Holt an ego the size of Toledo and a hard-on for purposefully ruining Hadley's day every time he spotted her.

Well, not today, Satan.

Tonight was too important for his stupid games. For the past two years, she'd worked her tail off at Kittsen & Sons Charitable Advisors just to get a chance to guide a minor client as they positioned their charitable foundation for the next level. Now, all of that overtime at the office, missed brunches with friends, and sleepless nights staring at the ceiling and wondering what she'd missed had come to fruition with tonight's event. There was no way she was going to let Will mess it up.

Her gaze narrowed on his too-wide shoulders as he walked into the Harbor City Grand Hotel ballroom like he owned the place. Well, he did, but that was completely beside the point. He may have snuck past security—or more likely gotten in with a quick hey-do-you-know-who-I-am—but he was not on the guest list and he was not staying. Period.

The half-a-size-too-small shoes she'd borrowed from her roommate pinched her toes as she hustled around the people on the crowded dance floor, but by the time she made it across, her prey had disappeared.

Standing off to the side of the stage, she ground her teeth as she scanned the crowd for Mr. Obnoxious.

Seriously, how hard could it be to spot the one man at a black-tie fundraiser in jeans and a hoodie like a Silicon billionaire instead of the Harbor City trust-fund baby he was? Pretty damn hard, considering everywhere she looked, it was tuxes and ball gowns. She sighed. He was here somewhere, and she would find him and kick him out on his billionaire ass, mark her words.

Keeping her eyes peeled for the evil twin, E.T. for short, Hadley checked in on the support staff who really made tonight work. The waiters, bartenders, cooks, security, registration attendants, and more were the engine that made any fundraiser go. As a charitable-giving consultant, she pulled all the pieces together for a fundraising event, but at the actual event it was a great support staff who made it all come together. Sadly, it wasn't until she'd finished her rounds before she spotted him again, by the coat check this time and looking over the crowd as if he were searching for a gazelle to separate from the pack.

Gotcha.

The safety pins on her size-too-big-but-it-was-on-sale-seventy-five-percent-off-so-she'd-make-it-work dress from ten seasons ago poked her in the ribs (because if it was too big everywhere else, it was definitely ginormous around her basically nonexistent boobs), but she ignored the pain as she fast-walked-without-looking-it across the ballroom because she had a bigger prick to deal with.

Will Holt.

Her bestie—and in a twist of fate that showed just how much of a sense of humor God had, Will's identical twin brother, Web—was not here.

That meant Will was here for her. Well, not *for* her, more like to torment her on the biggest night of her career, the one that would make or break her chances of promotion to bigger accounts, and thus really making a difference in the world.

Advancing on him like a guided missile, Hadley glued an almost-friendly smile on her face and girded herself for battle.

"What are you doing here?" she hiss-whispered as soon as they were shoulder to shoulder on the edge of the dance floor.

He snagged a mini bruschetta from a passing waiter. "Enjoying the hors d'oeuvres and charming company, obviously."

Oh yeah, she believed that about as much as she believed her outrageous Harbor City rent was going to pay for itself. "You weren't invited."

"Yet here I am." He popped the bruschetta

into his mouth and picked up two champagne flutes from the tray of another passing waiter, keeping one for himself and handing her the other. "Just like you and last week's rugby game."

She accepted the glass, suppressing the shiver of distaste when their fingers brushed—that was the only explanation for the way her heartbeat kicked up at the slight touch—and took a calm and dignified sip of the high-priced bubbly. It wasn't like she could throw the drink in his face, considering they were both faking being nice in a room full of some of the biggest philanthropists and gossips in Harbor City. A word here or there from any of them could devastate her reputation and ability to—eventually—start her own charitable-giving consulting firm. He knew it. She knew it. They were both playing their parts while seething on the inside.

"I went to the rugby game so I could cheer on Web." It was the same answer she'd given him a million times already. What was it with this guy that he couldn't accept that she and his brother were besties?

"When he hasn't even played for the last few games because his ankle was acting up? How very"—he paused, clinking his glass against hers—"friendly of you."

She sputtered something that barely even qualified as syllables, heat smacking against her cheeks. It was their standing weekly friend date. She and Web always had brunch after. She liked watching rugby. It was *interesting*. That's it. There was no other reason for her to go watch the games, definitely not the fact that Will played on the team, too.

Why does he always make me feel like I'm doing something wrong?

"You," she said, about a million epithets for "him" running through her head, "are the worst."

He shrugged his broad shoulders and looked totally unconcerned. "Just because I don't fall for your country-bumpkin, sweet-as-pie con job like everyone else?" He set his untouched glass of champagne down on the nearest flat surface. "I know exactly what you're doing with Web, and you won't get away with it."

Then, without even bothering to wait for her response—because why would the big jerk?—he strode off, disappearing into the coat closet that was packed full because of an unexpected summer downpour. No one wanted their black-tie finery to get drizzled on, so it was wall-to-wall raincoats and dripping umbrellas.

If he thought disappearing into there was going to stop her, he had another think coming.

Pinched toes protesting, pulse rocketing, and ire stoked to Mt. Vesuvius levels, Hadley marched in there and flung the door shut behind her. He stopped and did a slow-motion turn that wouldn't have looked out of place in the movies—except Will was anything but hero material. He crossed his arms over his chest, the move only emphasizing his thick biceps even in a hoodie— and raised an eyebrow in question.

The unmitigated cocky gall of this guy. *Ugh.*

It was beyond past time for this confrontation.

After nearly a year of having to deal with his bad attitude, she was more than ready to have it out.

"What. Is. Your. Problem?" She bit each word out as her stride ate up the space between them, until she was mere inches from him, finger jabbing him in his obnoxiously hard chest. She ignored the heat coming off him in waves and jabbed him in the chest again for good measure. "You have got to—"

The rest of that sentence was supposed to be "stop showing up unannounced" but he'd reached down and wrapped his warm, strong hand around hers, presumably to make her stop poking him, and the words froze in her throat as electricity zinged along her skin at the contact.

She tilted her chin upward, her lips parted in shock, and her breath caught—because Will fucking Holt suddenly looked like he wanted to kiss her until they both self-combusted.

And damn her mutinous body, at that moment she knew exactly how he felt.

• • •

The world froze for Will, shrinking down to the four walls of the tiny coat closet lit only by the dim light of a single wall sconce and Hadley Donavan. He'd meant to stop her from jabbing him again with her finger, but the second their skin connected, his entire brain short-circuited.

He didn't like her.

Hell, he couldn't stand her.

And yet…here he was, holding on by a

thread—a worn, raggedy, barely-keeping-it-together thread that was milliseconds from snapping. The last thing in the world he should do is kiss the woman angling to take his brother for every million she could.

His muscles tense, his lungs burning from holding his breath, he stayed immobile. One breath, one blink, one brush of her body against his, and he'd give up his half of the several-billion-dollar Holt family fortune to finish what they'd start with a kiss. Then she let out a shaky sigh and used the tip of her tongue to wet her lips before looking up at him with a lust-hazy gaze as she lifted herself up on her toes, and he was a fucking goner.

In a heartbeat, he went from fighting her every step of the way to meeting her in the middle. His lips crashed down on hers as if he'd been waiting years to kiss her. He hadn't. This was just a fluke of the moment, a crazy combination of timing and lust and frustration and all the other things building up since they'd met. It meant nothing. And he couldn't stop.

Her hands were in his hair, cupping the back of his head and pulling him down even as she strained upward, and he deepened the kiss. Sweeping his tongue inside her mouth, tasting her, teasing a little moan from her, and she eliminated any remaining space between them. She let go of his hair and he went to take a step back, but instead of taking the space he offered, she went with him until he was standing with his back against the wall. The damp raincoats surrounded them as they kissed. Was that even the word for what this was? It was more of a breaking of the dam as they gave in to what had always been buzzing under the surface of their bickering and teasing.

She slid her hands underneath his hoodie, her fingertips cool against his abs. How was it possible to not believe something was happening and want more all at the same time? He had no fucking clue, but he was right there. He wanted—needed—all of her even though he shouldn't. Words like "gold digger," "brother's so-called friend," and "enemy" zipped around in his head, but they had all the impact of a buzzing gnat, easily waved aside for the pleasure that was kissing Hadley.

He didn't mean to reach for her skirt, to pull it upward so he could slip his hand underneath, but there he was with his palm gliding up the outside of her smooth thigh and the round curve of her hip. Fuck, she felt good, better than he'd imagined too many times to count. He cupped her glorious ass, too much awesome to fit in his hands, and pulled her close so he could feel her heat against his hard cock straining against his jeans. Hadley let out a soft moan of encouragement, rubbing against him as she forced her hands between them and reached for the top button of his jeans.

A better man would remember why she was awful. Why she couldn't be trusted. Why this was wrong. But he wasn't a better man. Will was drowning in Hadley and he couldn't think of a better way to go.

Then a bright light cut through the semidarkness of the coat closet—a reality spotlight landing right on them—followed by a knowing, cruel chuckle that he was all too familiar with. Obviously startled, Hadley jolted away from him, but it was too late.

"Having some fun with the help, Will?" said Mia, his ex, a cold, close approximation to a smile curling her lips. "You know that's something I would have overlooked." She paused for dramatic effect, looking them both over with clinical detachment. "I'll leave you to get straightened up."

The door swung shut behind her.

He shoved his hands through his hair. Fuck. What had just happened? What had he done? Mia wouldn't keep her mouth shut. This would be the amusing anecdote of the fundraiser told and retold over cocktails and coffee. He had to protect Hadley somehow.

"Hadley," he said.

It took a second, but she turned toward him— her eyes wide with a what-the-fuck surprise and her fingers pressed to her kiss-swollen lips—and said, "Web."

A slap to the face would have been less of a blow than hearing her say his identical twin brother's name at that moment. The worst part being that it was a self-inflicted wound. He *knew* better. Of course Web would be her first thought. After all, it would be damn hard to scam a guy into falling in love so she could walk away with half his billions if she banged his brother.

You're an idiot, Holt.

"Yeah," he said, his voice deadly flat even to his own ears. "Exactly."

He swiped his raincoat off a hook and made it to the door in two strides, yanking it open and walking out, his steps measured, his breathing even, his heart going a million miles per hour. He never looked back.

Mia was already halfway to the bar when he spotted her, earning her keep as an impoverished (by Harbor City's high-society standards anyway) woman from a storied family who kept things entertaining with the latest gossip. There was no point in pursuing her, though; it would only add legitimacy to her story. The air moved behind him and the extrasensory alert that always went off when Hadley was near blared out a warning.

A little too late, don't ya think?

There was no point in talking to her—it wouldn't change anything. What could make a difference would be talking to her boss. No doubt Mia was angling to get Hadley fired. He wasn't going to let that happen, because it would make Hadley more sympathetic to Web and, therefore, make it easier for her to become a gold-digging success story.

And that's the only reason?

It was. It had to be.

And after that, he'd do whatever it took to stay the hell away from her from now on.

CHAPTER TWO

"You! Are! Shitting! Me!"

Hadley's roommate, Fiona Hartigan, stood in the middle of their galley kitchen, her mouth agog and her organic fruit smoothie stopped halfway to her mouth. Sure, it was a little overdramatic, but then again, so was Fiona in the absolute best way possible.

"I wish." Hadley filled up the Money Honey travel mug she'd gotten in a goodie bag at a philanthropy management conference a few months ago and added an extra shot of store-brand hazelnut creamer. "The Evil Twin stood there in the middle of the event that should have made my career and told my boss that Mia was slinging crap because he would never in a million years kiss someone as lowly as me."

Fiona's green eyes rounded to practically manga-character levels, and she took a long, loud slurp on her straw as she shot Hadley a considering look and then asked, "He used those words?"

Ugh. Okay, maybe she was being a wee bit over-the-top, too. "Okay, he didn't use *exactly* those words, but that was the gist of it. And you know everyone in my office just happened to be circling around the boss like a bunch of gossip sharks that smelled blood in the water. Everything about fundraising in this cliquey environment is about your reputation and who is in your corner."

"What did you say?" Fiona asked, leaning one hip against the smidgen of counter space in their teeny, tiny, way-too-expensive-to-be-this-cramped Harbor City apartment.

"What could I say?" She set her travel mug down and marched three paces to the end of the kitchen and three paces back, her cheeks burning at the memory of the look her boss had given her over Will's shoulder. It was the same look her mom had sent her way whenever she'd taken a practical joke too far and was in for it. "I got the hell out of the you're-going-to-get-fired-this-very-moment zone and did my job like the professional I am."

"So you hustled triple-time in order to be too busy to have an uncomfortable discussion with your boss?"

"Pretty much." Haley slumped against the fridge, the magnet clip holding up the invitation to her sister's wedding stabbing her in the back, and let out a miserable groan. "Oh God. I'm going to lose my job for being unprofessional. Whoever the hell I pissed off in a former life, I offer up all my apologies."

Fine. She was the overdramatic one. Right now, she was totally all right with that, because if kissing her nemesis and then having her entire professional world think she'd probably done a helluva lot more than that with him in the coat closet and was therefore banging her way into getting donations wasn't the situation in which one should be overdramatic, then she had no clue when it was.

Fiona tapped her straw against her chin. "Maybe this is fate working for you."

"By making me lose my mind and do something as ridiculous as kissing Will Holt?" Oh God. It sounded worse when she said it out loud.

"Well, that was probably just for giggles, but—" Fiona held up her hand as if to stop Hadley from protesting, which she totally was about to do. "Hear me out. What if this is a nudge from the universe to finally start your own consulting firm? You've been talking about it forever—maybe this is the time to make it happen."

Oh yes, The Donavan Agency. Somewhere in a box stuffed under her bed, she had business cards and everything. There was a fully formed business plan in her Dropbox. She'd even worked out a potential client list, determined a charitable-giving area of specialization, and had a finished website just waiting to be launched. What didn't she have? Money—for an office, for employees, for health insurance, for client acquisitions, pretty much for anything beyond the basics of food, shelter, and Netflix. Well, mostly.

"Yeah right." Hadley sighed and pushed off the fridge, going straight for her travel mug waiting for her on the counter because like it or lump it, she had to go into the office today if she wanted to get paid. "You need money to make money and in case you forgot, you're still waiting for my half of the utility bill."

Which was why she was depending on twice-run-through K-cups for her caffeine intake.

"Today's your payday," Fiona said. "I know it's coming."

Travel mug in one hand and phone in the other, Hadley gave her roomie and friend a quick hug, careful not to spill any weak coffee on her. And to think when she'd answered that ad for a roommate three years ago, her only hope was that she wouldn't be rooming with a serial killer. For once, the reality of her life in Harbor City had far exceeded her hopes. If only the rest of her big city existence had lived up to her dreams when she'd left her small-town Nebraska home…not that she'd be admitting that to her family back on the ranch anytime soon. They already thought she was a few hay bales short for leaving in the first place.

"What did I do to deserve such a sweetheart of a roommate?"

Fiona squeezed her back. "Obviously something spectacular."

It was true, and it had to have been in a past life because this one was kind of a mess—and definitely not the shiny, happy, perfectly Insta-gramable version she shared with her family. When failing wasn't an option, a person faked it until they made it. That had been her game plan since she'd arrived in Harbor City, and she had no plans to change it. As long as she could keep up that perfect-life pretense, it would happen.

"I'm putting that out there in the universe," she mumbled later as she rode the train to her office. "Again."

However, when she walked over to her cubicle—ignoring the curious looks and barely whispered comments from her coworkers—and found an empty cardboard box on her desk, she knew the universe was team Evil Twin. It had to be.

The light on her phone blinked on a second before her boss's voice came through on the intercom. "Hadley, can you please come see me?"

She didn't have to ask what about. The box kinda made that pretty apparent.

"I'll be there in just a minute," she responded, calling up the reserves of her fake-it-until-you-make-it pride that she wasn't sure she had enough of for this moment.

Then she packed up the personal items on her desk into her now-full box and carried it to her boss's corner office, head held high and sniffles on lockdown because if faking it had ever meant something, it was right now.

The only thing that kept her from losing her shit right then was the memory of Will's shocked expression when he'd realized what they'd done. If she could survive Will thinking for even a moment she was into him, she could survive getting fired.

She hoped.

• • •

The Holt family country home was two and a half hours north of Harbor City. It was also a million miles from the responsibilities of being one of the two most eligible bachelors and sole heirs to the fortune Jeremiah Holt had begun amassing during a crooked poker game in a half-burned-out speakeasy in the very woods Will was staring at while trying to figure out how to get his brother to ghost that woman.

She has a name.

No. He was not going there. Not again. He'd done that too many times since that kiss at the fundraiser and it had—without a single exception—ended up with him rubbing one out like he'd never made out with someone in a coatroom before. He had. Many times. Okay, that might be an exaggeration, but it wasn't like Hadley was special.

Shit.

Her name. He ground his teeth, the ache in his jaw attesting to how much he'd been doing that lately. This time he would not give in. He would not remember. He would not think about her soft lips, her needy little moan, her silky-smooth thighs, her— *Dammit, Holt. Get your shit together.*

His brother, Web, cleared his throat as he glanced down at the cutting board in front of Will as they both stood in the kitchen. "Now, I'm not much of a cook, either, but I think that onion is chopped."

Will looked at the minced-within-a-millimeter-of-its-existence onion for the chicken cacciatore. "Just making sure."

"And the grumbling to yourself?" Web took two beers out of the fridge, popped the tops, set one down next to the cutting board, and took a drink from the other. "I mean, if this is stressing you out, we can just order Thai."

"I was not grumbling to myself, and I'm not stressed," he grumbled.

Web just raised one eyebrow and pointedly nodded toward the onion Will was apparently chopping—again.

Will set down the knife. "The recipe says 'finely diced.'"

"Do you just want to talk about it?" Web asked, needling him the way only a brother could. "You know, unpack your feelings and admit you feel guilty that Hadley lost her job because of you and that I'm going out to Nebraska to be her plus-one for her sister's wedding."

There was nothing—*nothing*—about that sentence that didn't make Will's gut churn. Unpack his feelings? Admit guilt? Hadley? Nebraska? He grabbed the beer and downed half of it.

"It wasn't my fault. I talked to her boss." It hadn't gone well, but he'd done what he could to isolate Hadley from the fallout of a pissed-off ex-fiancée with an eternal grudge. "I can't help it if Mia, who is on the company's board of directors, made all sorts of assumptions." And, if the doorman-to-doorman gossip was to be believed, all but demanded that Hadley be fired. Thank God Web hadn't outright asked him if the gossip was true. Surprisingly, he seemed to think Hadley would never even consider making out with Will.

He was tempted to tell Web the truth about why Hadley was so determined to spend time with him, why she always brought up how she could really help steer the Holt Foundation in a better direction. How she was so focused on the money that she brought a full-on spiral-bound prospective report. Then, whenever she and Web went anywhere besides that hole-in-the-wall place after rugby games, Web always picked up the tab. That she was always short for the cab ride home when Web insisted on covering the full fare. Plus, there was all the dream apartment shopping she did online, down to posting pictures on Insta of how she'd furnish her fantasy place. And the way she always seemed to be mentioning that she was between paychecks? Yeah, it sounded a little too much like the way Mia had set Will up to play the sucker with the sole purpose of marrying him for his money. That's why he couldn't stop thinking of Hadley. He had to protect his brother.

He needed to come up with a better way to break up Hadley's gold-digging plans for Web.

Like admit to your brother that you kissed her?

Damn, he wished he knew why he couldn't, but no matter how many times he'd tried today, he couldn't get the words out, and that's how he'd ended up with micro-diced onions. "Why do you care so much about her anyway? I'm your brother. You should feel bad that I got dragged into it."

"You'll be just fine," his brother said. "And she's my best friend who lost her job."

The snort of uh-huh-sure came out before Will could stop it.

"Why is that so hard for you to believe?" Web asked. "What are you, some kind of asshole who doesn't think men and women can be friends?"

No, but had his brother somehow miraculously never set eyes on Hadley's ass? "Are you trying to say you aren't attracted to her?"

Web shrugged. "She's not my type."

Considering the fact that Web's type encompassed just about every woman, Will had a real fucking hard time believing that his twin wasn't into Hadley. The woman obviously had to have her claws firmly planted in his brother's balls if Web was willing to go to Nebraska, of all the godforsaken places, for Hadley's sister's wedding. And *that* was why he was dicing the shit out of onions to make Web's favorite dinner as a way of softening him up and getting him to see the light. If a good meal couldn't get Web to refocus his mind, then Will was going to have to do something drastic. He was the oldest, if only by five minutes, and the last living member of the Holt family besides his brother. Therefore, it was his responsibility to protect Web from what no one had been around to protect Will from: Hadley the gold digger.

Later that night, though, it was more than apparent that the most important thing to protect Web from at the moment was him dying of food poisoning. Will knocked on the bathroom door after the sounds of the latest round of gut hurling stopped.

"I swear to God, I didn't give you food poisoning on purpose." Sure, he was an asshole, but he wasn't a murdering asshole. "I feel fine."

Not even a twinge in his stomach, apart from

the sympathy gagging whenever Web made puking noises.

"Great," his brother said through the door. "So because you have the ability to ingest under-cooked chicken, then I'm at fault here?"

Fuck. That was not what Will meant. "I followed the recipe and used the meat thermometer. My chicken was cooked all the way through."

Web let out a long moan that would have sounded made up if he hadn't spent the past ten minutes puking his guts up behind closed doors. "I'll be sure to let my lawyers know."

"Nut up, Web. You're not going to die." People didn't die from slightly undercooked chicken, did they?

"I have a plane to catch tomorrow morning," Web said, sounding pathetic and weak.

It was like the clouds parted and the sun appeared after a month of rainy days. In a heartbeat, he was smiling big enough to make his cheeks hurt.

"So don't go." There, problem solved. He should have poisoned his brother sooner.

"Fuck you, Will. There is a thing called loyalty." There was more rustling behind the door, like his brother was shifting on the bathroom floor, and then a loud groan. "I promised Hadley I'd be her fake boyfriend at her sister's wedding so she wouldn't be so overwhelmed by her relatives. I can't leave her to face her family alone."

"What are they, cowboy zombies?"

How in the hell could they be worse than the woman herself? Short answer? They couldn't be.

"They're just a lot to take all at once." The sound of more groans came through the door. "I guess I'll just suffer through. If this lingers, I'm sure she'll take care of me. It'll give her an excuse to hang out alone with me so she can avoid her family. Really, you did her a favor."

Oh hell no. Abso-fucking-lutely not. Hadley wasn't going to tighten her hold on Web even more by being the one to nurse him back to health.

"I'll take your place." The words were out of Will's mouth before his brain caught up.

"No way," Web said, not sounding half as horrified as his words promised—no doubt he was trying not to throw up again. "You cannot be serious. And it's not like you can stay away from being the always-in-control CEO for a whole week."

"Why not? We used to switch spots all the time. And believe it or not, I can loosen my grip on Holt Enterprises for five days. The company won't fall apart in a week, and it'll give you a chance to recover from the food poisoning." And it'd give him a chance to break whatever spell Hadley had over his brother. He was a fucking genius.

"It's a crazy idea."

That's where his baby brother was wrong. So very wrong.

CHAPTER THREE

For Hadley, the temptation to hide out right here in the Denver airport rather than go home to the family ranch was pretty overwhelming.

It wasn't that she didn't love her family—she did—but being around all of them at the same time under the not-stressful-at-all (sarcasm alert) conditions of her little sister's wedding could shake the strongest of women. They'd want to do *everything* together, from making breakfast in the morning to brushing teeth at night—okay, maybe not the last part, but family togetherness and the ranching way was pretty much her family's motto. Simply put, Hadley's family was exhausting, and they would *all* be there for the festivities leading up to her sister's big day.

All.

Of.

Them.

Every single person, from all of twenty billion branches sprouting from the Donavan-Martinez family tree, would be at the wedding. More than that, most of them would be staying at the ranch. It would be wall-to-wall Donavans, Martinezes, and Donavan-Martinezes until the cows came home.

All of that meant that the family-mandatory-fun-time-togetherness was going to be at epic levels, leading up to Adalyn's wedding in a week. If it wasn't for how much she loved her baby sister and wanted to see her say "I do," Hadley would definitely be saying "I don't" to a full week wrapped in her family's well-meaning but claustrophobic embrace.

Her phone vibrated in her cross-body purse as she pulled up short to avoid getting run over by a group of people rushing toward the TSA line. She pulled it out and hit Talk, keeping her eyes on the constant flow of human foot traffic, hoping to spot Web walking out of the arrivals area.

"Oh good," her sister, Adalyn, said with a relieved sigh. "You haven't lost cell signal yet."

That would happen about four hours into the five-hour drive from the airport when she turned off the main highway and onto the long, gravel-covered county road leading to Hidden Creek Ranch. Service would get spotty and texting would become an imaginary dream of the future until she got about five miles out from the ranch and the signal from the towers improved.

"I'm still at the airport," Hadley said, dodging a seven-year-old pulling his own miniature wheely suitcase before it went right over her toes.

Adalyn—always the dramatic one—let out a groan. "You have to save me from Mom. She's lost it."

That was no surprise. No one wanted things to be perfect more than Stephanie Donavan-Martinez. There was no way her daughter's wedding would be any different. If the woman was sleeping at all between rounds of stress cleaning and prepping food for a small army of people, Hadley would go into shock.

"Is she recleaning the bathroom after Dad already did it again?"

"Worse." Adalyn took a dramatic pause. "She's stopped all cleaning and is locked in her crafting room."

Hadley jolted to a dead stop in the middle of the airport, her jaw slack. Their mom had gone into hibernation with the entire family about to converge on the ranch? This was very not good. "Oh God, what did you guys do?"

With the exception of herself, the suspects to get on Mom's last nerve were all there: her sister, her brothers Weston and Knox, and her dad in all but actual DNA, Gabe. Mom loved them all, but there was no denying they each had a special gift for making their mom a little batty.

"Me?" Adalyn asked, her pitch going higher. "Why would I have done anything?"

"Because that's what little sisters do. They cause trouble." She almost got that out without a giggle. Adalyn was forever the people-pleasing—if a little over-the-top—one. It was Hadley who was forever the child most likely to cause trouble.

"Nice try." Her sister laughed. "I am the good daughter while you are the one whose name is followed by a soft sigh and gaze turned heavenward."

"Just because I'm the only one to move out of the state." And didn't go into ranching or marry a rancher or listen to country music or…the list went on and on.

"Plus, you're single at thirty," her sister teased. Adalyn altered the cadence and tone of her voice to mimic their mom with damn near perfection. "Not that a woman needs a man, but…"

Hadley chuckled. "Don't do that again; you sound just like her."

"We all turn into our mother in the end."

"So we'll be badasses but the interfering, loving, drive-you-nuts kind?" Raising four kids as a single mom was no joke. Sure, she'd found Gabe and they'd had a whole Hallmark movie romance, but Hadley had been fourteen by then, her brothers twelve and ten, and Adalyn eight.

"Exactly."

"Don't worry—I'll be there soon." Hadley glanced over at the gate where all the arriving passengers would flow out, but only a few people trickled in, none of whom was Web. "Backup is on the way."

"Thank God. You have no idea how grateful I am that you came in early. I know getting off work for a week was tough."

Probably not as tough as it would have been had she not been fired after *the incident*. But no way was she sharing that news with her family. They still shook their heads whenever they mentioned her living in the "city."

"You're my sister." Hadley resumed her impatient pacing in front of the arrivals area. "Of course I was going to be here for the whole wedding-week shindig."

"Even if you had to bring your best friend to pose as your boyfriend because you want to ditch as much of the mandatory family fun time as possible?" Adalyn asked.

Hadley grimaced, guilt tickling the pit of her stomach. *Busted*. She opened her mouth to deny it, but who was she kidding? Everyone knew how weird all the family togetherness was to her. She couldn't help it. There was obviously some emotional piece she was missing.

"I promise, I'm shut away behind a locked door in the bathroom," her sister said with a sympathetic chuckle. "Your secret about why Web is really here is safe with me. Just don't even think about chickening out between the airport and home."

"I'm not scared." *Much*.

"Just get here, Trigger. Derek is getting all weirded out."

Something in Adalyn's tone when she said her fiancé's name set off Hadley's worry alert, and her shoulders tensed.

"Pre-wedding nerves?" she asked, trying to keep her tone neutral even as she was already plotting her sister's fiancé's death if he even thought about doing something that would hurt Adalyn.

"Maybe. I just…" Her sister's voice cracked. "Something seems off with him. I don't know. It's probably nothing. I'm sure I'm just worrying for no reason."

That wasn't what the tremble in her voice said, though. All of Hadley's big-sister protectiveness whooshed up like a brushfire in the wind, and she started pacing to get some of the raw energy out. Glancing over at the flight notification board, she noted for the billionth time that his plane had gotten in fifteen minutes ago. Where was Web? She needed to get to the ranch. Now.

"It's only jitters," Hadley said, hoping like hell it was true, since she hadn't met Derek yet. "Anyway, I pity anyone getting thrown into the Donavan-Martinez tornado for the first time, especially when you're about to marry into the family. We're a lot."

Her sister giggled, but it didn't have the same oomph it usually did. "That's true."

"It is," she said, using her all-knowing big-sister tone, hoping it would work. "So relax and don't hide in the bathroom for much longer or Aunt Louise will tell everyone that you've been pooping for too long and start sending the cousins to come check on you to make sure you don't need help."

That was the Aunt Louise Special. Yet one more bit of extra overwhelming family together-ness. Really. Let a person poop in peace.

"I will literally die of embarrassment if that happens," Adalyn said. "You're horrible for even putting the possibility into my head."

"Love you, Buttermilk," she said, using her sister's nickname.

"Love you right back, Trigger."

Hadley hung up and strolled by the bronze Elroy Jeppesen statue outside of passenger arrivals at the Denver International Airport for the fifty-second time. She sent up a big old fuzzy thank-you to the friendship gods for giving her a super-rich best friend who could come to Nebraska for a week.

That Webster "Web" Holt was willing to leave his cushy life in Harbor City to come to the Middle of Nowhere, Nebraska, for a week was amazing. Add in the fact that he'd agreed to help her keep her sanity with all the family together-ness, and it was easy to see why Web was pretty much her favorite person in the entire world. It didn't matter that they'd had to take different flights, since he had spent the past few days at his family compound hours outside of Harbor City and that his plane had been delayed for three hours. She was so grateful to have him here that she wouldn't even fight him for the last piece of Aunt Louise's Frito pie, which just happened to be the most magical comfort food in the history of forever.

Just when she was about to check the arrivals board for the zillionth time, passengers started flowing through the security doors on their way to baggage claim. Hadley scanned the crowd, looking for her bestie. If their positions had been reversed, Web would have had a helluva time trying to spot her in the sea of humanity. She always just got lost in the crowd. That was the curse of being of average height (five feet four inches on a tall day), build (on the chuffy side of the scale but not giving a shit because doughnuts were to die for), and hair color (bland brown because she had no time to go to the salon for highlights or anything else).

However, at six feet four inches with dark-brown hair, green eyes, and the kind of laid-back attitude that came with never having to worry—about money, a job, or what people thought about him—Web always stood out. And if he walked into a room with his identical twin brother? No one could look away.

Annoyance started bubbling in her stomach at even the thought of Will.

The way he was always smirking at her as if he knew something she didn't. Her chest tightened and she ground her molars together as that all-too-familiar tension locked her back tight. The pseudo-concerned crap he shoveled at her about not being born with the silver spoon of Harbor City's high society firmly in her mouth.

She closed her eyes and envisioned smacking Will upside the head with that well-polished utensil.

And—on top of all that—there was the fact that he was the reason she was now unemployed.

She cut herself off before her temper went into countdown mode.

Let it go, Had. The second-best part about spending a week in Nebraska is not having to see your bestie's completely horrible, absolutely awful, no-good twin. The first—obviously—would be your sister's wedding.

Adalyn deserved to have the kind of happily ever after she'd spent her life wanting. Hadley could understand that, even if rolling over in bed to get blasted in the face with the same guy's morning breath day after day, year after year, decade after decade was definitely not in her plans.

Hadley dreamed of adventure and freedom and total self-control all the days of her life.

But she didn't have time to dwell on that amazing thought right now as her gaze snagged on Web's tall frame coming through the security doors.

Her welcoming smile turned to outright amusement as the sight of him finally processed. The black cowboy hat that almost sat right on his head. Wrangler jeans so new, they still had a crease down each leg hugging his muscular thighs. And the boots? Good Lord. He was wearing the fancy, shiny kind that showed up only at movie premieres and would never see any actual work on branding day.

If there was a soft-focused holiday movie about a heifer with magical matchmaking abilities, the cowboy hero would look exactly like Web. He didn't even begin to look as if his clothes had come from Feed and Steer, the store where a rancher could get his entire wardrobe, a fully automated roping shoot, and a gallon of supplements to encourage the cattle to stay hydrated while increasing their food consumption.

She shouldn't laugh—Web was a child of Harbor City's richest of the rich and obviously was trying to fit in the best he could. His heart was in the right place. Still, her lips twitched as the giggles bubbled up inside her.

Get ahold of yourself, girl. This is your best

friend. The guy who flew across the country to stand by your side. Don't make him feel bad for cosplaying the kind of cowboy who exists only on TV.

"Hey, cowboy," she called out, her voice giddy with unreleased laughter despite her best efforts.

Web turned his head, spotted her, and tipped his hat like he was Curly in an *Oklahoma!* revival, then headed her way, a sly grin on his face.

That's when her oh-shit senses started buzzing. As he swaggered through the crowd, that warning sense grew from a low hum to a full-on-earthquake. Heart hammering and palms sweaty, her left eye started twitching as she held tight to the one truth that she had to believe: This couldn't be. This abso-fucking-lutely couldn't be.

She squeezed her eyes shut and forced out the oxygen that had been trapped in her lungs.

It was just a trick of the light or her pre-family-gathering jagged nerves playing her. That had to be it.

Please, whoever is the patron saint of women just trying to make it through the day without committing murder, deliver me from this vision of a totally fresh hell.

She opened her eyes right as he stopped in front of her. Searching his face for the tiny little markers that differentiated Web's face from Will's, she held on to that little ribbon of hope that everything hadn't suddenly gone pear-shaped. Then she noticed the tiny mole by Web's left eye was missing. Maybe she'd always imagined it had been there? She took in a deep inhale and was hit with the unique mix of musk, leather, and the kind of trouble mothers had been warning their daughters about for generations. It was a uniquely Evil Twin scent. There was no way she could deny what she'd known the moment she'd seen him move.

This wasn't Web.

It was Will.

She stopped breathing, the world stopped spinning, and every one of the forty bazillion people in the crowded airport disappeared. It couldn't. They wouldn't. Holy fuck, her stomach was knotting up at the realization that she was now in hell.

He gave her a slow once-over that, despite knowing better, made her body wake up and take notice—*stop it right now, boobs, or it will be all uncomfortable sports bras for you until the end of time*—and punctuated it with a half smile.

He tipped his cowboy hat like a man who'd practiced it in the mirror. "Howdy."

The way Will said it with that rough rumble that on anyone else would be sex personified made her twitch with annoyance. Oh God. She couldn't kill him in front of witnesses.

Hadley crossed her arms and glared up at his somehow-hotter-than-his-identical-twin's face. "Get back on that plane."

"No can do." He gave his head a regretful shake. "It's going on to L.A. and I have had my fill of actresses for the time being, but it was sweet of you to think of me."

Heated frustration shot up from the earth's

core and blasted through her. How did he always produce this hot, flushed, so-damn-bothered involuntary reaction just by existing in the same room as her? Every. Single. Time. Ugh. He was the worst, just the absolute worst.

"What are you doing here and where is Web?" she asked, practically biting off each word.

"In reverse order…" He held up two long fingers. "At our family place in the country puking his guts up, but don't worry, he'll be fine." He lowered one finger. "Coming to your rescue."

Ha! That would be the day. "I don't think so."

He smirked at her.

Yes, *smirked*, and it wasn't even the least little bit sexy. It was enraging—like shake-her-fist-at-the-wide-open-high-plains-sky-and-yell-"noooooooooooooooo" enraging.

If Will had any idea how he was affecting her, he didn't show it, just kept right on going like God's gift to humanity. "I'm tall, dark, handsome, and rich. I'm pretty sure I fit the bill of a knight; I just need my brave steed. And anyway, I look exactly like Web, so your family will never know the difference. He and I used to swap spots all the time in school."

Nope. This was not happening. "You can't come with me."

"Are you sure?" He shot her a skeptical look. "I was told this was an all-hands emergency. Web's words were that anything—I repeat, anything—would be better for you than going to this wedding alone. Now, my brother's not known for exaggerating, but there's a first for everything. Are you really saying that spending a week with me is worse than facing down your entire family as they question every life choice you've made since you left your teeny, tiny hometown?"

The questions would come from love, Hadley knew it. A little query here, a comment there, a concern uttered in hushed tones over the home-made enchiladas. She was bound to crack under the pressure, which was exactly what she did not want to happen. Losing her cool and acting like the metaphorical flaming bag of dog poop during her sister's wedding and thus ruining everything was pretty much a nightmare situation. She need-ed someone to have her back, to help keep her sane, and to give her an excuse to escape the con-fines of her family before she lost it.

She sighed and her shoulders sank. She *needed* Will Holt, and the big jerk knew it. "Don't make me regret this."

He tipped his hat at her again, as if this were some old western movie with him playing the part of the flirtatious gambler while she was the saloon girl with a heart of gold. "I'm all about leaving women happy wherever I go."

Hadley clamped her mouth shut before she told him exactly how he could make her happy. Not to go into it, but in the week since *the incident*, she'd developed a very in-depth revenge fantasy that included a deep hole, hot honey, fire ants, and itching powder. Instead of telling him that, though, she turned and marched toward baggage claim, not bothering to check if the wrong cowboy was following.

CHAPTER FOUR

If Will didn't love his brother, he'd try to kill him—on purpose this time for forcing him to go to these kind of ridiculous lengths.

The only positive in the current situation being that Country Barbie wasn't happy about him being there. Good. *Misery loves company.*

At least he had her away from his brother. The fresh-from-the-country, I-just-want-to-be-friends scam might have fooled his brother, but Will knew better. There was no way Hadley was as innocent as her big brown eyes and freckled cheeks promised. She was after something, and Will knew well and good that it started with a Holt and ended with his family fortune.

No matter how apple-pie-adorable Hadley looked, she was just one more in a long line of dubious advisors, greedy sycophants, and con artists who saw the orphaned Holt brothers as easy pickings. Just like everyone else, she wanted something from them. No doubt, access to the Holt Foundation funds was just the beginning. That's why she pushed so hard to be considered as an advisory candidate and why she'd made sure her dream home on Instagram always included a nursery. Alimony was one thing, but child support was guaranteed for eighteen years. Never trust anyone outside the family when it came to money, his dad had warned him before he'd died, but Will had been too young and naive to understand. Mia had worked the same sweet and innocent con on him, and it had almost been too late when he'd realized. He sure as hell wasn't going to let Web suffer the same nut punch of betrayal.

His phone vibrated in the pocket of his stupid-tight jeans. No shock at the name or the text.

Web: Be nice to my friend.

Yeah, he'd be just as nice to her as she was to him.

Will: What, no hello? No how was your flight? No don't get gored by a rogue bull?

Web: Again. Be nice to my friend or I'll tell her to lock you in the barn with the…what in the hell lives in a barn? Horses? Could a pissed-off horse hurt anyone?

City people? He and his brother? Oh yeah, most definitely. They were Harbor City born and bred with only the trips to the fully manicured and well-staffed upstate country compound as "roughing it" experience.

Will: When am I not nice to dear, sweet Hadley?

Web: Any time you two are in the same room.

No lies detected there—not that he'd admit it.

He weaved around another person in the crowded airport while he kept one eye on Hadley's ass as she marched through the terminal and the other on texting his brother back.

Will: I'll be so damn charming, her whole family will fall in love with me.

Web: Can you live stream that? No one will believe it otherwise.

Will: Very fucking funny.

Also, probably more than a little true. He wasn't exactly the Holt twin everyone wanted to hang out with, which was how he liked it. The Prickly Bastard Holt Twin label fit him fine.

Web: Just remember you are a fake boyfriend. Help Hadley maintain her sanity this week WITHOUT getting into her pants. The last thing I need is for my brother and my best friend to be hate fucking.

Web's words gave him a moment of joy. No jealousy at all implied. As much as Hadley might be after Web, his brother really did seem immune to her wiles. But that didn't mean he'd remain immune forever.

Will glanced up from his phone. The woman in question had finally slowed her power walk to a still-quick strut. Sure, he noticed that sweet peach of an ass of hers—he'd have to be dead not to— but that didn't mean he was interested. He wasn't, no matter how often he'd thought about *that* kiss. It had been unexpected, that was all. Who'd have thought the devil would have such soft lips?

He grimaced and typed a response.

Will: Not an issue. Trust me.

It wasn't. It wouldn't be. Hadley was the enemy.

Web: Have a fun drive out to the ranch.

Yeah, that wasn't going to happen. He fucking hated car rides, had since he was a kid. The only

thing that would make it tolerable was the unin-
terrupted opportunity to annoy the ever-loving
shit out of Hadley—for a good cause, of course.

As if she could read his thoughts, she stopped
by the baggage carousel and looked over her
shoulder, her lips curled in a scowl that didn't do a
damn thing for him. Really.

Then why do you keep thinking about that kiss?

It was an accident. A onetime fluke. A what-
the-fuck-is-the-universe's-problem-with-Will-
anyhow fuckup. It wasn't like he'd gone in there
expecting to kiss his nemesis. Hell, he'd gone in
that coat closet to get away from all the forced
cheer of everyone glad-handing for donations. All
he'd wanted was five minutes of peace and quiet.

Instead he'd ended up with Hadley kissing him
as if he were the man she'd been dreaming about
for her whole life.

Then it got worse.

Hadley had looked at him and said one word.
"Web."

Yeah. That had been a shot straight to the balls.

"Slow down, darling," Will said when he finally
caught up with Hadley near the edge of the crowd
encircling the baggage carousel. "You don't even
know what my suitcase looks like."

"I'm assuming as black as your soul." She
stopped next to a couple holding hands and glared
at him. "And what's with the 'darling' and the
outfit? Are you making fun of people who live out
here?"

He glanced down at his clothes. Jeans. Boots.
Hat. He'd turned down the pearl-button Western

shirt the on-call stylist at Dylan's Department Store had offered. "Just trying to fit in."

"Will Holt," she said, crossing her arms and jutting out a hip. "You stand out everywhere you go, and you know it."

He couldn't argue. That was the curse of being one of the Holt twins. Not only were he and Web decent-looking and rich, their family had been at the top of the Harbor City society food chain since the Gilded Age. That meant his entire life since the time his and Web's birth announcement had been splashed across a double-page, full-color spread in *Harbor and Cove* magazine had been lived out under a microscope. Add in the tragic backstory of their parents dying young, boarding school after boarding school, and a grandmother who had barely tolerated them before she died and left them a fortune, and it was a gossip's dream.

He fucking hated it.

Of course, he wasn't about to tell Hadley that. A man didn't admit weakness to a gold digger he was planning on taking down before she could hurt his brother.

"Are you flirting with me, Hadley Donavan?" He took a step closer, using his nearness to distract her enough that she wouldn't notice he was changing the subject.

"Why, because everyone does?" She scoffed before biting her lip and looking back up at him, concern filling her eyes. "How is Web really?"

The quick conversation switch made sense. Of course she'd want to pretend to care about how his brother was doing. "He'll be fine. The doctor said he just needed some rest."

She took a half step back to allow plenty of room for the woman in the wheelchair to pass by. "Is it the flu?"

"Sorta." Will looked over at the couple holding hands as nonchalantly as possible.

"What's that mean? Did you poison him?" she asked, her voice as sugary as her words were tart.

"Not on purpose." He grimaced at her. "The chicken didn't make *me* sick." He left out the fact that he'd only had a few bites because he'd been too fixated on trying to figure out what to do about *her*.

The light blinked on top of the baggage carousel, announcing the bags were on their way, and saved him from more questions. He spotted his hard-shell suitcase—yes, it was black—and managed to squeeze through the crowd standing elbow to elbow to grab it. When he turned around, he caught Hadley averting her focus from ass level up to his face. Her jaw was clenched but her cheeks were pink.

Well, wasn't that fascinating.

"Were you checking out my butt?" he asked, strutting over with his suitcase, ready to pounce on the opportunity to needle her.

Her brown-eyed gaze dipped down and to the left. "No."

"Are you sure?" He stopped in front of her, just on the edge of that invisible do-not-cross edge of her personal space. "It seems like you were, and you're definitely turning red."

"It's warm in here." She pressed her hands to her cheeks. "I don't blush."

"Ever?" The question was out before he could stop himself. It wasn't his business. He wasn't here to find out all about the secret life of one Hadley Donavan.

She shook her head. "No."

"Interesting." But it wasn't. Who cared if someone blushed a lot or a little or never? He was a guy. He didn't give two shits about that. Still, the fact that she was getting worked up brought out the part of him that just wanted to meet the challenge in her eye. "I knew a woman once who would turn tomato red right before she came. It happened every time, no matter the position or…" He paused, letting her hang for a second as she obviously fought between telling him to fuck off and wanting to know what he'd say next. "The activity. We tested it out one long weekend. We started off with—"

"Oh my God, enough." She pressed her palm to his chest, her eyes going wide at the physical contact before she jerked her hand away and rubbed her fingers together, as if she'd felt the same zing he had. "I don't want to hear about how you have sex with other women."

"Why?" He glanced down at her lips, so pink and soft and glossy, fisting his hands to keep from reaching out for her. "Do you only want to consider me having sex with you?" Watching as she snagged her bottom lip between her teeth, her gaze going hazy, it took a lot to remember that kissing Hadley—again—was off-limits. "It's totally normal and healthy to consider what people are like in other, more naked situations."

There was a red splotch at the base of her throat to match the pink in her cheeks now, but her nipples were hard, too, two twin peaks pressing against the thin cotton of her T-shirt. At least he wasn't the only one affected.

She stared up at him, the brown of her eyes darkening to almost black. "I might just have to leave you on the side of the road once we're a few hours into the drive."

"Very funny," he said, amused by her attempt to scare him. "Like the drive is going to be hours."

For the first time since he'd walked out of the passengers-only area, Hadley smiled. "Web didn't tell you?"

His stomach sank, and that old familiar gurgle in his gut started. "Didn't tell me what?"

Her smile got even bigger, transforming her entire face and making her eyes sparkle with undeniable glee. "We're going to be at my family's ranch all week."

"Yeah, I knew that." Cows. Grassland. Saddle sores and barn stink.

"It's a five-hour drive from the airport."

Each word came out slowly, like a tiny little bomb that hit harder than she could have realized. Since childhood, he'd been able to make it two hours tops before the car got to him and he puked his guts up. After five hours? His stomach was already rebelling at the hell that was before him.

Web had set him up, no doubt as an oversize punishment for Will giving him a slight case of food poisoning. So much for brotherly love.

"You're kidding," he finally managed to get out.

"Not even close." She giggled, and the sound scared him more than anything else. "Get ready, city boy—you're about to take a long drive in the country."

This was not going to end well.

CHAPTER FIVE

The look on Will's face when she'd told him how long the drive was going to be had been priceless. Seriously. Not even *he* could have afforded it. Hadley was going to treasure that oh-shit-what-have-I-done expression for the rest of her life.

Served the big jerk right, even if after an hour on the highway, he'd gone quiet and— She glanced over, and her stomach dropped. He had a distinctive green sheen to his face, his jaw had gone from square to rigid, and he kept flexing his fingers but otherwise remained perfectly still.

Oh shit.

"Are you okay?" she asked, breathing a sigh of relief when she spotted the GAS STATION AHEAD sign, regret snipping at her for not noticing earlier that he was obviously in real misery, not the spoiled and bored kind.

"Perfect." He gave her the smallest nod possible, maintaining a stick-straight posture. "As always."

Lord have mercy. What, was he too rich and privileged to get car sick? Of course he would think so. The sun rose and set on his command.

"Are you ever not full of shit?" And to think

she'd felt bad for him for a whole half a second before he went all Will Holt on her.

He turned in his seat, winced, and then let out a shaky breath. "Like you're one to talk."

She side-eyed him. "What does that mean?"

"We both know why you are so-called friends with Web."

"Because we actually are?" They had been pretty much since they met and bonded over their mutual hatred of candy corn and love of office supply stores.

"Yeah." Will let out a weak chuckle. "As long as he has all that money in the bank, you're friends."

He couldn't be serious. She glanced over from the long, straight highway that went on forever and glared at him. He didn't flinch. That's when realization struck. *That's* why he hated her? He thought she was after Web for his money? Disbelief and righteous indignation whipped through her, making her whole body sizzle. What a total and complete jerk.

"Oh no," she said, sarcasm thick in her tone as she turned her attention back to the road. "You caught me. I'm really just softening him up so he'll fall in love with me and then *bam*, I'll steal his money and have an affair with the pool boy and the upstairs maid." She shook her fist in mock frustration. "And I would have gotten away with it, too, if it wasn't for you being an interfering jerk who assumes he knows everything." She stopped shaking her fist and flipped him off. "Breaking news, you don't."

He snorted. "Don't bother denying it. I know all about how you're always talking to Web about moving the Holt Foundation money over to your client list. I know about the meals and cab rides where he picks up the check. I know about all the planning-for-tomorrow IG posts with photos of homes that only someone in our income bracket could afford. You're good, I'll give you that—it's never too over-the-top. It's as subtle as the way you always point out that the expensive outfits in the storefronts near the rugby field are gorgeous but that you'll never be able to afford them without winning the lottery—or marrying a millionaire. I doubt Web has even noticed the way you're working the long con and planting these little ideas. Plus, if you can't get your money by marrying into it, you can use Web's money to climb the corporate ladder. I suppose you look at him and see the perfect mark."

What. The. Ever-loving. Hell.

"Are you deranged? I talk to Web about working with the Holt Foundation because I'm damn good at my job. As far as the rest of that bullshit goes, I'm not even going to justify that kind of ridiculousness with a response, beyond that as far as climbing the ladder, I'd need a job for that. Remember, you kicked the good ol' corporate ladder out from underneath me in that coat closet. Or wait! I suppose what happened at the fundraiser was part of my master plan?" If it were, she truly sucked at being a gold digger. Almost banging her target's brother would be a seriously shitty ploy.

"How can I know what goes on in your mind?" Will shrugged. "Maybe you've decided to switch targets."

"You seem to think you know a lot about my motives." Of course he did. He'd always been like this with her—a judgmental asshat. She squeezed the steering wheel tighter as she punched back the urge to holler in frustration. "Knowing me, I probably finagled it so that the meanest woman on the charity circuit walked in on us at the very worst moment."

She blushed at the memory of her hands reaching for his zipper. His hands going up underneath the hem of her dress. Everything hot and sudden and beyond want into gotta-have-you-or-I'll-explode territory. Hot annoyance and slick desire mixed together in an instant, making it hard to figure out if she should pull over the car to yell at him or finish what they started in that closet.

"Maybe you were hedging your bets," he said, no longer even looking her way but instead at the cornfields as they sped past.

"More like the three sips of champagne I'd had on an empty stomach—unless you counted a couple of canapés—had affected my usually very good judgment." Her cheeks burned at the memory of the door opening, light flooding in, and the cruel disdain on Mia Cardin's face. "Then, like a virgin in a slasher movie, I paid for my momentary lapse in judgment when we walked out with everyone watching, thanks to an early alert from Mia. Amazing forethought on my part to ensure you were still tucking in your shirt at that moment so no one would be left doubting what had happened in the coat closet and, thus, furthering my evil plan."

"I tried to fix that," he said, almost sounding like he meant it.

"Is that what you call it?" She let out a harsh chuckle to cover the hurt that cracked like a whip against her skin. "You told my boss that the whole situation was being blown out of proportion. Any fool, and I quote, would know that a guy like you with your social status would never actually be with some poor chick who'd moved to Harbor City with everything she owned packed into three suitcases. Then you laughed." The memory of that humiliation burned like lava through her veins. "And everyone else laughed."

"That's not exactly what I said."

"Close enough."

She swerved with a hard jerk of the steering wheel to avoid a pothole, and Will let out something that sounded like a mix between a miserable groan and a curse before clenching his jaw tight enough that she was surprised it wasn't followed by a tooth cracking. Despite knowing that he was the last person in the world who deserved any sympathy, it slid in between the cracks of her protective shielding anyway.

"Okay, cut the crap," she said. "You're carsick, aren't you?"

"As long as I keep my eyes on the horizon, I'll be fine," he said through clenched teeth.

"Okay. Whatever." If that's how he wanted to

handle motion sickness, he could. See if she cared.

That, of course, lasted all of about thirty seconds.

Way to go, Hadley. Do you really hate him enough to want to see him puke his guts up in the rental?

Because she was still pissed enough that she was doing what her mom called her "huffy breathing," she had to stop to consider it as they barreled down the highway. After all, he *was* the reason for one of the more humiliating experiences of her life, and now she knew he thought she was friends with Web only for his money. Still, her mom had raised her better than to leave a person—even a total asshole—to suffer, so she started scanning the road up ahead for signs advertising a decent place to stop. Well, that and the fact that she didn't feel like driving for three more hours in a car that smelled like upchuck.

"Sorry," she said, not even close to meaning it. "I had no idea you got car sick."

He closed his eyes tight. "Web did."

"Oh!" She gasped. "He set you up."

Her lips twitched, and she bit the inside of her cheek. She wouldn't giggle. She wouldn't chuckle or guffaw or snicker. She'd been raised better than to laugh at people who were obviously in misery. Clamping her jaw shut tight, she kept her eyes on the road and told herself to stuff a sock in it.

"Go ahead and laugh," Will said. "I won't hold it against you. Your perfect family probably never pulls this crap on one another."

She snorted and took the next exit, heading

straight toward the last big gas station before the miles grew longer between towns and then the towns totally disappeared. "One time my brother Knox replaced my shampoo with Nair, not realizing that it was impossible to miss the very distinctive scent of the hair remover."

"What did you do?" he asked.

The tension in the car lessened at his question, eased by the common ground of sibling pranks, and the tightness in her shoulders gave a bit. "Whatever makes you think I'd take my revenge?"

That got a chuckle out of him, if a weak one. "I've met you."

"I Saran Wrapped the opening of his bedroom door and then woke him up in the middle of the night screaming there was a fire. He ran smack into it, and I got the entire thing on my phone."

"Nice one," he said.

She pulled into a parking spot next to the convenience store / gas station / restaurant / trucker shower stop hybrid. "Hold on. I'll be right back. Don't puke in the rental—that smell will only make the motion sickness worse."

He squeezed his eyes shut and pinched the bridge of his nose. "Thank you very much for that mental image."

"Sorry," she said as she lowered the windows before getting out of the SUV and hurrying inside.

It took only a few minutes to buy a couple of cans of ginger ale and a snack-size box of saltines as well as some over-the-counter Dramamine, but by the time she got back out, Will was standing outside the car, leaning against it with his boot heel on the tire and the brim of his black cowboy hat dipped low. Replace the highway in the background with grassland and it would look like the start of a cheesy cowboy movie. All he needed was the single strand of straw hanging from the corner of his mouth.

It wasn't fair that he could still manage to look so hot even while looking like a basic-cable-cowboy rip-off. That he did and she still noticed just revved her up in the way being around him always did.

It made no sense.

He looked exactly like her best friend—duh, they were twins—but she had never been tempted to kiss Web. Just the thought of it made her make the "ew" face.

But with Will? It was always half hate and half lust swirling inside her at even the mention of his name, which pissed her off to no end. Why didn't being around Web make her body react like that? It would make her life so much easier. The whole situation just drove her up a wall.

"I got you this." She shoved one of the cans of ginger ale and the box of crackers into his hands, covering up her inconvenient attraction with a surly attitude, per usual. She opened the box of Dramamine and threw a pill at him. "Take this, too. This is pretty much the end of the line for places like this. We'll hit a couple of small gas stations between here and the ranch, but if you need anything, you should get it now."

"I'm good," he said, sounding more like his

usual cocky self, but took everything she'd held out.

She gave him a nod and got back in the driver's side, syncing up her driving playlist with the car stereo again and making her way down the highway.

"Thanks for the ginger ale and crackers," he said, settling back in the reclined passenger seat and closing his eyes. "That plus a nap should get me through this."

Of course he was snoring quietly before they'd gone five miles. The spoiled and the rich never needed to worry about anything. It had nothing to do with the Dramamine, she insisted to herself.

The rest of the drive, while not quick by any means, went about as fast as it usually did. Growing up out in the sticks, a person either had to learn to deal with a lot of time in the car to get to a mall, the movies, a supersize grocery store or they had to spend their life at home and hope that UPS would deliver even though their address was a PO Box at the closest post office.

Some people loved it, relished the rugged individualism of it all. That was not Hadley. She'd had moving feet since birth, and by the time she was fourteen when her mom married Gabe, she'd already planned how she was going to ditch the sticks for Harbor City. She'd have a gorgeous apartment with a view, a glamorous job, and a thriving social life. At least, that's what she'd promised everyone.

What she'd ended up with was a fifth-floor walk-up with windows looking out on the brick side of the building next door, a frustrating but rewarding job that she'd just lost, and a social life that usually consisted of Netflix and the occasional work-related party. Except for Fiona and Web, she didn't have many friends. Acquaintances? Sure. Friends? Not so much. And she was lonely.

It was a real transition to go from her hyper-involved family on the ranch to the city where people didn't even make eye contact when you accidentally plowed into them on the sidewalk.

But she wasn't pathetic. She hadn't failed to make her dream a reality. It was just taking longer than expected was all.

So she'd kept her mouth shut about the realities of her life in Harbor City when she talked with her mom and let everyone think she had it made. She stuck to her plan to fake it until she made it in Harbor City. No one—especially not her family—needed to know the real situation.

Will woke up as soon as she made the left turn off the paved two-lane highway and onto the gravel road leading to the ranch. "Where are we?"

She tried not to watch out of the corner of her eye as he extended his arms in a stretch that showed off all his muscled glory. The man's forearms should be illegal. They could cause an accident.

She forced her attention back to the road. "We're almost home."

He looked around, his green eyes widening as he no doubt realized the landscape went on for practically forever without a single building getting in the way. "So what's the backstory of our relationship, or do you just want me to wing it?"

Her heart sped up in panic at the idea of Will winging it.

"Web and I were sticking close to the truth." Because that was the way not to get caught in an embarrassing lie. "We started out as friends, and it just morphed."

He nodded. "I can work with that."

"It's not serious, though. I'm not bringing 'the one' home to meet my parents," she continued. "Web was just giving me a buffer, an excuse to not spend all my time with my family. I love them, but they're just…a lot to take. And they never understood why I left for the city." She sighed. She hated lying to her family, but she also didn't think she could take a whole week of "helpful" nosiness, either. Especially not now that they didn't know she'd been fired.

Her jaw clenched at that memory, and she grabbed on to the anger like a life raft. "It's your fault I got fired, which my family knows nothing about, so really, you've got no one to blame for this mess but yourself."

He cocked one arrogant eyebrow at her but gladly didn't argue.

They drove in silence until they crossed underneath the sign for HIDDEN CREEK RANCH. It only took a few seconds before Hadley spotted the three cowboys in the distance. They were sitting on their horses on a slight rise in the land. Something soft and good settled in her belly right then—that sense of being home.

She didn't have to be up close to know their boots were dusty, their jeans worn in, and their hats weren't just for decoration. Her stepdad, Gabe, and her brothers had obviously come to the lookout to see if they could spot her. Just like old times, she hit the horn three times, each one a short burst of sound that would be carried on the breeze that never seemed to ever stop blowing out here. One of the three—probably Weston, the sentimental one of the bunch—raised his hat in acknowledgment, and then they all took off, disappearing in the horizon.

Damn, she hadn't expected the hot happy tears she was blinking away or the lump in her throat. Even though she'd never move back, there was no beating the feeling of being here with her family. They were overwhelming and nosy and constantly finding fault, but she never, not for one single instant, doubted that they loved her or that she loved them.

And she was already planning to ditch them whenever she could. Worst of all, she was doing it with the biggest asshole snob she knew. Her gut dropped and her heart went into overdrive with the spike of panic shooting through her veins.

What if he behaves around them in the same shitty way he acts around me?

"Look, we need to get something straight." She pulled off to the side of the road, a cloud of dust settling in their wake. "I appreciate you doing this when Web couldn't, but this is my family. They make me nuts, but I love them." And she did. She might live a four-hour plane ride plus a five-hour drive away, but that didn't change her feelings even one bit. "They are amazing and frustrating and some of the best people you'll ever meet." She turned to face Will, needing him to see on her face just how 100 percent serious she was. "And if you do anything to make them feel bad about not being rich Harbor City high society, I'll cut your balls off. We own cattle. I know how to do it."

Okay, she didn't, but he sure as hell didn't need to know that.

He raised an eyebrow and toasted her with his empty ginger ale can. "Duly noted."

And with a final evil-eyed glare, she pulled back onto the road, feeling pretty good about things—right up until she drove into the yard in front of the house. There were nearly a dozen family members waiting on the front porch, eager to get all the constant family togetherness started.

Oh God. What in the blue blazes had she done?

•••

There were a million people waiting for them when Hadley pulled up in front of the house.

It was a big place, two stories with a wrap-around porch that had an honest-to-God metal triangle hanging from the ceiling that someone could bang the attached rod against, the clang alerting everyone it was time to head home—just like the old black-and-white cowboy movies he used to watch as a kid. It sat alone on the top of what could barely be called a hill, since it was more of a roll in the land. Big leafy trees surrounded the house like guards around the four walls. Off in the distance, he spotted the red metal roof of a barn or bunkhouse and several smaller houses between the big building and the main house.

The whole thing was about as country sweet as you could get—especially considering the place had managed to spawn the ball-threatening Hadley Donavan. Maybe she moved in late in life.

"Were you born here?" Will asked.

"Not out here." She put the SUV into Park and turned off the engine. "I grew up in town. Didn't move out here until I was fourteen when Mom married Gabe."

"There's a town?" Okay, he'd sacked out, lulled to sleep by the Dramamine and never-ending interstate, but he definitely would have woken up with stop-and-go city traffic.

"Yeah, we drove right through it." She reached for the door, exhaling as if to gird herself, and opened it. "We were lucky and the single stoplight on Main Street was a blinking yellow when I drove through." She paused and shot him another glare. "Remember what I said about my family. Do not fuck with them."

"The thought never crossed my mind." No, he'd been too busy having dreams about literally fucking Hadley, which just went to show how much the drive had messed with him.

He took a sly peek at her ass as she got out of the car. Yes, he was a glutton for punishment in the no-touch zone, but he wasn't fully awake yet and had absolutely no interest in Hadley, no matter what lies the lusty twitch in his dick tried to tell as he watched her strut around the SUV's hood.

Damn. He was going to have to get all of this "not interested" under control if he was going to make it through this week without getting distracted. He was a man on a mission, and he wasn't about to let his brother fall into the same trap that had gotten Will once before. No pretty face or sweet ass would come between the Holts and their money ever again.

Although Will was going to have to be careful about how he went about convincing Hadley that even if Web might be an easy mark, Will would do whatever it took to protect him. There were a lot of places to hide a body out here—not that anyone looked particularly murderous, but if there was one thing he understood more than anything else, it was the power of family loyalty. Judging by the happy tears, hard hugs, and general joy from Hadley's family as they rushed to greet her, he had no doubt her family understood it as well.

Unable to put off this ridiculous plan any longer, he channeled his twin and put on his friendliest smile before getting out of the car and joining the throng of mostly women surrounding Hadley.

"You must be Webster. I'm Hadley's mom, Stephanie," Stephanie said, turning to him with a friendly, if reserved smile and holding out her hand.

He accepted her handshake and managed to cover his shock at the strength in her grip. "Everyone but Hadley calls me Will. She loves to give me a hard time about my name."

Hadley shot him a death glare. So they hadn't discussed the name thing, but he was right and he knew it. It was only a matter of time before he failed to answer to Web and then the gig would be up.

Adalyn, judging by her Bride-To-Be T-shirt, cocked her head to the side, her face twisting with confusion. "Isn't that your bro—"

Her question was cut off by a well-timed elbow from Hadley followed by a speaking glance that said, *Shut the hell up.*

"My brother's nickname for me, yes," he covered.

"Well." Stephanie paused for a second, not looking the least bit appeased. "Will. It's good to have you here for this special occasion."

"Thanks for having me, and please let me know what I can do to help." The polite words came out almost as a reflex, because the answer was always no when it came to big events that were always catered and planned by professionals.

"Don't suppose you can cook?" Stephanie asked.

Considering she probably didn't want her entire family slightly poisoned by undercooked chicken, there was only one answer he could give. "No, but I can wash dishes like you wouldn't believe."

"Good." She gave him a real smile this time

that had the corners of her eyes crinkling. "You've got a job."

As everyone started to walk inside, Hadley pulled him back half a step. "Do you even know how to wash dishes?"

"I can load a dishwasher." Occasionally he even did it. Usually, though, the cleaning crew took care of all that at his Harbor City penthouse.

"But have you ever actually *done* that?" She took a step closer, looking up at him with a knowing little smirk—the one that told him she knew just how full of shit he was. "Have you ever washed dishes by hand?"

"I'm not a complete spoiled jerk," he said, sounding exactly like one even to his own ears.

She just lifted an eyebrow.

God, she was pushy—something that should have been annoying. Really, it was annoying. Completely. Utterly. Without a doubt. That was the only reason why he couldn't drag his attention away from that smart mouth of hers because he couldn't believe what words came out of it.

"Okay, fine." He closed the distance between them, using the advantage of his height to look down at her. "No. I haven't, but I'm sure I won't have a problem excelling at it just like I do everything else."

"Oh really?" she asked, not giving an inch. "I suppose you can also excel at all the ranching chores, like help check the fencing and gather eggs and muck the stalls, too."

"Of course," he said, his mouth running without his brain because all he could think about was how badly he wanted to kiss that knowing grin off her face right now. "By the end of the week, your relatives will be thinking of me like I'm just another cowboy in the family. They're gonna love me."

Hadley scoffed. "No. Fucking. Way."

"Wanna bet?"

He had no idea why he was doing this. Proving her wrong about his abilities to wash dishes or muck fences or mend stalls or be a beloved member of her family wasn't on his agenda. He was here for one reason: to convince her to take her gold-digger hooks out of his brother. She was priming Web, softening him up for the taking. He'd seen it before—lived it—and the pattern was the same as what Mia had done to him. Start with friendship, add in some damsel-in-distress bullshit like her I-really-need-you-to-go-to-my-sister's-wedding ploy, and then go in for the multimillion-dollar kill.

"So do we have a bet or not?" he asked.

"Bet on what?" she asked as she pantomimed pulling finger guns from a holster on each side of her round hips and shooting them into the air like a trick shot. "That you can become a rootin' tootin' city slicker cowboy much beloved by my family in a week? It'll never happen."

Oh, it was definitely happening now. Winning was his specialty. There was no way he'd lose to her. "If you lose, you leave my brother alone. If I lose—which isn't going to happen—I'll never mention you being a gold digger again, and I'll get out from between you and my brother."

Hadley released a dramatic sigh and pressed the back of her hand to her forehead. "Oh no, all my plans to marry a billionaire are in jeopardy."

Such a smart-ass.

"Is that a yes?" he asked.

She crossed her arms, cocked her hip, and considered him for a moment before saying, "You bet your never-seen-a-cow-patty-before boots."

Then, in a repeat of what had happened at the airport, she turned and walked away, going up the steps of the ranch house's front porch.

She was confident, he'd give her that. Too bad for her, he was a man who never lost—not in business and not when it came to protecting his family.

Hadley Donavan was about to find out first-hand just how good the bad Holt twin could be.

CHAPTER SIX

Hadley was going to love watching Will have to shut up already about his totally wrongheaded belief that she was friends with Web only because she had plans to steal his money. Really, how many bad movies had he watched to come up with such an inane plot? All of which would make seeing him end up falling on his tight-Wranglers-wearing ass at the end of the week even sweeter.

Petty?

Her?

In this case, she so very much was and could accept that about herself. If anyone deserved to come down a few pegs, it was Will Holt, CEO of Holt Enterprises and perpetual pain in her ass.

"That's some smile that fella has you wearing," Aunt Louise said as she stood by the screen door in her usual uniform of jeans, a seed company T-shirt, and worn baseball cap with her iron-gray hair pulled back into a French braid that reached all the way down to the middle of her back. "I like to see it."

Oh, this was perfect. Her aunt Louise—who'd run her small ranch by herself since her husband, Dexter, had passed away forty years ago—would talk Will's ear off about all things ranching related. By the time she was done, his brain would be filled with so much cattle-related minutiae that he'd admit defeat on the bet before it even got started.

"Aren't you sweet for saying so," Hadley said. Could this get any worse? But she knew for sure they couldn't sell "serious relationship" with how often her family was going to notice they wanted to kill each other. Time to change the subject. "However, he is really interested in learning everything there is to know about the cowboy life," she said, lacing her voice with enough oh-my-gosh-gee-willikers insincere sweetness that there was no way Will would miss that she was setting him up.

"Really?" Aunt Louise's eyes lit up with interest and she turned her full attention to Will. "What do you want to know?"

He didn't even hesitate. "Everything."

Of course he said the exact right thing. God. This week was going to be hell.

Aunt Louise clapped her hands together. "Well, you have come to the right woman." She nodded at Hadley. "This one never did take to anything about ranch life."

"Gotta say, I'm glad about that," Will said, putting his arm around Hadley's waist and tucking her up close against him. "If she had, then she never would have come to Harbor City and I wouldn't have met her."

His fingertips brushed against the roll that always made an appearance as soon as she buttoned her pants and—on instinct—she sucked in her gut before realizing what she was doing and letting it all back out again. Will was the last guy she was going to put on a front—or Spanx—to impress. So what if she had so-called unsightly bulges, unfortunate chin hairs that reappeared no matter how many times she plucked them, and unpainted fingernails trimmed down as far as possible? He could pretend to date her as she was or he could go jump in an irrigation ditch. Either way, she'd be happy.

"Aren't you just the sweet talker?" she said, unwinding herself from his light hold and ignoring the tingling sensation imprinted on her skin.

"Only when it comes to you." Will tucked a stray hair behind her ear, his fingertips gliding over the shell of her ear and then lightly down the side of her neck as if he were so far gone for her that he couldn't help but touch her at every opportunity. "You just bring out the best in me."

"Oh, there's nothing quite like young love," Aunt Louise said with a grin.

Then her aunt hurried off, which was good because there was no way Hadley could stop herself from nailing Will with a death stare. That whole cow-eyes look was not the plan. Plus, there was not to be any touching whatsoever.

"What are you doing?" she asked through gritted teeth.

"Thinking ahead. Web said you needed help taking a break from all the immersive family time, so if they think we're so into each other that we can't stand to be apart, then they'll be even more likely to give you some space. Brilliant, right? It's okay to admit it."

She would not, even if it were true. A woman had to have some pride, especially when it came to Will. Him hot for her? Ha. That would be the day.

Every time she saw him, he shot snarky little comments at her that only she could hear, as if she wasn't more than aware that he didn't approve of her friendship with his brother. Well, he could go stuff it. The second she and Web had met in the world's longest and slowest coffee line, they'd bonded over the superiority of warm chocolate croissants, the need for subtitles on any show where the cast had a Scottish accent, and the fact that if Bill Bryson and Mary Roach had nonfiction book babies, they would be the most interesting books ever written.

Then she'd made the mistake of going to one of Web's rugby games and discovered his brother, who was also on the team, was actually his twin and his twin was actually evil. Will had hated her on sight and wasn't shy about letting her know— at least not when it was just the two of them. There were snarky comments, questions about her background, and disapproving looks whenever he spotted her. She had no idea when or how she'd peed in Will Holt's cornflakes, but apparently she had, and he and his sexy wink, cute dimple, and too-smackable-for-his-own-good ass could go hump it.

As if he knew what she was thinking and wanted to rub it in that she couldn't do anything about it, Will took her hand in his and then lifted it so he could kiss the back of it. It wasn't much, just a quick brush of his lips, but it made her breath catch all the same.

Damn that man. It wasn't fair.

"Good Lord, you two, I feel like I could make fried bologna sandwiches just from the heat coming off you," Aunt Louise said, peeking out of the screen door and fanning herself with her hand. "Some of us are having to deal with menopausal hot flashes. Come on inside—I need to get some sun tea to cool me off."

Once Aunt Louise had her back to them, Hadley yanked her hand from Will's barely there grasp and shot him a dirty look. The jerk just winked at her and held open the screen door for her to walk through. As she passed by, she would have laid her hand on a stack of Bibles and sworn that it felt like walking outside right before a thunderstorm, when the whole world felt electric. She didn't mean to look up at him at that moment, but she did anyway, and her heart sped up. She'd never, ever admit it out loud, but there was something about him that had that effect on her. No doubt he knew exactly what he was doing with the little touches, and he was probably going to continue to push her buttons the entire week.

That was okay. She could take it.

After all, it wasn't like she was in any danger of falling for him. Will Holt was the most bullheaded, annoying, frustrating person she'd ever met, and no amount of hotness wrapped up in Wranglers was going to make her forget that.

• • •

He wasn't flirting; he was a man with a plan—at least that's what he kept telling himself as he flexed his still-buzzing fingers and followed Hadley inside. Maybe it was because he'd been distracted by watching her walk in front of him, but it wasn't until he was standing in the middle of the open-concept living room that the full beauty of the house hit him.

This was not the kind of ranch house he'd been expecting. Too much TV had planted the idea that it would look like a log cabin on steroids. Oh, there was plenty of wood and antlers on the walls, but it was the floor-to-ceiling windows at the back of the house that grabbed his attention. The outdoors looked bigger out here. The nearly flat green land with its gentle rolls seemed to go on forever, and the puffy white clouds that hung in the atmosphere almost looked painted on against the clear blue sky. As a guy who'd grown up with Harbor City's Center Park as the biggest green space he'd ever seen in person, the view was awe-inspiring.

Hadley stopped beside him, taking in the sight, a slight smile curling her pink lips. "A little bit different than the view from your penthouse, right?"

"I could get used to this," he said, imagining himself out on the range painting fences or tracking gophers or whatever it was that someone did on a ranch. "Might need to get a place out this way. I have the clothes for it now."

That pulled her attention from the view to him, which would have been more ego-boosting if it hadn't resulted in her looking at him as if he were wearing a head-size belt buckle.

"Please, you'd freak out as soon as you figured out you couldn't get your favorite Chinese place to deliver."

"So I'd learn to love pizza delivery." There. He could be a man who compromised.

Hadley laughed so hard, she snorted. "Let me know when you make the call for an extra-large pepperoni. I want to be there to hear how hard they laugh when you give them the address."

Oh really? He was going to have to pull the rich-guy helicopter-food-delivery option out of his back pocket? Determined to prove her wrong about not being able to get pizza to the front door, he pulled out his phone. That's when he spotted notification after notification rolling in now that they were within a cell phone service area again. As he scrolled his brother's Instagram posts, realization dawned with a smack to his face. Web hadn't just set him up for a long and miserable drive in the country.

"Have you seen this yet?" he asked Hadley.

"What?" She took a step closer, her hip brushing his leg, and peeked at his phone screen. "You don't think he faked it?" She looked up at him, her pink lips parted and her eyes wide. "He wouldn't." She glanced back down at the photo of his didn't-look-like-he'd-been-sick-for-even-a-minute brother. Her eyes narrowed. "I'm gonna kill him."

Shaking his head, Will grimaced. "You'll need to get in line."

Then they stood there in a silent what-the-fuck moment, staring at the photo of a very healthy Web out on the family yacht with a handful of people in cowboy hats and bathing suits behind him. Web was obviously having the time of his life. The caption read: *Celebrating the two people I love most in the world finally getting to spend some time together. That definitely calls for a little vitamin D! Yeehaw.*

She made a sound that bordered on a growl. "He faked having food poisoning."

"Looks like it." Will might be the bad twin, but that didn't mean Web didn't get into plenty of shit himself.

"But why?" she asked, looking up at him as if they were on the same side for once.

The combination of her closeness and that nonhostile expression on her face was disconcerting. It made his fingers itch to reach out and run a thumb across the line of her jaw, tilt her face back, dip his head down, and— *Whoa there, Holt. Remember who you're looking at and why.*

Rubbing his palm across the back of his neck, he tried to steady his pulse. "Guess someone wants us to be friends."

Hadley snorted. "Not gonna happen."

"Finally," he said, not meaning to but somehow dropping his gaze to her glossy pink lips. "Something we can agree on."

But that wasn't the only thing they'd agreed on.

A week ago, they'd agreed on that kiss, that stick-your-brain-in-a-wind-tunnel-and-let-it-get-blown-away-because-you-aren't-using-it-and-you-don't-care kiss. As if she were thinking about the same moment, Hadley lifted her fingertips to her mouth and let out a shaky breath.

"Enough with the gadgets—come on into the kitchen," Stephanie called from the area behind them.

He and Hadley jolted apart, the air coming back into the room with a whoosh, and looked away from each other. After a few seconds, Hadley led him from the living room. Everyone had gathered around the huge kitchen island and was eating handfuls of a Chex cereal, peanut butter, and chocolate mixture that they called Puppy Chow. There was Hadley's mom, her sister, several people introduced as cousins ranging in age from six months to late teens, and one older lady who'd spent a lot of time staring at his junk and then unashamedly giving him a wink when he caught her.

Note to self: Do not dance at the wedding with the old lady. Possible package grabber alert.

The radio was tuned to a country music station, but with so many people talking at once, he only caught a half a verse here or there. It was loud enough, however, that Hadley was moving along to the beat, her hip occasionally bumping up against his as they stood next to each other on one end of the island that separated the kitchen area from the living room.

"Don't be a chicken," Hadley said, nudging

toward him the bright-green bowl everyone was snacking from. "It's made from only the best organic dog food."

She was giving him a hard time—he knew this because what was in the bowl looked like a giant vat of Muddy Buddies. Still, her cocky we're-on-my-home-court stance had him second-guessing himself, something he never did.

He dipped his hand into the bowl and scooped up a few pieces. "You're giving me shit, aren't you?"

Hadley elbowed him in the side, shooting him a what-is-wrong-with-you look, at the same time her mom cleared her throat.

"Language, young man," Stephanie said, her tone cutting him not even an ounce of slack.

He winced. Cursing in front of the family was definitely a mistake Web wouldn't have made. "Sorry, ma'am."

"Yeah, I'm Stephanie. There's no reason for that ma'am stuff." She rolled up the sleeves of her denim work shirt, never taking her eyes off him, as if he were the kind of person who needed to be kept track of at all times. "Now, Web—sorry, Will, we haven't heard hardly anything about you except that you're a fabulous dancer."

That was one of the talents he and his brother had in common. Their grandmother had insisted on lessons, which he'd hated then but got the most possible use out of now. Women loved a guy who knew how to move on the dance floor.

"Mom," Hadley said with a groan. "Don't interrogate him; he just got here."

Stephanie grinned. "That seems like the perfect time. He's tired out from the trip and vulnerable."

"Now I see where Hadley gets her instincts." Will gave Hadley's mom his best charming smile and it had absolutely no impact at all. Okay, then. Maybe it only worked on women from the city. Maybe that's why Hadley had always blown him off. "I grew up in Harbor City, and I work in the family business."

Usually, this is when he dropped the Holt Enterprises name and people got dollar signs in their eyes. That didn't seem right here. Not because of Hadley's warning but because everyone here seemed genuinely nice. They weren't looking at him like they were wondering how they could use him to their advantage. It was more like they were considering *him*. It was weird, and he kinda liked it.

"What do you do for fun?" one of the cousins—Raider?—asked.

"I play rugby." When they gave him a look that all but screamed *weirdo sport*, he continued. "It's like football, just take away the pads, change the rules completely, and swap out the ball."

"So how did you two meet?" Stephanie asked, obviously still sizing him up going by the friendly-but-not-really tone in her voice.

"Yes," Adalyn said with a happy sigh. "Tell us everything. I love these meet-cute stories."

Tension poured off Hadley in waves as she stood next to him, biting down on her bottom lip. He could understand why. He had all the power right now. One word from him and he could have her family believing that she met him at a nudist beach or at a vegan grocery. He was more than just a little tempted to do it just to mess with little Miss Perk and Perfect—but he'd promised Web.

"I was in the coat check room at a party hosted by her company and in walked Hadley." There. That was close to factual, and the plan was to stick to the truth as much as possible.

Hadley's eyes went wide and her foot came down on the toe of his right boot. "And that's the end of the story."

Everyone in the kitchen looked from Hadley to him. The old lady who up until then couldn't keep her attention off his junk was leaning forward in her chair as she popped one piece of Puppy Chow after another into her mouth. The pressure on his toes increased, though, and for as much fun as it would be to tell everyone about that kiss just to watch Hadley get all worked up, he couldn't do it. The woman was going to know where he was sleeping for the next week, and he had no doubt she would use that information to her advantage by smothering him in his sleep. So he just shrugged and kept his mouth shut.

The crowd let out a collective groan of disappointment.

"You're no fun," Aunt Louise said, settling back in her chair, her disappointment obvious. "How can you say you don't want to get serious with this one? I swear, I'll never get you, Trigger."

Next to him, Hadley groaned.

What was this? An embarrassing childhood

nickname? Oh yes, he was going to have to find out more—just to get under her skin, of course.

He turned to Hadley. "Trigger?"

His pretend girlfriend shoved a handful of the surprisingly delicious Puppy Chow into her mouth, pointed to her puffed-out cheeks, and shrugged as if answering was beyond her abilities at the moment. Luckily, her mom wasn't as hesitant to give up the goods.

"When we first moved out to the ranch, the kids were all scared of the horses. So to try to help them get used to their new surroundings and the animals, Gabe and I gave the kids nicknames of famous horses to make them seem friendlier," Stephanie said. "Hadley is Trigger. Adalyn is Buttermilk after Dale Evans's horse. Knox is Goldie and Weston is Buckshot."

"So it's not for your temper?" That really did seem to be the most likely possibility to him.

"No." Aunt Louise cackled. "But it could be."

Everyone had a good chuckle about that—including Hadley. Relaxing his guard, Will took another handful of the Puppy Chow, which really was amazingly good. All of Hadley's relatives were talking over one another again, happy and at ease. It was so strange compared to what he was used to.

After his and Web's parents had died, their grandmother had raised them. She was not the chatty sort. When they'd come home for break while attending boarding school, she'd mainly stayed in her wing of the mansion that took up a huge chunk of a city block near Center Park.

Other than Grandma, there were a few distant cousins, but that was it. He'd never sat around in the kitchen and shot the shit with his family ever and had no idea that he'd been missing all of this.

Hadley was lucky, not that he could tell from looking at her. While everyone else was smiling and having fun, she was hanging back, her face carefully neutral. What the hell?

"So yeah, we'll be having game night, a bonfire, and Gabe's been setting up a cowboy obstacle course," Stephanie said, talking to Aunt Louise, her voice carrying over the din. "It's going to be so much fun this week."

Now, if all of that didn't sound like the perfect way to make her family fall in love with him so he could win his bet with Hadley, then he didn't run a company that controlled more cash than the GDP of a small country. The joy of a plan coming together flooding through him, he wrapped an arm around Hadley and pulled her close.

"That sounds amazing," he said. "We can't wait to do *all* of it."

Hadley made a sound that reminded him a lot of a feral animal growling, but it was too late. Her mom was beaming at both of them as if Christmas had come early.

"Oh, that's wonderful! Usually we have to guilt Hadley into participating. This is going to be a blast. Now, you guys must be tired," Stephanie said. "Let me take you where you're staying, and you can clean up and maybe take a nap." She led them out the back door. "We have the grandparents and older relatives staying in the main house, so you guys are in one of the outbuildings that Knox has been renovating."

Will followed along in silence, but the gleeful look Hadley sent him over her shoulder at her mom's words didn't reassure him. If he ended up spending a week sleeping on a bunch of hay, he really was going to train his grandmother's dog to trip Web every time he walked by.

Again, the reality of the ranch didn't fit with what he'd imagined. He figured the barn or workshop or whatever would be steps away from the house. It wasn't.

Instead, once they cleared the trees along every side of the house except for the one with the huge windows, they walked out into a big expanse of open space. A ways off, there was a barn, another huge building with doors big enough to drive a city bus through and park it inside, and then a bit farther off from that were three small cabins, all but one of which looked like they were minutes away from being blown over by the wind.

He didn't usually have to hurry to keep up with anyone thanks to his long legs, but Stephanie had the stride of an NBA center and Hadley matched it.

"Trigger," hollered an older man walking out of the barn as they approached it. He hurried over, followed by two younger guys, and wrapped Hadley up in a huge hug that lifted her off the ground. Then he swung her around before setting her back down on her feet. "How was the drive?"

She cut a glance Will's way, and he expected

her to expose his whole car sickness humiliation, but instead of sharing the fact that he spent the drive nursing a ginger ale, she just said, "It was fine."

"You must be Hadley's boyfriend, good to meet you. I'm Gabe Martinez." The older man gave him a firm handshake while the guys who had to be Hadley's brothers just stood behind Gabe, their arms crossed, looking like the unwelcoming committee. "And the chatterboxes behind me are Knox and Weston."

"Nice to meet you," Will said as he held out his hand to the nearest unsmiling man in jeans and a cowboy hat.

After a second's hesitation, Knox accepted the handshake with a hard enough hold that Will's knuckles banged together. Careful to keep his expression neutral, he squeezed back, allowing himself just the smallest of smirks after the other man's eyes widened. After that, Will turned to Weston, who pulled Will into that manly back-slapping hug, his palms landing like blows from a sledgehammer.

"Watch yourself," Weston said, his voice low enough that there was no way it would carry beyond the two of them. "Fuck with her and I'll come all the way out to the east coast to kick your city ass. They don't call 'em shit kickers for nothing."

Before he could issue a retort, Weston stepped back in line with his brother and they both gave him matching glares that reminded him more than a little of a certain grumpy brunette who he was sure had designs on his brother's trust fund.

Hadley sent him a told-you-so smirk.

Okay, winning over those two might take a little work, but Will was up for it.

"Well, now that the introductions are out of the way," Stephanie said, "let's get you two where you're going."

He and Hadley followed Stephanie as she led them past the barn to one of the cabins.

"This was one of the ranch's original buildings, but Knox has been renovating it," Stephanie said, walking through the front door. "He hasn't started on the other three yet, but this one's done and it'll make a nice stand-alone place for him when he moves out of the main house. I'll hate to have him leave, but at least he won't be half a country away."

Zinger delivered, her mom gave them the general layout. The cabin wasn't big by any means, but there was a living room with a fireplace, galley kitchen, a bathroom, and a closed door at the end of the narrow hallway had to be the bedroom.

"So this is your place for the week," Stephanie said. "Towels are under the sink, sheets are on the bed, and the hot water heater is small so don't go taking any long showers."

"There's only one bedroom." Hadley, her eyes rounded, turned to her mom. "I thought Will would be staying in the barn."

"Nope, that's booked up, too. The older cousins are all up in the loft like it's a giant sleepover." Stephanie looked from her daughter to Will and back again. "Is there something you want to tell me, Hadley? I figured since you guys are close enough for you to bring him out here for the wedding, it would be okay. The couch folds out into a bed."

Okay, he'd already checked out the couch in the living room and even when it was transformed into a bed, his feet would be hanging off by at least a foot, but he'd live.

"This seems perfect to me," he said, draping his arm across Hadley's shoulders and twirling a strand of her silky brown hair around his finger. "Don't you think, Trigger?"

Hadley gave a stiff nod as she "accidentally" stepped on his foot again.

"Okay, I'll leave you two to it, then," Stephanie said, heading toward the front door. "Dinner's at six. Don't be late."

They held the pose until her mom was out of sight of the cabin's front window, and then they broke apart—not that there was really anywhere either could go. They were for all intents and purposes trapped together in a tiny cabin for the next week.

Hands on her hips, mouth formed into a flat line, Hadley didn't even give him the opportunity to say anything. "The couch is yours."

He had already been planning on taking the couch, but admitting that seemed like the wrong move in this game. So instead, he did the one thing that would drive her straight up the wall— he gave her a slow smile and tipped his hat in her direction. "Whatever you say."

If she had been anyone else, he would have

very much enjoyed the sight of her ass in those tight jeans as she turned in a huff and strutted down the hall. As it was, she was Hadley and he was Will and there was no common ground there—even for ass appreciation.

The last thing he expected was to see her marching back his way a few seconds later, looking like she was about to smite him. "There's no bed. The whole room is filled with Knox's tools and workbench."

Will glanced down at the couch that had just gone up in value about a million percent. He sat down on it lengthwise, his boots hanging over one armrest, and settled back, using the other armrest as a pillow. He tilted his hat down and closed his eyes.

"Guess you should've called the couch," he said, not bothering to hide his smirk.

CHAPTER SEVEN

Hadley cracked her eyes open. What parts of her body weren't heavy with sleep were aching from the uncomfortable crash of consciousness—calling it a nap was too generous—in the single overstuffed chair in the living room. She had no idea how much time had passed, but the sky had turned pinky orange and the scent of hamburgers on the grill was wafting in from the open window.

"Welcome back to the world of the not-currently-snoring," Will said from his spot on the couch. "I've never heard anything like it before. It was like the cross-harbor train was hiccupping but louder."

Ignoring the fact that his light-brown hair was mussed to just the right amount of took-a-nap-but-am-still-crazy-hot, the deep dimple in his cheek as he grinned at her, and the way his shirt clung to his muscular chest—okay, *mostly* ignoring it—she lifted her chin.

"I don't snore," she said, a declaration that probably would have carried more weight if she hadn't been trying to subtly dab at the drool on the corner of her mouth while she said it.

"I thought you might say that." He got up from

the couch and crossed over to her before squatting down next to her chair and holding out his phone so they could both see the screen. "That is why I recorded it."

He hit Play and—

Damn those tech people and their need to constantly improve the video quality of cell phones.

The image on the screen showed her with her mouth open wide enough to catch a swarm of horseflies, her hair going every which way, and a very distinctly glistening line of moisture going from her mouth to her chin. It was bad. It wasn't like grab-a-horse-and-ride-off-to-the-farthest-pasture-for-the-rest-of-eternity bad, but it was still very not good. Then it got worse because of course it did. Will clicked the volume control button and took the phone off mute and a low, loud, stuttering rumble of a snore filled the room.

Hadley closed her eyes, but it only made the snores louder in her head. Great. Exhaling, she opened her eyes and looked up at Mr. Bargain Bin Halloween Costume Cowboy himself. The big jerk was grinning down at her, his cute-boy dimple doing its best to distract from his evil nature.

She shrugged. "So it happened once."

Will slid his phone back in his front pocket— how there was enough room, considering how tightly they fit, she had no idea—and stood upright, his attention never straying from her face.

"By the end of the week, we'll know for sure," he said.

Ah yes, they were stuck sleeping together. Well, not *together*. They'd be in the same room—

one that was small enough that if she got up right now, she'd have no choice but to stand within touching distance of him.

Not that she wanted to touch him.

Ugh.

That was the last thing she wanted even if he had one section of hair in desperate need of being brushed back and a day's worth of scruff on his jaw that looked like it was the perfect mix of sandpaper and silk to the touch. Nope. She was keeping her hands to herself, clasped right in the middle of her lap, and her ass firmly planted on the damn uncomfortable chair because what had happened in the coat closet at the fundraiser had been an accident.

Pure chance.

Bad luck.

An obvious sign that she'd done something horrible in a previous life.

"I have no idea what's going on in that head of yours, but it looks like steam is about to come out of your ears." He leaned down and put his hands on the chair's armrests on either side of her. "You thinking about all the hot dreams you had of me?"

No!

But now she probably would be, damn her easily suggestible subconscious.

Not that she'd admit that the coat-closet kiss had been an *ahem* inspiration that might have— all right, had—required the purchasing of new batteries. The man's ego was out of control enough as it was. Plus with Will here, there was not enough privacy on the whole of Hidden Creek Ranch for her to use the vibrator she'd tucked into her suitcase. Somehow the man would figure it out. And he'd call her on it. And oh my God why was it getting so hot in here and why were her nipples suddenly so achingly hard?

Do you really need three cowboy guesses for that one, Hadley?

"We need to head out for dinner before Aunt Louise sends one of the cousins to see if we are doing something we aren't supposed to," she said, the words all coming out in one fast rush that still managed to sound breathy and desperate to her own ears.

There was no way Will would miss it—or the probable reason for her discomfort.

He stood up and took a step back, but the intensity of his attention remained on her like a yearned-for-but-unspoken-about touch. "You mean like finishing what we started in the coat closet?"

"That *is* finished." *Say it enough and it's gotta be true.*

His green-eyed gaze dipped down to her mouth, lingering and hot. "Too bad for me."

She exhaled a shaky breath. "Yes, it is."

His gaze flicked up to her eyes, and the air practically crackled between them. "I don't doubt that for a minute."

Needing to move before she reached out and did something dumb, she all but jumped up from the chair and started pacing in the small space, her heart hammering against her ribs as desire threaded through her, warm and addicting. "Why are you saying things like that? There's no one here to see it."

He cocked his head to the side, genuine curiosity softening his hard features. "Don't people just flirt with you for fun, not because there's an audience?"

She snorted. "No."

He stepped into her path, forcing her to stop walking or ram right into his hard chest. "Why not?"

A million reasons. She was too bitchy, too mousy, too soft, too hard, too round, too flat, too loud, too quiet, too country, too out of place in the world she thought she'd wanted to be a part of since she was a kid decorating her room with pictures of Harbor City. No matter the reason, she wasn't the type of woman people flirted with. She was the one they usually ignored—except for Web. He hadn't flirted; there was none of that between them, but she hadn't felt that tug with him anyway. It really had been the weird kind of instant friendship that sometimes happened where after five minutes it was like she'd known him forever.

She was saved from any of that spilling out, though, by the knock at the door that had to be a cousin sent by Aunt Louise to find out what was holding them up—and, therefore, everyone's dinner.

Hadley switched directions and headed toward the door. "We've gotta go."

"I want to finish this conversation later," Will said.

"It's good to want things," she responded as she yanked open the front door and nearly plowed into her cousin Marco in her hurry to put some space between her and the Evil Twin.

She didn't run off the porch after that. She was a grown adult woman and didn't run away from uncomfortable truths. No. She quick-walked because hamburgers on the grill meant baked potatoes, corn on the cob, and German potato salad along with no-bake cookies and homemade popcorn balls. It would be heaven on a paper plate. Her speed had nothing to do with getting out of the cabin before that man tempted her any more and she did something foolish. Nope. Not a damn thing.

• • •

Will settled in next to Hadley at one of the three picnic tables behind the main house. Everyone was talking and laughing as they carried their plates loaded down with food and grabbed a can of beer or pop, as all the Donavan-Martinezes had called soda, from the gigantic cooler. Well, all of the family members were, with the exception of Adalyn, who was standing off to the side of the house, talking on her phone and looking like she just might nut whoever was on the other end of the line.

"So," Gabe said in between bites of a delicious-looking burger that was the size of a small country. "Hadley was telling us that you secretly wanted to learn how to be a cowboy."

Of course she was. He wouldn't expect anything less—anything to get under his skin. If she wasn't trying to set his brother up for a seven-figure sucker punch, he'd probably admire her for it.

"I'm not sure those were my exact words?"

"Don't be shy," Hadley said with a sweet smile he knew meant anything but good things. "You said you couldn't wait to learn how to be a real cowboy."

Oh, she was playing dirty.

"That would be great," Will said. "But don't tell them *all* my secrets, darlin'."

A hint of pink touched her cheeks, highlighting the freckles across her nose that he hadn't noticed before. "Not *all* of them."

"Oh yeah," Knox said as he slathered butter over his corn on the cob. "Just the ones about your pure-gold toilet and ten ex-wives."

Will almost flinched, but years of going toe to toe during cutthroat business negotiations when Holt Enterprises had been on the verge of collapse had taught him to keep his outward reactions in check. He covered with his usual cocky nonchalance. "Regular toilet and only one ex-fiancée."

Next to him, Hadley stiffened. "You were engaged?"

"Only for a few months." All but seven days of which had been a living hell once he'd realized how he'd not only fallen for a shark, he'd nearly lost the family business and most of his money. "Turned out she loved my bank account quite a bit more than she loved me."

Hadley pursed her full lips and looked down at the half-eaten burger on her plate. More than likely she was trying to figure out how she'd have to change her run at Web, since it was harder to play a mark if someone watching out for them had been in the game before.

That's right, darling. Get ready. I'm coming for you, and you might as well realize it now.

Will didn't knock Web for not realizing why his new friend was acting the way she was. His brother wasn't soft, but he was trusting. He looked at the world and saw only the possibilities, which was why he headed up the family foundation while Will had taken over the family business and the mantle as the head of the family. He'd gone into Holt Enterprises, saw the shit it was in financially, and had done everything he had to in order to set it right again. He'd learned to read the room at a glance so he could push through his vision when no one thought he had the experience or the know-how to turn the company around. He'd learned how to gauge the mood of the worriers on the company's board of directors so he could tailor his message to allay their fears. He'd discovered how to spot a competitor's tell; then he'd hit them in their softest point during negotiations so he could swoop in and turn that to his advantage. He'd figured out—too late, he'd admit to himself—how to detect the truth (given rarely) and ferret out the lie (the more common human response).

And that skill was how he'd first figured out

that Hadley was up to something. Web may not have noticed the little fibs, the conversational diversions, and her general shadiness, but Will had, and he wasn't about to forget it just because Hadley knocked him off-balance every damn time he saw her. It didn't matter, though, because he was on to her.

"I was young," Will said, flashing an it's-no-big-deal smile at the table even while his hands were curled into fists in his lap. "Live and learn."

Gabe nodded and looked over at his wife, his gaze softening. "There's something to be said for life experience."

Stephanie chuckled, the hard-ass Will had met this afternoon transforming into…still a hard-ass but one with the edges rounded a bit. "And a willingness not to run for the hills when the woman you asked for coffee blurts out that she has four kids at home."

"Any man who'd do that is an idiot," Gabe said, looking at Stephanie as if she were the only other person in the world. "And I'm grateful for each and every one of their dumb asses."

"Language," she said, but there wasn't any heat in the objection.

Gabe shrugged. "Guess how much I love you just gets the best of me sometimes."

Knox let out a melodramatic groan that would have marked him as the youngest even if he didn't have a baby face. "We are sitting right here, you know."

Gabe didn't even bother to look over at his youngest stepson. "So you should look away, because I'm gonna kiss your mom now."

And he did, a quick kiss that left Stephanie hazy-eyed. Will tried to remember a time before his parents died when they'd ever held hands, let alone kissed. He couldn't. They weren't physically affectionate people when it came to each other or their kids. No doubt they would have seen the kiss between Hadley's parents as gauche.

Cutting a look to the side, he tried to gauge Hadley's reaction. Like the rest of her family, she was rolling her eyes at the PDA, but the upward curl of her lips gave away her true feelings. The only person who wasn't watching the interaction between Stephanie and Gabe without an indulgent smile was Adalyn, who'd finished her call and joined them at the table.

She let out a sigh. "Looks like Derek won't be able to make it down for a few more days. His boss has him practically chained to the desk," Adalyn said. "So what did I miss?"

"The usual old-people PDA with Mom and Dad," Weston said.

Knox sat up straighter and leaned forward. "And Will here wants to learn how to be a cowboy."

Adalyn looked at him and shook her head. "I'm sure Knox and Weston can help you out there. I'd do it, but the wedding stuff has me out of the saddle until after the honeymoon."

"Hadley couldn't show me the ropes?" It really would be the perfect revenge for pawning him off on her brothers.

Everyone at the table—including Hadley—

laughed at that.

"Hadley is pretty much a town-only kind of person," Weston said. "But I'm sure Knox and I could teach you a thing or two. You're not afraid of a little hard work, are you?"

The smug, raised-eyebrow, hey-city-slicker look Hadley's oldest brother gave him telegraphed all too clearly exactly how much work the brothers thought he did. If they only knew. His days may not be as physical as theirs, but he was still up at four, in the office by six, and after that it was in back-to-back meetings until dinner, schmoozing potential investment partners until he got home and fell asleep reading emails in bed at around midnight.

"Hard work has never scared me," Will said.

"Great," Weston said with a curt nod. "We'll start in the morning. Be ready by dawn, and we'll take you out on snipe patrol."

Out of the corner of his eye, he caught Hadley glaring at her brothers. Of course she didn't want him to win their sorta bet that her family would fall in love with him. Well, she was going to have to get used to losing on that front, too, because Will always won—no matter what.

Stephanie cleared her throat, silencing everyone at the table. "Not tomorrow, I'm going to need Hadley and Will to go on down and get PawPaw for the wedding festivities."

Was that a dog? A peg-legged possum? He was about to ask a follow-up question when he noticed Hadley's glare had transformed into a shit-eating grin that would look perfectly in place on a lottery winner's face.

"You don't mind coming with me to get my granddad, right?" she asked. "For some fun family togetherness?"

The sweetness in her tone should have warned him about the trouble ahead, but the always-needs-to-know-the-answer part of his brain had just taken a hit of that's-the-answer dopamine. "No problem—anything for you."

"So sweet," Hadley said, resting her head on his shoulder and really playing up the fake-girlfriend role. "It's only a three-hour drive down there, so we should be fine to leave in the morning and be back home by dinner."

Fuck me.

She got him. Again. There was no way to back out of it now without admitting weakness—a definite not-gonna-happen if there had ever been one. He'd concede this battle to her, but she'd better enjoy this victory while she could, because it was going to be her last one.

And that determination made it all the way through dinner, toasts to the bride-to-be, and Adalyn's favorite dessert—s'mores over the firepit. However, as soon as they got back to the cabin and he saw Hadley's shoulders slump at the sight of the chair she'd napped in, he gave in—for strategic purposes, of course. It was smart to keep your competition off-kilter by throwing some no-strings-attached free will every once in a while.

"You can have the pull-out."

Now, this was where she'd feign protest for politeness's sake—that fake generosity would be the smart move for someone trying to slyly move in on his brother for all the dollars in his bank account.

Hadley didn't even hesitate before grabbing ahold of her suitcase and rolling it behind her as she walked down the short hall toward the bathroom. "We'll take turns. Me tonight, you tomorrow when we get back from driving PawPaw home."

With her, it was always what he didn't expect. Just like how she'd managed to get him to agree to another gut-wrenching drive. "You set me up with that."

"I did," she said, glancing over her shoulder and winking at him.

Will was in a pair of sleep pants and brushing his teeth over the kitchen sink when Hadley sauntered back into the living room in a silky red tank top and matching shorts trimmed in lace. Most of his blood went south before the realization settled in that she'd packed those pajamas thinking it would be his brother who'd see them.

A good man would have pulled himself back from the edge and remembered a gold digger played the long con. He recalled that last bit all right, but he was still balancing right there on the edge of lust and loathing without a clue which side to fall on, while he watched her set up the fold-out bed and slip between the sheets already on it and promptly closing her eyes without ever looking his way or uttering a single *good night*. He would have thought he would have gotten his ability to breathe back again, but no.

"You gonna turn out the light?" she asked in a bored tone, "or are you just standing there in the kitchen with a mouth full of toothpaste and staring at me while I'm sleeping—because that's not creepy at all."

Face hot at getting caught, he swallowed the toothpaste without thinking. It tasted like mint-flavored poor choices. "I'll be done in a second."

She didn't answer, just rolled over and tucked the sheet up high under her chin. By the time he kicked his boots under the pull-out mattress so he didn't trip over them in the middle of the night and sat down in the chair, Hadley's breathing had already evened out as she slept. Without the usual annoyed expression she wore when she saw him, she looked softer, sweeter, somehow even sexier than usual. Hell, she looked every bit like she was the kindhearted person she presented around Web. But she wasn't. And Will couldn't—Web couldn't—afford to forget that.

CHAPTER EIGHT

Will's neck was never going to be the same.

As he sat up, he rolled his neck and shoulders, working out the aches from sleeping mostly upright in a chair that was about as comfortable as the middle of the back seat of a subcompact car. Sunshine cut through the blinds in the cabin's big front window, landing in a bright puddle in the middle of the empty pull-out bed. The sheet was still a twisted, rumpled mess, as if she'd slept about as well as he had—but there was no Hadley in sight.

That probably wasn't a bad thing, considering he'd seen plenty of her in his dreams—correction, his nightmares last night. And in every single one of them, she'd been wearing those silky little pajamas, and the strap holding her top in place kept slipping off her shoulder. It was just enough to give him a perma-hard-on while he slept, but that was it. Thank God.

"So are you sure everything is going okay in Harbor City?" Hadley's mom's voice filtered in from the porch through the half-opened front door. "I worry about you being out there all alone."

"I'm not alone," Hadley said softly. "I have friends and a job I love doing, if not the people I do it with."

"And now you have Will," Stephanie said.

Feeling like some kind of cartoon villain, Will tiptoed over to the window, getting almost there before his little toe got snagged on the foot of the pull-out bed. He kept moving forward but his toe went backward and the stupid iron bar stayed in place. Pain shot up his leg and he clamped his jaw shut to keep from yelling out, reflexively lifting his leg and spinning around.

That's when he saw it. Immediately, he froze with his injured foot in the air and fear clamping down on his balls.

Snuggled inside the tangled sheets bathed in a pool of sunshine was a fox or a coyote or a baby wolf or an alien animal that only lived on this ranch. Hell, this could be the snipe Knox and Weston had been talking about last night at dinner, even though he knew, like the rest of the world with internet, that they weren't real. This thing, though, was very real, even if he had no clue what it was. All he knew was it was an animal he'd never seen in any of the Harbor City parks. About the size of a cat, it was gray with orange on its sides. It flicked its bushy tail, the black tip landing right up against its snout. It had one yellow eye cracked open and was staring right at Will. Its lips curled back, revealing pointy little teeth, and let out a low growl.

Cold panic slid down Will's spine. "It's okay, boy," he said, holding up his hands while still balanced on one foot. "I'm allowed to be here."

The low growl turned into a medium one.

"Hadley," he hollered, not sure if this was a pet or a rabid animal ready to rip his face off. "I think I might have found the snipe your brothers were going hunting to find."

The front door opened and Hadley walked in. She was still in her pajamas, her long brown hair pulled into a high ponytail that bounced as she moved. She took one look at him frozen in place with his hands out, his right foot off the ground, and what he was pretty damn sure was a very manly look of pure fucking what-the-hell on his face before breaking out into giggles.

"That's not a snipe," she said, her arms wrapped around her belly. "It's Lightning."

"What is a lightning?"

"He's a greedy old swift fox who would steal the hard-boiled egg off your breakfast dish and poop on whatever he claims is his, but he wouldn't bite you," she said, coming closer and scratching the fox behind the ears. "Gabe found him as a tod years ago after he'd been injured protecting his sister, who'd gotten cornered by a coyote. She made it. Lightning lost a leg, but thanks to Gabe's quick thinking, he survived. He's been coming and going of his own free will since then."

Right on cue, the fox got up on his three legs, pulled off a perfect downward dog, and then leaped off the bed before trotting past Stephanie and out of the now fully opened front door.

"He's not aggressive," Hadley said. "He's just a geriatric three-legged friendly thief who always finds a way to sneak in, and he's gone now, so you can go ahead and put your foot down."

Will lowered his foot, trying to ignore the way Hadley was grinning at him and the you-poor-thing expression on her mom's face.

"Morning, Stephanie," he said, feeling like twelve kinds of ridiculous.

If Web were here, Will never would have heard the end of it. He'd be getting fox gifts for the rest of his life.

"Morning," Stephanie said. "I was just telling Hadley that breakfast will be ready at the main house in about half an hour so you two can have some before getting on the road."

Oh yes. The three-hour drive. Just when he'd thought the low point of his day was going to be thinking a possibly rabid three-legged fox was going to eat him. It was past time he got out of here so everyone could more easily pretend this morning had never happened.

"I'm going to go ahead and shower now," he said, grabbing his grooming kit and heading down the hallway, ignoring Hadley's satisfied little smirk.

A few minutes later, under the steaming-hot water coming out of the showerhead, Will was not still ignoring the triumphant look on her face. Fuck. He wished he was. Instead, he couldn't get the sight of her hard nipples pressing against her tank top when she'd walked in from the porch out of his head. There was no way he could spend three hours in the car with her wondering what sound she'd make if he rolled them between his fingers as she lay naked beneath him.

Get it together, Holt.

Right then, though, under the merciless spray, with both hands pressed firmly against the tile wall in an effort not to give in to the lust riding him hard, he didn't give a shit. He wanted her. He wanted to see her go soft and wanting, he wanted to feel her squeeze him tight as she came, he wanted… Christ, he just fucking wanted.

Telling himself—just like he had the other times he'd come thinking about Hadley—that it would just be this once, he curled his soapy hand around his hard cock, stroking up and down slowly, as if that were going to offer any relief at all. What he needed was a tight grip—her grip—around him, teasing him, drawing the pleasure out, knocking him nearly to his knees with want.

This wasn't right. He couldn't stop. He didn't want to.

So with a long exhale, he closed his eyes and pictured her mouth swollen from kisses like it had been that night in the coat closet. His balls tightened and lifted as he sped up his strokes and imagined it was Hadley jerking him off while she told him how wet she was in a low, throaty whisper. Fist flying up and down his length as images of her flew through his mind, he edged closer and closer to coming. Her head tossed back as she laughed. The sway of her hips as she strutted across the room. The absolute joy in her eyes when she got the best of him yet again. He bit down, grinding his molars together, to keep the involuntary moans from escaping as the pressure built.

She was dangerous.

She was the enemy.

She was his brother's friend, in it only for the potential payoff.

Still, Will wanted her. It was a need he couldn't seem to shake. And in that half of a breath between his body locking in anticipation of the inevitable and his orgasm hitting, he was in the coat closet with her again. Only this time when she looked up at him, instead of saying his brother's name, she said "Will." Then everything went dark as white-hot pleasure shot through him.

Breathing hard, Will opened his eyes and redirected the shower spray to the wall. There wouldn't be any evidence left for Hadley to find, but that didn't change the fact that he knew what he'd done—and that he was pretty damn sure he'd do it again.

He had to get this woman out of his life—out of Web's life—for both of their good.

Rushing through the rest of his shower, he went through all of Hadley's suspicious behavior that had added up to reveal her true motives. The way she'd insinuated herself into Web's orbit so suddenly, there was no way it had been an accident. How she politely objected to Web picking up her tabs around town but then always gave in.

The fact that she avoided sharing any information about her family or where she'd come from with anyone but Web—okay, at least not with Will. Her unsubtle hints about how nice it would be to live "the good life" of someone who didn't have to worry about cash flow.

Then there were all her ideas about the Holt Foundation and how its charitable efforts could be improved. She'd obviously done her homework on his brother, investigating until she found out what made him tick and how much he really, honestly cared about helping people with the foundation. Really, she was following the same path Mia had with him, right down to acting like she gave a shit about his work. There must be a gold-digger playbook somewhere that outlined it all.

By the time he'd wrapped the towel around his waist and had finished mentally cursing himself for forgetting to bring fresh clothes into the bathroom with him, he was back to his regular self, no longer obsessed with how much he wanted Hadley. Determination renewed, he opened the door and strode out, nearly running down the woman haunting him.

"Oh, sorry," she said, jumping back. "I didn't mean…"

Her words died off as her gaze traveled over him, not missing a single inch of bare skin. Lust, tangible as the towel he was holding in place with one hand, rolled off her in waves, tempting him beyond measure. The way she bit down on her bottom lip as her brown eyes darkened didn't do a damn thing to help him maintain his equilibrium around her. He glanced down, clocking her towel and change of clothes. No doubt she'd been about to knock to see if the shower was free yet.

She'd be naked under the water soon. Hands soapy. Body wet. Alone only for a few minutes. Would she take advantage of the privacy, too?

"Bathroom's all yours," he said, his voice sounding rougher than he meant it to as he stepped out of the still-steamy room so she could walk in.

She paused just inside the bathroom, her hand on the door. "I put your suitcase in the bedroom so you can get dressed without having to worry about someone walking in."

He nodded, not sure he could do more than that at the moment. "Thanks."

One long, lingering look later, she closed the door, leaving him alone in the hallway, already halfway to forgetting why he was here.

Fuck. He was in so much trouble.

• • •

The drive had seemed like a better idea last night. Now all Hadley could picture as they sped down the stick-straight highway was the water droplets clinging to the dusting of hair on Will's obnoxiously well-muscled pecs. If it had been anyone else, she wouldn't have had a moment's hesitation. Her panties would have been floor-bound.

But, *of course*, it had to be Will.

And, *of course*, the towel he'd had wrapped around his hips had been deliciously small.

So that meant, *of course*, she'd just spent her entire shower weighing the benefit of masturbating and releasing all that totally inappropriate tension versus the just-her-luck likelihood that she'd slip at exactly the wrong moment and would be found— by Will—knocked out cold on the shower floor with her fingers on her clit.

In her moment of shower indecision this morning, she'd opted for imagined dignity over orgasmic relief. Regrets? Oh yeah, she had lots. All of which added up to her being overwhelmingly horny and stuck in a car for three hours with the man she totally hated all while she couldn't help thinking about all the ways she'd climb him like a tree if given the chance.

But lucky her, she only had an hour and a half left of the three-hour drive with a guy who—she glanced over from the corner of her vision—was starting to turn green and had a white-knuckle grip on the can of ginger ale he'd grabbed from her mom's fridge. Good. He was her nemesis and he could stand to be as miserable as he'd made her after *the incident*.

So Hadley kept her mouth shut, just as it had been since they got into the car and she turned on her playlist. *Still…* Guilt started to pluck at her resolve. *Still…* Yes, he was an asshole; everyone who met him would probably agree to that. *Still…* She started to scan the highway signs for just how many miles were left until The Stop Inn so Will could get out of the car for a few minutes and his stomach could settle.

Why? Because she was still salty about what had happened after *the incident*—and she had every right to be.

Seriously, she had former coworkers who were no doubt repeating what Will had said about what a loser she was to potential clients, which meant when she started her own consulting firm—and damn it, she was going to do that—there was no way she'd ever land their accounts.

If being single in the city didn't already have her mom worried, being unemployed and single in the city would send the woman into a flurry of criticizing-out-of-love activity. That was exactly why she gave her mom and everyone else in her family a very *curated* idea of what was going on in her life. Everything was fine. Always. No complaints. No whining. Absolutely no failure.

"Hadley," Will said, sounding less like a multimillionaire from birth and more like someone on the verge of losing his breakfast. "Can you stop for a minute?"

"Are you going to puke?"

"No." The denial would have come across more believable if he hadn't said it while wincing in misery.

"You look like you're going to puke." Did she have to poke him at this moment? Probably not, but she needed to distract him until she got to the next exit.

He flexed his jaw and stared up at the car's ceiling with an intensity that bordered on desperation. "I do not do a damn thing I don't want to."

Bypassing her blinker—there wasn't a car around for miles—she turned right onto the main street of the blink-and-you-miss-it town of Myrtle. "Spoken with the determination someone would expect from the likes of Will Percival Holt, the youngest CEO of Holt Enterprises in five generations and the wonder of the stock market."

"How do you know my middle name?" he asked, sitting up straighter and pivoting in his seat to look at her.

"I told Web he had the dorkiest middle name ever, and he corrected me."

"That really hurts, Trigger." A half smile curled one side of his mouth upward. "I'm not going to puke."

He sounded more confident that time—maybe because she'd pulled into the parking lot of a gas station / grocery / diner called The Stop Inn.

"Whatever you say, Percival. Let's get you some fresh air and after I pick up my sister's wedding gift, we can get you another ginger ale." She cut the engine and took a better look at him. The man was definitely close to the color of day-old guacamole. "And maybe some Dramamine."

He looked around and then stared back at her, total confusion making his forehead wrinkle. "You're buying a wedding present at a gas station?"

"This isn't just any gas station. It's The Stop Inn." Not that she expected him to understand what that meant, but for her entire high school life, this place had been about as close to magic as it got.

When a person grew up in the sticks, there were limited entertainment options. They could cruise up and down Main Street. They could have beers and a bonfire in someone's back pasture.

They could come to The Stop Inn for coffee that
was more non-dairy creamer than java and make
detailed plans of exactly how they were going to
escape their small town. She didn't have to glance
over at Will to know he didn't get it. How could
he? He grew up rich in the big city where his
every want was granted.

"And The Stop Inn means?" he asked, following her inside.

The smile that broke out on her face started in
her heart. "Stacey and Kristine."

. . .

Maybe Will should have been more worried when
he heard the chain saw, but he was so damn glad
to be out of the car that not even the fact that he
was walking through an aisle of cinnamon-scented
car air fresheners located right next to porcelain
figurines of semis being driven by reindeer while
Santa's sleigh was on the roof made him think
twice. Plus, there was the fact that he couldn't stop
sneaking looks at Hadley's perfect round ass as he
followed her through the gift shop part of the
building that also contained a small diner
complete with bright-yellow Formica tables. It
wasn't until they were past the novelty T-shirts
that said things like *Country Built* and *Farm
Tough* that the unmistakable revving he'd only
heard in horror movies sounded. And when
Hadley walked through a glass door hidden
behind the sign labeled TRUCKER SHOWER ONLY,
the noise hit him in the face loud enough to make

his teeth rattle.

A rangy woman with a military-grade short haircut was wielding the chain saw, going at a large log that looked like a half-carved bear. She wore a band T-shirt with the sleeves cut off and the kind of safety goggles he hadn't seen since he'd done chemistry experiments in boarding school. As soon as they cleared the doorway into what seemed to be a courtyard with a huge steel building on one end, he and Hadley walked around so she was in the other woman's line of sight.

A slow smile curled the woman's mouth upward and she turned off the chain saw, laid it down, and raised her safety goggles onto her forehead. "Trigger?"

"Stacey!" Hadley crossed over and gave the other woman a hug. "It's been forever."

"Too long for sure. Hey, Kristine," the woman yelled in the general direction of the big outbuilding. "Come look what the cat dragged in." A second woman, hair pulled into a tight ponytail, came out of the building and took one look at Hadley before breaking into a quick jog and joining in on the hug. After that, it was the kind of rush of talking only old friends had, a sort of coded language like he had with Web—except with these three, it was punctuated by giggles, hugs, and something about getting caught breaking curfew. Hadley showed off a few pictures on her phone of Harbor City while the other women held hands and oohed and ahhed at the appropriate intervals.

Once the three of them finally took a breath, Kristine turned around and gave him an assessing look. "So are you going to introduce us?"

Hadley stepped closer to him, pulling him into the trio's gravitational pull. "This is my friend Will Holt. He came with me for Adalyn's wedding. Will, these are two of my oldest friends, Stacey and Kristine Van Camp."

He shook the other women's hands, and then they all went over to a porch outside the huge building, where there was a pitcher of tea and a cooler filled with ice and sodas.

"You reliving old high school memories coming all the way out here?" Stacey asked after they'd all caught up.

"Actually, we were on our way to get PawPaw, and I was hoping to buy the perfect wedding present for Adalyn. She's been searching for just the right hope chest for a while, and I figured you two might have something in stock."

Kristine nodded. "We picked up a few in an estate auction out in Central Kansas. They'd be over in the furniture section. Go on and look your fill. You know we'll give you the family discount."

Will followed Hadley past the huge dragons, wolves, and deer carved out of wood and into a building roughly the size of the big barn on her parents' ranch. It took him a second for his eyes to adjust after coming in from the bright sunshine. Once he did, though, his jaw fell open. The place was huge and filled with what had to be half a million dollars' worth of oddities and antiques, all in various states of refinishing.

"What is this place?" he asked. "Is that an iron lung?"

Hadley followed his gaze to the big metal tube. "I think it is."

Of all the things he'd expected to see in flyover country, he never pictured a collection like this. There were wagons, Victorian-era furniture, what looked like an actual buckskin suit, and family photographs that had to date back from the pioneer days.

"Who are these people?"

Hadley started off toward the far corner of the building to the area that had furniture. "Stacey and Kristine ended up at an estate auction by accident on their honeymoon and they got hooked on finding unique pieces. They got so much good stuff that they opened up an online shop and ship their finds out to places around the world. It's the perfect place to get something unique for Adalyn. Help me look through the hope chests and see if you can find one that doesn't top a hundred dollars."

Less than a hundred dollars? Ouch. Everyone knew the more expensive the gift, the more love there was behind it. That's why every holiday from boarding school, he and Web came home to extravagant gifts from their grandmother, even if she had to spend the holiday elsewhere. She said what she needed to say with cash, not hugs. "I thought you liked your sister."

Hadley shot him a no-duh look. "I love her."

"So shouldn't you be spending more on her wedding gift than a piece of old random stuff from a high school friend's garage?" How else was she going to know?

"Number one, who in the world bases how much people love you on how much they spend on gifts?" She must have seen the truth on his face because she wrinkled her nose in disbelief and then shook her head with a pitying sigh. "And that works for you? Does expensive stuff make you feel loved?"

What the hell? Why was she making him feel so weird about how the world worked? "It's just the way things are."

She scoffed. "Not everyone judges things by the price tag."

"You're saying you'd work for free?" Not likely. Who in the hell would take that kind of sucker's bet?

"If I could, yes. I love what I do. I get to help great causes that really do make a difference for people. If I hit the lottery, I'd start my own foundation so I could fund those things. Well, that and I'd make sure my family was taken care of. Ranching has been good to them, but you never know when an early ice storm or a hundred-year flood is going to change everything."

Yeah, that was a likely story. If it were true, she was the one in a million who'd actually go through with it. He'd spent too much time in his life rubbing elbows at fundraisers to believe that for the vast majority of people, their donations were anything but a tax write-off. It all came down to the bottom line. Everything had a price tag. Even the dark-brown wooden hope chest she was trying to pick up.

"Can I help?" He waited for her to agree and then lifted the dark wood box the size of an office moving box. That's when he saw it. It had horns, was plugged into the wall, and stood surrounded by old gym mats. "What is that?"

Hadley followed his gaze and then let out an evil chuckle that would have done the Grinch proud. "The perfect way for you to earn some of the cowboy cred you bet me you'd earn by the end of this trip."

By riding one of those bucking bronco machines? "You're not serious."

She smiled up at him, more of a dare than any form of encouragement. It was like pouring gas on a fire. He just about went up in flames.

Hadley winked at him. "Time to cowboy up."

"And what does that mean?"

"Doing the thing that may be a little uncomfortable, but it's the right thing to do, and you'll be glad as hell afterward that you did."

He didn't believe that definition for a second—more than likely it was all about making a fool of him, but he let himself be suckered in anyway. "Fine." He strolled over, as if there was nothing weird about riding what was basically a metal tube covered in fake cowhide that was hooked up to a motor. "Let's do this."

Really, how was this even hard?

"You sure you know what to do?" She had that look on her face, the one that said he was going to land on his ass.

There was no way in hell he was backing down

now. "I hold on to the sticky-up part of the saddle with one hand and don't fall off. Is there more to it than that?"

She let out a sudden cough that sounded a lot like a strangled laugh. "Nope. That's pretty much it."

Shoving the unease down with an extra dose of forced confidence, he strutted over to the bull. He put one foot in the stirrup and pulled himself up, then threw one leg over to the other side. Fucking A, he'd lost the plot. He was supposed to be destroying Hadley's plan to fleece his brother, not riding a motorized cow. Before he could change his mind, though, Hadley started counting down.

"Three."

His heart rate jumped to oh-my-God-what-are-you-doing-Holt levels of speed.

"Two."

He grasped the standup part of the saddle with a suddenly clammy hand.

"One."

He had about two seconds of rocking back and forth like a teacup ride run by a drunk carny before it sped up and the laws of physics jerked him out of the saddle and dropped him in the pile of blankets surrounding the mechanical bull.

"Ready to give in?" she asked from her spot by the on-and-off switch, a grin transforming her face to one of unadulterated joy.

Never. The surety of privilege and a lifetime of always getting his way because he never gave up revved inside him like the purr of a race car's motor. He didn't give in. He didn't admit failure, let alone that he'd made a bad call.

He stood up and started back to the bull, determination in every step. "I'll get it this time."

Fifteen minutes and not a single solitary successful eight-second ride later, and Hadley was flipping through the pictures on her phone and giggling. He couldn't help but chuckle along with her, despite his now-sore ass.

She held up her phone so he could see the screen. "I could sell that picture for a million dollars."

It was a joke, he knew that, but it was the perfect reminder of why he was here in the first place.

"Now, let's get that Dramamine and ginger ale."

"Look at you being all devoted, just like a real girlfriend," Will said, trying to sound nonchalant when he wasn't feeling it at all.

"More like watching out for you so Web doesn't kill me for breaking the big family CEO."

"Web wouldn't hold a grudge, and our grandmother is the only other relative. She'd probably strong-arm the board of directors into selling the company off. It's not like we're close."

Try as he might, he couldn't keep the undercurrent of something prickly out of his tone. He strode a little too fast to the gas station / grocery / diner's door and yanked it open, standing to the side so she could go in first. Hadley brushed her hands on the sides of her jeans and walked inside, giving him a smile of thanks as she passed by. If she was any other woman, he'd think twice about that look on her face, but he couldn't. The best thing he could do right now was put an end to this little truce of theirs before he forgot his mission completely.

They made their way to the sodas chilling in the back. He grabbed two ginger ales and offered her one.

"You make it seem as if you and Web rarely see your grandma," she said after they paid for their drinks. "That's hard to even wrap my brain around. I mean, mine live half a country away, but it still feels like they are constantly involved in my life. Plus, you guys were just at the family compound."

"Web and I were, but our grandma was not." And there it was, the fishing for information. She was subtler about it than Mia, but there was no doubt in his mind that she was on a mission just as much as he was. He stalked over to the cash register. "Her yearly visit isn't until she stops in for fashion week in the fall."

He walked out of the gas station / grocery / diner so fast, she had to practically jog to keep up.

"I don't understand," she said, pointing the key fob at the rental and clicking the unlock button.

"Maybe you're not supposed to." For the first time since the conversation had taken such a weird turn, he looked over at her, letting his expression be as hard and unforgiving as he wished he felt inside. "It's not like it's your family. It's not like you'll be a part of it, which begs the question: why are you so interested in who is involved in Holt Enterprises and how our family works? Why the interrogation, Hadley?"

Her eyes rounded. "I'm just making conversation."

"Or gathering intel." He jerked the door open and got into the car.

For a moment, all Hadley did was stand there with her mouth hanging open, staring at the spot where Will had been. Then she marched over to the car, the gravel in the parking lot crunching under her shoes, and yanked open the car door before sliding in behind the wheel, keys held tightly in her grip.

"What in the hell was that supposed to mean?" she asked.

He snorted and didn't even bother to look her way. "It's always better to know everything about a target before you strike."

"The gold-digger thing? Again?" She let out a frustrated groan. "You have got to put that to rest, because you couldn't be more wrong. You ever think that Web and I are friends because he's not you?"

Exactly. He wasn't Web. He was more cynical, more experienced with deceptions and people going after him for money. Everyone did. The photographers wanting exclusive pictures. Their grandmother valuing the family money above all else. Mia and her brazen cash grab.

"We have another hour and a half to go." Hadley shoved the key in the ignition and turned it with more force than necessary. "How about we just get it out of the way, get PawPaw, and get back to the ranch so you can go try to learn to be a cowboy and I won't have to see you."

"Sounds good to me," he said, popping the top of his ginger ale.

The faster they made it to her pawpaw and then got back on the road so this endless road trip could be over, the better. There was not anything that would get him to deviate from that course.

CHAPTER NINE

After an hour and a half of the world's shittiest music—somewhere there was a crappy coffee house missing its fuck-everyone acoustic playlist—Will breathed a sigh of relief as they pulled into the guest parking lot at the Sandhills Senior Living Village. The village was actually a four-building apartment complex with a clubhouse, pool, and large green area with walking paths and a working community garden.

When they got out of the car and headed for the double glass doors of the clubhouse, Hadley still wasn't speaking to him. That was just fine with him, because it only showed that she was pissed for getting caught sticking her nose where it didn't belong. He couldn't fault her for trying. Information was power—especially when it came to someone trying to worm their way into another person's life.

Mia had done her research when it came to him. It wasn't until after everything blew up that Will had discovered just how much legwork she'd done. His grandmother. The majority of Holt Enterprises' board of directors. Former girlfriends. Shit, even the doorman at his building had been the target of one of Mia's flirty interrogations.

They were both fast-walking for the door at the same time—no doubt she was as determined to win as he was—when it burst open and an older man flanked by two women walked out. After giving each of them a quick kiss on the cheek, the older man walked toward Will and Hadley with a huge smile on his face. He was lean and leathery, with a shock of white hair cut close. He had a swagger that had either come from a lifetime of riding horses or successfully charming women— possibly both. As soon as he was within arm's reach of Hadley, he wrapped her up in a hug.

"Trigger, what in the world are you doing here?" he asked, taking a step back. "You look like you're ready to take on the world per usual. I hope I'm not the one you're gearing up to do battle with."

"Nope, just doing Mom's bidding," Hadley said with a chuckle. "You ready to head out?"

"I thought you weren't coming until tomorrow," PawPaw said as he turned to Will and held out his huge meat hook of a hand, complete with well-earned callouses that hadn't gone away even though the man had to be in his late seventies or early eighties. "You must be her special friend, Web."

"That would be me, but everyone calls me Will."

"Good to meet someone else whose name isn't their name. My real name is Paul but this one"— he hooked a thumb at Hadley—"couldn't quite manage Grandpa Paul when she was little so she started saying PawPaw, and it stuck."

"She does like to get her way," Will said, smiling at her as if that was just an adorable quirk of her personality.

"Ain't that the truth," PawPaw said with a shrug. "But unfortunately, I can't give in on leaving today. It's the Summer of Love dance tonight. I broke out my tie-dye. Plus, Marion, Alice, and Cat would skin me alive if I ditched them."

"You have three dates?" Will asked.

"Do you know what the ratio of men to women is in a place like this?" PawPaw leaned in close and said in a stage whisper, "Very good odds, if you get my drift. I do better than others because I still have my original hips—which tends to come in pretty damn handy."

Okay, that was more information than he needed, but good for PawPaw. He glanced over at Hadley, who was staring up at the sky as if she wished she was anywhere but here, finding out about her grandpa's dating life.

Hadley shook her head and made a *tsk-tsk* sound. "You're going to have to call Mom and tell her we're not coming home today."

"That seems extreme—especially when it comes to news she's not gonna want to hear. I'll text." PawPaw took out a brick of a phone and started thumb typing. "You two are lucky that I've got more than enough tie-dye to share and that I've got a spare room, because Rochelle is having a family reunion and there are Burgesses packed into every hotel room for miles."

Hadley's eyes went wide. "We can drive home

tonight and come back tomorrow."

Will's stomach took a ten-story nosedive at the idea of driving back three hours today only to do it all over again tomorrow.

"Don't be silly, Trigger." PawPaw hooked his arm through Hadley's and started walking with her toward the green space. "Plus, this way we'll get an early start in the morning. I already told your mom we'd be there by lunch. So now you two can have a little dinner and dancing. What could be better than that?"

Okay, Will could think of about a million things better than that—especially since he and Hadley still hadn't said a single word to each other since she'd tipped her hand with all those questions in the convenience store. However, saying that wasn't part of his plan.

"I can't think of anything better," he said, falling into step with Hadley and PawPaw.

"Looks like it's a plan, then. Don't you worry, Trigger, I bet one of the ladies has an extra tie-dye outfit you can borrow." He looked over at Will. "I've got a couple of Grateful Dead T-shirts that should work for you."

Will wasn't usually a costume kind of guy, but if it meant not getting in the car again until tomorrow, then he'd wear a chicken suit if necessary.

• • •

How had this happened? How had Hadley ended up wearing a tie-dyed micromini dress as three of her grandpa's girlfriends wove daisies in the single, loose braid flowing down her back? This was nuts. Totally bananas.

"Are you sure I shouldn't wear my jeans with this?" she asked, tugging down on the hem that barely reached mid-thigh.

Marion gasped, whipping her head around so fast to stare at Hadley in shock that her no-nonsense bob, dyed a dignified brown, took a heartbeat to catch up. "And ruin the look?"

Alice added a final daisy to Hadley's hair and stood back to admire her work. "When my cousin sent me this dress all the way from California all those years ago, my daddy forbade me from wearing it." She let out a sigh that spoke of could've beens and if onlys. "I've had it in a trunk ever since. Don't you dare ruin this dress's coming out by wearing it with jeans."

Cat smoothed the dress's Peter Pan collar and then locked eyes with Hadley in the mirror. "Just be careful how you sit in it or you'll be showing the world your good china."

Great, something new to worry about beyond the fact that she was going to have to dance with Will. She'd tried to work out a way to avoid it and had come up totally blank. Taking a deep breath—and offering up a quick prayer that the fifty-year-old seams of a one-size-smaller-than-her-belly-liked dress would hold—she had to admit defeat. She hated that. But there was no way around it. She was going to have to get up close and personal with the big jerk who happened to be saving her ass.

Luckily, Alice, Cat, and Marion had just the thing to settle her pre-dance nerves—Ensure spiked with vodka. She'd questioned it at first, but after one drink, it was obvious these older women knew what they were about.

"This was really nice of you guys," she said, lifting her glass in a toast. "Thank you."

Cat fluffed her steel-gray curls that went down to her shoulders and gave her a smile. "It's not every day we get to kidnap one of Paul's granddaughters and dress her up."

Hadley had no idea how to respond to that, so she just smiled at the three self-appointed fairy godmothers and let them get on with her transformation.

"Shoes! You need something besides…those," Cat said, finishing by pointing at Hadley's running shoes and wrinkling her pert little nose in disappointment.

"I have just the thing, one minute." Marion disappeared into her bedroom, moving quickly despite her cane that had tennis balls on its three-pronged base. She returned a moment later with a pair of woven wedges. "My granddaughter left these last time she visited. You two look to be about the same size."

Hadley slipped on the shoes and then did a quick walk around the small kitchenette. They were about half a size too small, but she wasn't going to be wearing them for hours. They'd make an appearance for PawPaw's sake and then get out of there. One dance—max—and that would be it.

"So what do you think?" She did a spin for her fairy godmothers and executed a quick curtsy as they clapped. "Thank you for letting me borrow it. It's a fabulous dress."

"It's not just a dress, you know," Alice said. "It's self-determination, control, power. You kids now with your Amazon Prime delivery and Instacarts, you have no idea what it was like to wait weeks for a package to arrive. I held my breath opening it up. I was one of those kids who hated tearing the wrapping paper on my Christmas presents, so imagine that but with the heavy tape they used to seal parcels."

"You are still like that, Alice," Cat said before taking a drink of spiked Ensure.

"I timed you on your birthday," Marion said. "Your quickest unwrap was three minutes."

"If it bothers you so much, don't watch next time." Alice brushed her fingertips across the shoulder of the dress, picking off a piece of lint Hadley would have sworn didn't really exist. "This dress was everything I wanted to be and couldn't at the time. Then life happened and I forgot all about it. By the time I remembered, there was no way it would fit me anymore."

She stepped back, crossed her arms over her rainbow-colored T-shirt, and let out a happy sigh. Hadley might be within the other woman's line of sight, but it sure didn't seem like Alice was seeing her.

"Are you sure you're okay with letting me wear this?"

"Oh, honey." Alice stepped forward and gave

Hadley a quick, surprisingly solid hug. "Dreams are meant to be unwrapped and worn proudly—and I'm glad mine is finally getting its time on the dance floor."

"Like she needs dreams when she has that tall drink of Cherry Coke," Cat said with a wink directed at Hadley.

Alice rolled her eyes. "Not everything is about getting a man."

"No, but it sure is nice to be able to warm your toes on those cold nights," Cat countered as she threaded a belt through the loops on her tie-dyed shirtwaist dress.

Oh God. This was going somewhere she did not want to go, considering the person warming Cat's *ahem* toes (along with Marion's and Alice's, going by how they'd been talking) was Hadley's pawpaw. Could she sneak out the door without them noticing? Since they were standing in front of it, probably not, but it just might be worth the effort.

"Just use that electric blanket I got you for your last birthday," Alice said, pulling on the light rainbow-colored cardigan.

"You are such a dear, but I wasn't really talking about my toes." Cat turned and must have seen the embarrassment on Hadley's face. "Sorry. I lost my filter when I turned seventy-six. Best thing to ever happen."

"Catherine," Marion said with an indulgent sigh. "I've known you since you were twelve. You never had a filter."

And Cat didn't look the least bit upset about it.

Hadley had to admit her pawpaw had great taste in girlfriends. These three were a riot, if more than a little TMI.

"Oh my gracious," Alice said. "Look at the time. Time to hit the bricks, ladies."

Hadley's dress was short enough that she'd feel the breeze on her panties when she walked, but she had an extra spring to her step anyway as they walked along one of the paths to the clubhouse. One dance, then she was out of there. Maybe it was the dress and Alice's sweet advice, but she couldn't help but feel like everything was going to go perfectly according to plan.

And that lasted right up until they walked into the clubhouse and she spotted Will. If her dress was a bit small, since it was sized for a high-school-age Alice, the T-shirt PawPaw had given Will must have belonged to a middle-school version of her grandpa. "Tight" didn't begin to cover it. The cotton clung to Will, from his broad shoulders, across the hard plane of his chest, and tapered down to his waist as if it were painted on. If she looked long enough, she'd probably be able to count each one of his six-pack abs.

And if that wasn't bad enough, he was heading straight for her. They hadn't spoken to each other since he'd gone all weird in the gas station / grocery / diner and now she wasn't sure she could form words. Anticipation danced across her skin, and her breath caught when she saw the way he looked at her—as if he knew and totally endorsed every naughty thought she'd had about him during her shower this morning.

He tipped his cowboy hat at her fairy god-mothers, which they answered with a set of harmonized giggles, then turned to Hadley. "Can I have this dance?"

If she could have said no at that moment, she would have. Instead, she took his hand and walked out onto the dance floor.

• • •

Will should have agreed to driving back to the ranch tonight.

Then he wouldn't be wearing a ridiculously small T-shirt, holding Hadley in his arms, and swaying to "Lay, Lady, Lay" by Bob Dylan in the middle of a geriatric dance party. Her arms rested on his shoulders, her fingers twined loosely behind his neck, while his fingertips lay lightly on the small of her back.

Feeling her move against him as Dylan sang made it hard to remember why he was here in the first place. Other dancers around them chatted and smiled while they glided around the floor. Not them. They were like those big statues on Easter Island, silent and unsmiling.

It wasn't suspicious at all.

He dipped his head down, bringing his mouth close to her ear. "If you don't at least pretend to be having fun, everyone is going to know that this whole thing is fake."

"Oh really?" She tensed in his arms. "I hadn't considered that at all."

"So what are you going to do about it?" he

asked as he spun them through the crowded dance floor.

Hadley lifted a shoulder and let it fall. "Develop a headache that means I have to go to bed."

The mention of the word "bed" filled his brain with enough bad ideas to make him miss the beat. She looked up at him, her eyebrows raised in question, and the futility of the situation hit him hard. Despite it all, he wanted Hadley. Why? Because he was the king of fucking bad ideas at the moment.

"Oh yeah," he said, laying on the sarcasm thick. "That won't be weird at all."

"Why are you like this?" She let out a huff of frustration. "From the day Web introduced us, you've either ignored me or insulted me. And don't throw that gold-digger ridiculousness at me again. We both know that's not really it."

The only answer he had to that was too close to the truth to be comfortable, which was exactly why he kept his mouth shut. It didn't help, though, because with each inhale, he got the scent of the daisies in her hair and a hint of something sharper, much like the woman herself—delicate on the outside with an inner mettle that everyone else seemed to overlook.

But not him. He'd noticed it from the beginning, as obvious as a flash in the dark.

From that first moment, he'd kept his distance and watched, waiting for the *real* her to make an appearance, just like it had with Mia. He hadn't been vigilant before. He was now.

"One, who in the hell could ignore you?" He

sure as fuck couldn't. She all but haunted him no matter what he did. For the past year, she'd squeezed her way between any two thoughts in his head until she was the constant undercurrent of his day. "Two, I never insulted you. I just pointed out all the ways you were wrong about how the Holt Foundation should be awarding its grants."

"Really?" She came in closer so their bodies were touching, from the insanely short hem of her dress to her mouth right up against his neck, so every word became a touch. "So in addition to graduating at the top of your business class, having three masters, and being the CEO voted most eligible bachelor in Harbor City, you had time to double major in nonprofit management and philanthropic studies like I did, plus gain more than five years of real-world experience? Wow. Impressive."

"So you looked into me?" Yeah, that was pretty much his big takeaway from her dressing down, and he wasn't even sorry about it.

"Yes, I cracked open the *Harbor City Post*. You're in it multiple times a week."

He opened his mouth before he realized he didn't have a retort for that. She wasn't wrong. Then again, it made for a convenient cover story for why she knew so much about him and Web.

"You always make assumptions about people," she said, sliding her truth shiv home right between his ribs. "You might want to rethink that practice."

He gritted his teeth, annoyance at how well she thought she knew him making his muscles tense. "My gut instinct is what helped turn Holt Enterprises around."

The entire board thought he was nuts to invest in an app that provided real-time parking information. They'd called it niche. However, unlike the rest of the board, he didn't have a driver and had to fight for parking spots himself and knew it was a winner. Thanks to Holt Enterprises' investment, the app changed how every driver in Harbor City thought about parking. That had been his first foray into technology but not his last. They'd picked up the dating app Bramble, invested in a few other start-ups, and were neck deep in beta testing for the next big dating app for dog lovers called Bark Up.

"It might serve you well in business, but people aren't the same," she said. "You have to give them a chance. Of course, you're just going to ignore that advice, aren't you?"

Okay, maybe she did know him a little bit. "It does seem a little biased—especially coming from someone who can't even trust her family enough not to lie to them."

Hadley flinched in his arms. "It's complicated."

"When isn't that the case?" Which was exactly why he liked the numbers side of business—spreadsheets, actuary tables, business valuations—that were logical and followed an unbiased formula.

"It's not complicated with us." Hadley looked up at him, her chin set at a stubborn angle and her gaze filled with 98 percent certainty. "We don't get along, end of story."

It was her 2 percent of doubt, though, that grabbed his attention, promising possibilities he shouldn't ever consider.

"Is that really all there is to it?"

Hadley lowered her gaze, suddenly seeming to find the collar of his stretched T-shirt completely fascinating. "Yes."

"Whatever you say, Hadley." But they both knew she was wrong, even if neither of them was going to do a damn thing about it.

CHAPTER TEN

Hadley lasted five dances past when she should, and every single one of them had been with Will. Now they were back in PawPaw's apartment, and she was in the guest bathroom trying to reach the zipper tab on her dress without ripping it or popping her shoulder out of the socket. She reached behind and did a back bow deep enough to crack her spine but couldn't reach it.

Blowing back the strands of hair that had come free from her braid during "Twist and Shout," she changed tactics and went high, reaching over her shoulders that she'd slumped forward in an effort to reach the zipper. Still nada.

She'd worn sweaty sports bras that were easier to peel off than this dress.

Okay, there were three choices here. Sleep in the dress, ask Will for help, or gnaw off her own arm like a coyote caught in a trap. While option one was tempting, she couldn't imagine that Alice would appreciate getting back a wrinkled, slept-in garment in the morning. That left only one realistic prospect—asking for help.

Biting back her distaste of having to ask a favor from the evil twin, she called out, "Will, can you help me with this zipper real quick?"

She barely got the words out before he was in the doorway, filling it up and making the already small bathroom seem minuscule.

"I can't reach the zipper," she said, trying—and failing—not to react to the fact that he'd already taken off that ridiculously small T-shirt. It wouldn't have been so bad if he'd put another shirt on. He hadn't. It was just him in a pair of jeans that hung low on his hips, showing off the tops of those vee marks on his hips that made forming words really fucking hard. "Can you just get me started?"

"Sure." He closed the distance between them until he stood directly behind her as she faced the mirror over the bathroom sink. "Here, let me get the flowers first."

Touch gentle, he tugged the ponytail holder from the bottom of her braid and then ran his hands through her long hair, combing out the long-stemmed daisies so they fell, landing in a circle around her bare feet. There wasn't a sound in the room, as if the rest of the world had fallen away. His fingers combed through her hair until it was smooth and loose, then pushed it to the side, exposing the back of her neck. Watching him in the mirror, there was no missing the tension in his jaw or the way he swallowed hard before reaching for the zipper.

She held her breath as he paused, her heart hammering against her chest. Then he inched the zipper down, the fabric of the dress falling away as he did so. The muscle in his temple pulsed as he stood frozen behind her, looking down at her bare skin, want and need swirling in his green-eyed gaze.

The thrill of anticipation made her skin tingle as she watched it all play out on his face. Gone was the usual smirk, the cocky self-assurance. He was a man at a breaking point. He wasn't alone in that.

An hour ago, Hadley would have known exactly what to do in this situation. She would have walked away with a cutting remark and one single triumphant look back. But now? She wasn't going anywhere. Desire, warm and demanding, had her bare nipples puckering beneath the dress as she felt the back of his knuckles skim down the length of her spine at a leisurely pace that stole the air from her lungs, not stopping until he brushed the scalloped edge of her panties, sending a shiver of lust over her.

It was all she could do to stay upright as a languorous warmth flooded her body. Holy hell, she clenched her eyes shut and inhaled a deep breath in a desperate attempt to remember why this was a bad idea. But when she opened her eyes again, she found him looking back at her in the mirror, and all her best intentions melted away.

He raised an eyebrow in question, his fingers hovering over the edges of her open dress. One shake of her head and she knew he'd walk away. Both of them would act as if this moment had never happened—as much as that would be possible. It's what she *should* do, because despite whatever was going on now, she knew Will Holt wasn't for her.

They weren't potential lovers. They weren't friends. They barely tolerated each other. Yet here she was, practically burning with want and nodding her consent.

There weren't words or an acknowledgment; he simply used the slightest touch to nudge the dress off her shoulders and down over her hips until it pooled on the floor. His sharp intake of breath thundered in the small bathroom as he reached around and cupped her bare breasts with his strong hands. The last bit of her hesitation faded away when he took her nipples between his fingers and rolled the hard peaks, tugging them lightly and sending pleasure shooting through her—the kind that made her knees buckle as she bit down on her bottom lip.

She planted her palms on the sink to help keep her balance under the blissful torture. There was just something about watching him tease her with slow, sure movements as they stood silently in front of the mirror that knocked her off balance, sped up her pulse, and left her yearning for more. It had to be the strangeness of the situation. It couldn't be because of Will; that wasn't even something she could consider.

It was just a case of right moment, wrong man—one with magical hands.

She'd just about gotten a handle on how fucking good it felt to have him touching her, sending the best kind of little shocks from her nipples to her clit, when he leaned down and kissed the spot right behind her ear, moving with deliberate intent down the side of her throat. Electric desire sizzled along her skin as he kissed and licked and sucked and nipped his way down to where her shoulder met her neck. That, in addition to the way he was tweaking her nipples, was exactly the kind of world-tilting teasing that had her holding on to the sink so she wouldn't slide off the side of the earth into oblivion.

He lifted his head, and the mix of intense lust and surprised wonder on his face as he looked at her in the mirror knocked her back to rights. What in the hell was she doing? This was Will Holt. He was the worst. They couldn't stand each other. She should stop things now and—

The tips of his fingers glided down her stomach, not stopping until he brushed the edge of her panties. Anticipation whipped through her. This wasn't a good idea—but she nodded anyway. And when his fingers slid under the elastic band, she promised herself this wouldn't change anything.

• • •

Will hadn't walked into the bathroom with any plan beyond helping with Hadley's zipper. He'd never meant to touch her silky skin, feel the way she responded to his touch, or let things get to the point where she was all but naked and he was sliding his fingers between her legs. God, she was soft and slick and so ready for him. And the look on her face when he circled her clit? The raw, honest desire was the hottest thing he'd ever seen.

He could watch her like this the whole night, take her right up to the edge and then back off. "Tempting" didn't even begin to cover it, but he was a greedy bastard and he wanted more. He wanted to watch her come.

Fingers slick with her, he moved against her, keeping rhythm with the rocking of her hips and the tightening of her body in anticipation. He lowered his mouth to her neck, kissing and nipping his way up to her ear, taking note of each time her breath caught, every barely perceptible sigh escaping her lips, and exactly how tight her grip on the sink became as her body moved closer and closer to that edge. And when he circled her clit again with two fingers, pressing with just enough pressure to make her bite down on her full bottom lip, she collapsed back against him.

Reaching behind her, she slid her hands between them, gripping his hard cock through his jeans. His entire body stiffened, and he let out a desperate hiss, the quiet sound booming in the otherwise silent bathroom. His gaze locked with hers in the mirror. She tugged her lip between her teeth and shot him a challenging, teasing look as she squeezed him tight.

Fuck. That's how she wanted to do this? Two could play at that.

He increased the speed of his fingers, sliding through her wet folds and circling her swollen clit, getting her right to the edge and pulling back. By the time he stopped a third time, a flush stained her cheeks and she had a wild, desperate look in her eyes. Before he knew what she was about, she turned so she was facing him and she was unzipping his fly. His jeans were halfway down his thighs before his brain could catch up, and by the time it did, it was too late. He yanked his wallet out of his back pocket and took out a condom. While he rolled it on, Hadley turned back around and placed her hands on the sink again. What an inviting sight. If there was anything that could tear him away from watching her in the mirror, it was seeing his hands gripping her hips as he lined himself up. Sliding inside her, he ground his molars together, desperate to keep it together longer than a few short thrusts.

He would have stayed still inside her for longer if he could have, but she was too tight, too warm, too fucking perfect. He had to move. Thrusting forward, he sank into her before pulling back and doing it again and again. There weren't any words, but they didn't need any. She met him halfway on each advance, and when he reached around in front of her and dragged his finger over her clit, she responded by gripping him so tight, he nearly came on the spot.

"Say my name." The demand came out rough and hard. It wasn't fair to ask things of her when she was on the edge of her climax, but he needed her to say it. He needed to know she wasn't thinking of Web while getting off on his dick. "Say it."

"Will," she said, half begging and half demanding more.

That was all he needed to hear. He'd give it to her—everything she wanted in this moment, it was hers. Finger circling her clit, he thrust inside her, fucking her in a slow, steady rhythm that had her quaking in his arms before she came hard enough that he had to catch her with an arm around her waist so she didn't collapse onto the floor.

It was all he could do not to fall over the edge with her right then, no matter that he wanted to extend the moment—delay falling back into who they were to each other outside of that door. But he was too close, and when she squeezed his cock in the aftershock of her orgasm, he knew the battle was lost. He thrust into her slick warmth, once, twice, three times, burying himself as deep as he could go before coming, his jaw clenched tight to muffle the sound.

Watching her in the mirror as he came back down from that high, the unspoken hint of possibility hanging in the air, he took in all of her—the rosy pink of her nipples, the tangle of her long brown hair, the full, round curve of her hips—and wondered if maybe he'd been missing what was right in front of him all along.

He opened his mouth to say something— anything—but that's when he glanced over at the mirror and saw her staring right at him. There was no missing the regret in her big brown eyes. It sliced through him, sharp as a serrated knife, shredding whatever he thought could have been.

Silent as he'd been since he unzipped her dress, he stepped back, breaking their connection, and moved over so she had a clear path to the door. "Just give me a second to clean up."

"Yeah, of course." She scooped up her clothes, not looking at him, and walked out. "Take your time. I'm all done in here."

Yeah. He just bet she was.

He shut the bathroom door behind her, turned on the shower, and got in before it even had a chance to warm up. Right now, he needed the frigid water to beat against him so he'd stop feeling her soft skin. Then he'd be able to block out the memory of how she trembled right before she came, her fingers gripping the sink like it was a lifeline. He'd be able to see the reality of the situation. Life was transactional. His grandmother. Mia. Hadley. None of it meant anything to them; it was just a means to an end.

Closing his eyes, he stepped fully underneath the icy downpour and didn't even flinch. Fuck. He was so damn tired of it all.

• • •

There was only one bed in the guest room at PawPaw's because of course there was. Thighs jellified, she put her underwear back on and threw on the T-shirt she'd been wearing earlier. For half a second, she worried about the fact that she wasn't wearing pajama bottoms, but after what had just happened in the bathroom, the time for that was well past.

What in the hell had she been thinking? She hadn't, and that was exactly why when she looked at Will in the mirror and realized that this was what there could have been between them, she'd never regretted anything more in her life. Instead of the sniping and the snarking, they could have… well, they could have at least been friends instead of nearly instant enemies. That thought, though, was immediately shown for the absolute bullshittery it was by Will's reaction. It was like a switch had been flipped and he'd gone back to being Sir Supreme Dick.

And you thought you could at least be friends with him?

She was totally blaming the post-coital happy hormone rush for that bit of ridiculousness.

So yeah, not having PJ bottoms was pretty far down on the list of shitty things right about now, because she'd just fucked a guy who hated her guts. And she couldn't stand him, either. He was the worst—unless she took into consideration what he could do when naked. Of course, that was best forgotten.

Pulling back the covers to the guest bed, Hadley made a promise to herself that she wouldn't be fooled by a fabulous orgasm and abs she had serious regret about not having licked. Will was still the evil twin. He just happened to be one with a fabulous dick.

She closed her eyes and evened out her breathing so when Will walked out of the bathroom a few minutes later, he didn't even attempt to talk to her before getting into bed. And the fact that he left a solid foot of open space between them? That was perfect. Abso-fucking-lutely perfect. Touching him again was the last thing she wanted. Once was definitely enough.

CHAPTER ELEVEN

Going by her horny subconscious, once was definitely not enough for Hadley. In her dreams last night, it had them doing it everywhere but on horseback while galloping off into the sunset. But when she cracked open her eyes the next morning, she was alone in bed—not that she cared.

Now, the fact that the corner of her pillow was damp because she'd spent the night drooling on it, and probably snoring, did dent up her pride. So her nemesis had seen her naked, made her come in a bathroom, and had been serenaded with the song of her wet-chain-saw snoring. Aaaaaaaaand she was going to get to spend three hours shut up in a car with him on the drive back to the ranch.

Please, God, let PawPaw be in the mood to tell every story he knows…

That would fill up the drive for sure. Hell, that might even get them through dinner. Of course, that left tonight. In the cabin. Alone.

She grabbed Will's pillow and held it to her face so she could groan into it—only to be hit with the unmistakable scent of sexy, off-limits Evil Twin. A better woman would have tossed the damn thing across the room. She was weak. She took a second and a third inhale. The sound of the bathroom door opening registered two seconds later than it should have.

"Are you smelling my pillow?" Will asked.

She didn't have to lower the pillow to see the smirk on his face, since there was no missing the self-satisfaction in his voice. As tempting as it was to just go ahead and smother herself with his pillow, she wouldn't give in and let him win.

She sat up and let the pillow drop. "I was screaming into it."

While true, it would have sounded more convincing if her voice hadn't squeaked in the middle of the word "screaming." Some reactions, however, couldn't be helped—especially now when it came to seeing Will wearing only a pair of zipped but unbuttoned jeans that were being held up by the patron saint of regrettable sexcapades. There was just something about the bare feet, muscled chest, damp hair, almost-totally-naked combination that gave him a sexy, vulnerable vibe that was her catnip. Obviously her better judgment needed to wake the fuck up because if there was anyone who didn't fit that bill, it was the Evil Twin himself. They'd only been arguing every time they met for the past year. She knew better than to get fooled by the happy trail that disappeared behind his zipper.

"That was some quiet screaming," he said, lifting an eyebrow. "I guess I shouldn't be surprised. You were very quiet in the bathroom last night."

And there it was, the reminder of what kind of

an egomaniacal prick he was. That was why her heartbeat had picked up, her nipples were poking against her cotton T-shirt, and why her gaze kept dropping to his zipper, wondering for how much longer it would hold.

"We're not talking about that," she said, her cheeks burning. "Ever."

"Really?" He thumbed the button of his jeans but didn't fasten them. "That's what you're going with?"

She forced her gaze up past his sinewy chest to his face. "Yes."

"Ouch. A man of lesser ego would be crushed right about now." He buttoned his jeans, grabbed his T-shirt from where it lay across the bottom of the bed, and pulled it on. "Seriously, though, we do need to talk, just to get everything out on the table. Last night was fun and all, but it's not a good idea for it to happen again."

"Wait. What?" She sat up, her jaw hanging so far open, she coulda caught flies. Who in the hell was he to tell her that? She was the one who was going to tell him that! "*You* don't want a repeat?"

He reached over and plucked that black cowboy hat of his off the dresser but didn't put it on. "I mean, we can both agree that getting naked together isn't in either of our best interests."

"What interests are those?" she asked, trying not to get distracted by watching his long fingers on the soft brim of his hat and remembering where they'd been last night.

One of his brows shot up. "Are you saying you want to have sex again?"

Damn it. That's what she got for getting distracted.

"No," she said, her voice sharp.

"Good. Glad that's all cleared up," he said, looking back down at his hat before glancing back at her and giving her a wink. "Now I'm going to go grab some breakfast. That bacon smells so good, my stomach started growling in the shower."

Without even looking her way, he strutted out of the room, cowboy hat dangling in his grasp.

What in the hell had just happened? Hadley flopped back, swiped Will's pillow from the bed, held it to her face, and let loose with a prolonged and frustrated groan. How had he turned this into *her* wanting to have sex with *him* again?

She didn't.

She wouldn't.

It was beyond inconceivable no matter how many very vivid, very specific bad ideas she might be having right about now.

• • •

An hour later, Will was back to clutching a preemptive can of ginger ale and staring at the rental car as if it were an acid-drenched carnival ride from hell. Hadley didn't even look his way before she got in on the driver's side.

Great.

Perfect.

Everything was going exactly to plan—if his plan had been to forget everything he knew about Hadley's objective to fleece his brother and instead to fuck her like a man who hadn't been thinking about anyone except her for the past year—which he *had* but that wasn't the point. He'd been thinking strategically, not with his dick. At least he had been up until last night. And now?

He couldn't glance her way without wanting to do it again, which was not the reason why he was out in the Middle of Nowhere, Nebraska, about to get into a car for another long-ass ride to a different part of the Middle of Nowhere, Nebraska. The state never fucking ended. It was just one flat, straight highway that continued indefinitely. It was hell.

"Are you sure you don't want the front?" Will asked PawPaw as he opened the front passenger door.

Delay? Him? Absolutely. If giving up the front seat gave him an extra two seconds outside of the car, he'd consider it a win.

"Why, so I'll be in the splash zone when you blow chunks while sitting in the back?" PawPaw shook his head. "No, thank you."

What sounded like a giggle disguised as a cough came from inside the car, but by the time he sat down, Hadley's lips were compressed into a straight line and she only had eyes for the road ahead.

"Let's do this," she said.

The engine roared—okay, as much as a rental could—and they were off. He popped the ginger ale before they'd even pulled out of the Sandhills Senior Living parking lot.

"So," PawPaw said a few miles later. "What was

your first impression of our Hadley?"

Hadley let out a groan of embarrassment. "PawPaw."

"What? A grandfather has a right to know what is going on in his grandkids' lives and who they've let into theirs."

"It's not fair to put Will on the spot like that."

PawPaw snorted. "Like I give two pink figs about anything beyond saying what's on my mind. You never have to guess what I'm thinking."

Will pivoted in his seat, taking a look at Hadley and her grandfather. The two obviously shared more than just a pointy chin and the same big eyes. "Seems to be a family tradition, because that is exactly what it was like when I met Hadley."

The old man rubbed his hands together with glee and leaned forward. "Do tell."

"She came to my standing weekend rugby match."

He'd just come off the pitch when he'd spotted her. The wind was whipping her long brown hair around and she'd wrapped her arms around her waist against the cold. She'd been watching the play but had turned and looked at him, and it was like finding out a secret. She'd waved and he'd nearly walked right into his brother, and that's when he realized Hadley was waving at his brother and not him.

"I was there to cheer on your brother," she said, one hand on the wheel and the other twisting a strand of hair around her finger. "He's one of my best friends."

Yeah. Friends. That's what she liked to call it. He knew better. The way she looked at Web, so cautious and careful when he wasn't looking and then morphing into Miss Perfectly Perky when he was, had told Will everything he'd needed to know. *Always be on the lookout for false faces*, that's what he'd learned from Mia. Of course, he hadn't noticed that at first. All he'd seen was the first woman who'd made him look twice since he'd almost lost half his trust fund and controlling interest in Holt Enterprises to Mia.

"So she's there," he went on, working to keep the bitter edge out of his voice. "It's one of those fall days when it's in the seventies one moment and then high fifties the next. I offered her my coat."

Hadley let loose with a loud bark of laughter. "You told me everyone knew to dress in layers that time of year, and then you shoved your coat at me before you even knew my name."

Okay, he might have said something along those lines—he'd *probably* said something along those lines—but it didn't change the fact that he was right and though he'd had a perfectly good coat, she'd looked at him like he was holding a tennis ball that had been thoroughly dog slobbered all over.

He kept going without addressing her comment. "She tells me she doesn't want my jacket even though she has her arms wrapped around herself and her teeth are chattering despite all the coffee she was drinking from this leaky thermos that dribbled every time she took a sip."

"I wasn't *that* cold and my teeth weren't chattering. I've used a blow dryer to open a car door that was frozen shut before; I know what cold is," she said with a soft chuckle. "Anyway, I was wearing an old long-sleeve T-shirt, so it didn't matter if I dripped on it."

"Then my brother comes by and gives her his ancient hoodie covered in stains and she puts it right on."

Really, their grandmother's Pomeranian would have turned up its spoiled nose at the grimy sweatshirt, but not Hadley. She'd smiled up at Web and put it on with a thank-you. That's when Will had realized something had to be up.

"I used his sweatshirt because if I spilled on that, it wouldn't matter, unlike your coat that probably cost as much as my rent," Hadley said.

It would have been better for Will if she hadn't been right about the cost of his coat. He hadn't thought about it that way before. If he had, he probably would have given her the benefit of the doubt instead of that moment being the trigger for his suspicions. Web had always been adamant that they were just friends, but things changed, and Will had come across his distrust of people's motives honestly.

"And you started dating after that?" PawPaw asked.

It took all Will had not to scoff out loud. More like at that point, they started facing off against each other every time they met. He couldn't say anything that wouldn't set her off and she couldn't seem to do anything that didn't seem suspicious, from suddenly starting to show up at what had been brothers-only brunch to offering unsolicited advice about how the Holt Foundation should be operating, she seemed to have her nose in everything—just like Mia had.

Hadley cleared her throat. "Around then."

PawPaw looked at them skeptically. "Well, since Hadley's never brought a man around before, I guess it must be serious. Maybe you're even getting ready to announce you're getting married."

Hadley gasped, and the car swerved over the yellow line before she righted it. "Us? Married?"

"What?" PawPaw shrugged. "It's a logical assumption. I mean, the only other one is that the whole thing is a giant head fake and you two aren't dating at all."

Will froze, that oh-shit buzzing sensation of a negotiation about to go pear-shaped making his ears vibrate. He glanced over at Hadley. Her face was perfectly neutral as she drove eighty, going past the cornfields on either side of the highway, but she was white-knuckling the steering wheel.

"Why don't you think we're dating?" Will asked.

"Because I wasn't born yesterday." PawPaw snorted and rolled his eyes. "Are you telling me the others all think that you two are actually dating?"

Testing the water of were-they-really-in-trouble-or-was-the-old-man-fishing, Will turned on his you-can-trust-me grin. "What makes you think we aren't?'"

"Are you telling me that the instincts and experience my eight decades on God's green earth are wrong?" PawPaw asked. "Or the fact that you two can barely look at each other unless the other one is looking somewhere else isn't a dead giveaway? There are sparks as big as those wind turbines Gabe allowed to go up on the western edge of the ranch, I'll give you that, but you two are too naive to notice them, I'd guess."

Hadley's shoulders slumped as she let out a long sigh. "You can't tell anyone else."

PawPaw let out a triumphant holler. "I knew it. I'll keep my trap shut, but on one condition," PawPaw said. "You're both on my team for game night."

What the— "Game night?" Will asked.

"It's a family tradition, a sort of a game Ironman. Rummy. Monopoly. Scrabble," Hadley said, sounding every bit as if someone had run over her three-legged swift fox.

Okay, he was obviously missing something. "What's so bad about being on PawPaw's team?"

"Who said there was?" the older man asked with an indignant huff, but he didn't make eye contact.

Yep, something was definitely going on here.

"PawPaw," Hadley said in that über-patient tone people used with toddlers who refused to grasp the realities of logic. "I love you, but you know no one wants to be on your team. You take it all a little too seriously."

"What is the point of playing a game if you're not doing what it takes to win?" PawPaw asked.

Will couldn't argue with the old man.

"You end up mad at whoever is on your team." She glanced at her grandfather in the rearview mirror and held up her hand to stop him before he could interrupt. "And before you fib and say 'not me,' I want to remind you of that game night four Christmases ago when I refused to turn my hat inside out like a rally cap when we were down to our last five hundred dollars and rolling to get past Park Place. You retaliated by putting coal in my stocking."

The older man sank down in his seat. "You can't prove that was me."

Hadley let out a little chuckle. "PawPaw."

"Fine, it was me, but that doesn't change anything." His gaze bounced from Will to Hadley. "If you want my silence, you're on my team."

There weren't a lot of times when Will had ever felt like he was in over his head or that he couldn't read the room's undercurrent. At this moment, though? Yeah, there was obviously family history here, and the game night must have some really high stakes. Hadley's beseeching gaze slid over his way. He shrugged.

She let out a sigh. "We'll be on your team."

"Excellent." PawPaw's smile was wide enough to cross both lanes of the highway. "Did I ever tell you about the time I danced with Dolly Parton while I was dressed up *as* Dolly Parton?"

And that was how the rest of the drive went, with PawPaw telling one farfetched story after another until they were on the gravel path leading to Hidden Creek Ranch and then pulling into the drive in front of the main house.

"Before we get out, are you sure you don't want to just come clean?" PawPaw asked, leaning up close to the front seat, his voice low, as if the people inside the house might hear him. "You could tell them things didn't work out, and no one would say a word."

"Yeah, that'll be the day when this family doesn't have an opinion to offer. We're not a couple. We never will be a couple, but Mom doesn't need to know that," Hadley said a little too fast for Will's ego.

PawPaw muttered something that sounded a lot like "young fools" but didn't press it further. Will had just gotten out and Hadley had crossed the front of the rental to join them on the way to the house when Adalyn came hustling out of the house and down the stairs, her smile huge but tight at the corners.

She stopped in front of Hadley. "Try to remember all the reasons you love Mom."

Neither of them got a chance to ask why, because that's when Stephanie walked out onto the porch.

"There you are!" Stephanie said, shooting an apologetic glance at Hadley. "Look who stopped by out of the blue."

Right on cue, a man who looked like a smug version of the Marlboro Man if he Juuled followed her through the front door.

"Matt?" Hadley asked.

The man strutted down the stairs and across the gravel, ignoring PawPaw, Adalyn, and the fact that somehow in the middle of all this Will had started holding Hadley's hand. When had that happened? He had no fucking clue, but he wasn't letting go now.

"Hey, Hads." Matt leaned down and gave her a quick kiss on the cheek. "You know I couldn't pass up an opportunity to come by and say hi." He turned to Will, holding out his hand. "Don't suppose you're the Web everyone keeps telling me about. Hads and I used to date eons ago. Nothing to worry about at all."

"I'm sure there's not," he said, dropping Hadley's hand to shake the man's offered one. "My friends call me Will."

"Good to know," Matt said and squeezed his grip before letting go. "Web."

Grinding his molars to dust, Will watched as Matt slung an arm around Hadley's shoulders and walked with her back to the house. This was a good thing. A very good thing. Really. And if he said it enough, he'd start to believe it.

He fisted his hand and hung back by the rental, going through all the ways that the appearance of her ex-boyfriend would be good, as if that would make his gut twist less. The biggest being that if she went for the guy, then Will wouldn't need to worry about exposing Hadley's gold-digging ways to save Web. Hadley would be off his radar and not his responsibility. He started toward the house, pulverizing the gravel under his boots with every stomping step. What the hell did he care if she ended up ripping a hole into Matt the Asshat's bottom line? That would be all the better.

If that's the case, then why do I want nothing more than to punch his lights out?

At the front door, PawPaw looked back at him and shook his head. "Well, this should get interesting."

Why did Will suddenly feel like he'd chewed glass the whole trip, and that was going to be the best part of his day?

CHAPTER TWELVE

Once inside, Hadley made a beeline for the kitchen while everyone headed out back for a game of horseshoes.

She found her mom peeking into the oven to check the two pans of Frito pie baking. Hadley almost forgot why she was there when the smell of melted cheese, seasoned ground beef, corn chips, enchilada sauce, and beans hit her. This was heaven in food form. Damn, that wasn't fair. Her mom had definitely planned her move well. It was hard to concentrate on being annoyed that her ex had finagled his way inside with her favorite comfort food in the oven. She took a deep inhale, closed her eyes, and could almost taste the salty crunch of the chips.

Rubbing her now rumbly stomach, Hadley sat down on one of the barstools at the island. "Is that Aunt Louise's recipe?"

"You know it is." Her mom tossed the flour sack tea towel over one shoulder and moved to the celery sticks by the sink.

"With the secret ingredient?" The one her great-aunt had lorded over everyone at every family gathering where food was involved since the dawn of time.

Stephanie nodded. "Yep."

This was epic. They were finally in possession of the only family secret any of them had ever managed to keep for longer than a week. "If you share what it is, I'll forget all about Matt being here."

Stephanie snorted in amusement and handed the rinsed celery to Hadley. "Good luck with that."

"Mom," she said as she started to chop the ends off the celery. "What were you thinking? Why didn't you kick him out?"

Stephanie didn't look even the least little bit embarrassed. "Honestly, I tried to get him moving, but he came all the way out to personally deliver the mason jars your sister said had to be a part of the wedding decorations. It's not like I invited him."

"Mom, you know I'm not interested in Matt."

"No one said you should be," her mom said. "Although who would object to Matt is a mystery to me. He's the kind of man who stays close to home, talks to his family on a regular basis, and isn't embarrassed by where he came from."

"I'm not embarrassed about where I'm from." She wasn't. It's just that she wanted to live in a place where everyone didn't know absolutely everything about her from the time she was born.

Stephanie looked up from the mixture of peanut butter and honey she was spooning into the celery sticks and raised an eyebrow. "Aren't you?

How many times had they had this conversation? At least a million since she had left for college. It never changed. Her mom just kept repeating the same lines, praising the virtues of small-town life over and over again, never understanding that despite all the open space, being out here crowded her in. In Harbor City, she had the freedom granted by anonymity and the opportunity to try new things or meet new people. Out here, it was the same faces, the same scenery, the same old same old every day until you died. Arguing about it would never change that, so what was the point of fighting about it?

"Mom," she said, the word coming out as an exhausted sigh. "I love you, so let's just change the subject."

"Fine. You know Matt's been asking Gabe and the boys about you every time they stopped in to Feed and Steer." Stephanie arranged the celery sticks on the plate. "I might have mentioned to him when you'd be coming home, and I guess he decided to shoot his shot. Sorry about that. You know Aunt Louise is waiting for an announcement from you two."

Yeah, Hadley didn't need three guesses to figure out what kind of announcement.

The buzzer on the oven went off before Hadley could deny it, but not before an image of Will in the bathroom last night flashed in her mind. Damn. It took all of half a heartbeat for her body to go from primed for a fight to primed for Will. Ugh. This was not how this was supposed to go. Last night didn't change anything. The man was…well, he was the evil twin who was convinced she had gold digging on the brain. The man did not get a place in her spank bank, he did not get to be in consideration for another roll in the metaphorical hay, and he most definitely was not husband material, no matter what Aunt Louise wanted to be true.

"Wait a minute." She gasped, realization making her jaw drop. "Did you promise to help her nudge Will and me along the matrimonial road? Is that how you got the secret ingredient?"

Her mom set the steaming hot casserole dish down on a trivet shaped like a steer and shrugged. "All's fair in love and Frito pie."

There were no lies in that argument—at least not when it came to the food. Hadley was sprinkling fresh corn chips on top of the melted cheese when Gabe strode in through the back door.

"You guys coming out with the food or are you going to keep quiet-fighting in here?" he asked from at least two arms' reaches away. The man was no doubt not taking any chances.

"We're not fighting," Stephanie said, rolling her eyes at her husband.

"Yeah," Hadley agreed. "It's a discussion."

"Uh-huh." Gabe took a few steps closer, taking a deep inhale of the Frito pie. "Well, whatever you want to call it, we're all starving. Can I at least take out the ants on a log? We need a distraction, because it looks like Derek isn't going to make it tonight, either."

Hadley's heart ached for her sister. Adalyn was

not a fan of being the center of attention, to the point that she'd skipped her own high school graduation so she didn't have to do the whole walk-across-the-stage-in-front-of-everyone thing. That's part of what made it so strange that she'd decided to put together such an elaborate wedding. It must have been Derek who'd insisted on the full shebang. Who would do that to Adalyn and then not be here to take some of the weight off her?

"What I would say if I could," her mom said, tone as hard as the frozen prairie in January.

There were few insults from her mom that were stronger than her mom being willing to hold back on saying exactly what was on her mind at any given time. It was one of the few things they had in common. And if she was keeping her mouth shut about Derek, then things were pretty grim.

"How's Adalyn doing?" Hadley asked Gabe.

He shrugged and let out a sigh that spoke of all the words he was keeping bottled up, too. "She's holding up, but Aunt Louise is like a coyote with a rabbit when it comes to getting every little detail out of Buttermilk."

God love Aunt Louise, but she had that whole blunt-Midwestern-bulldozer thing down pat.

Gabe put on the oven mitts, picked up the casserole dish, and started toward the door. "We better get out there."

By the time Hadley made it outside with the tray of peanut-butter-and-honey-filled celery sticks, everyone was already seated at the picnic tables. And because the fates were against her, every seat was taken except for one—the empty spot right by Will and across from Matt.

She set down the tray on the table and squeezed in next to Will, the brush of her hip against his when she sat down sending a teasing little buzz of attraction across her skin. Her brain was a hard no, but the rest of her? Oh God, the rest of her was softening like butter in July. And for the first time ever, the Frito pie tasted like shredded paper because every sense in her body was tuned in to the man sitting next to her.

And just when she thought it couldn't get worse, PawPaw stood up and pulled out a pair of handcuffs.

Hadley's stomach sank, and it took everything she had not to holler out "no."

"I had brought these for Derek and Adalyn," PawPaw said.

Maybe her sister had given her fiancé a heads-up. What PawPaw had planned was best avoided at all costs.

"However, after a discussion with Louise," he went on, "we think we came up with the perfect alternative for the family tradition."

Unease creeped across her skin, and Hadley's stomach sank. It took everything she had not to slide under the picnic table and hide.

Her grandpa beamed at her. "Will and Hadley, these are for you."

Oh God, kill me now.

• • •

Dinner had just moved into creepy no-one-can-hear-you-scream-out-here territory. Will might have made a break for it, but he was hemmed in on the bench by Weston on one side and Hadley on the other.

"Oh my God," Hadley grumbled under her breath. "Why is my entire family so embarrassing?"

Will leaned closer to her and lowered his voice. "Embarrassing or homicidal?"

She shot him a side-eye glare, then turned her attention back to her grandpa. "PawPaw, it doesn't work like that."

"Like what?" Will asked, wondering which direction he needed to go running to get to the highway and if he could manage a decent pace in these damn cowboy boots.

PawPaw shrugged, his grin amiable. "Sometimes you have to improvise, Trigger. This is the only way to kick off a game-night Ironman."

"Who made up that rule?" Hadley asked as she looked around at the rest of her family who were eating their Frito pie and—going by their amused expressions and unabashed gawking—obviously enjoying the free floor show.

PawPaw grinned, playing his part like he'd been born for it. "I did."

Will's palms were getting sweaty, and even though he knew it probably wasn't bad in the family-of-serial-killers kind of way, still he had no clue what in the world was going on. "Can someone please explain to me what this is about?"

"It's the couple's riddle," PawPaw said, as if

that explained everything. "Now, hold out your arm."

Everyone except for Hadley had their gaze glued to Will, pinning him to the hardwood bench of the picnic table. Stephanie and Gabe had that adoring look parents in the movies had when their kid went to prom. Adalyn was smiling at them, but her lips were pressed so tight together, they were lined in white. Knox, Weston, Aunt Louise, and the cousins were all staring at him with the glee of someone in one of the popcorn-eating gifs.

"Not sure I want to do that." Translation, there was no way in hell he was going to do that.

"It's nothing bad, just...well, my family." Hadley sighed and held out her arm toward her grandpa. "Go ahead and do it."

There was no way this was a good idea, but if she was willing to go with it, he wasn't going to chicken out. Pushing aside his misgivings, Will held out his arm so it was next to Hadley's. PawPaw didn't waste any time, snapping the handcuffs closed around their wrists.

"And we have our official couple to solve the riddle. I hope it goes better for you than it did when Hadley and Adalyn had to solve their riddle," PawPaw said, shaking his head. "It took them three hours."

Hadley let out a laughing gasp. "We were twelve."

"It was what was black and white and read all over," PawPaw said.

"PawPaw," Adalyn said with a chuckle. "We read news apps, not newspapers, and back then we didn't even do that."

"Enough yapping. Give them the riddle," Aunt Louise said before popping a corn chip in her mouth and crunching it loudly.

PawPaw rolled his eyes at his sister who, by the looks of things, had been telling him exactly what she thought he should be doing with his life for the better part of sixty years; then he turned back to Hadley and Will. "You ready?"

Hadley let out a sigh of resignation. "Yes."

"I sizzle like bacon and am made with an egg," PawPaw said. "I have a backbone but not a single good leg. When I peel like an onion, I still manage to remain whole. And even though I can be long like a flagpole, I can fit in a hole. What am I?"

"Diner food," Will said without even having to consider.

Easy answer. The key with riddles was to never overthink it.

PawPaw made a loud, blaring horn sound. "Wrong."

"Shhhhhhhhhh!" Hadley nudged him in the ribs with her elbow just hard enough to get her point across. "We only get two more guesses. No more answering without consultation."

"How was I supposed to know that?" he asked, scooting in closer to her so they were too close for a repeat—the fact that they were now aligned thigh to hip to shoulder was an unavoidable side effect. It wasn't the reason he'd moved closer. Although, yeah, he'd shot Matt a how-you-like-me-now smirk when he'd done it. He never told anyone that he wasn't an asshole. "It's not exactly a common occurrence to handcuff two people together until they can solve a riddle."

"Exactly," Hadley said, her voice a little breathier than it had been a minute ago. "Welcome to the family."

He spent the rest of dinner hyperaware of Hadley. The brush of her shoulder against his. The citrusy scent of her shampoo. And the weight of the metal handcuff against his wrist went from cold and strange to familiar by the time he was eating the chocolate cake. He and Hadley were still finishing up dessert when the rest of the family started clearing the table and going inside to set up for game night.

He lifted his cuffed left hand, picking up her right with it. "So what happens now?"

"We're stuck together until we solve it or tonight's game ends, whichever comes first," she said but didn't scoot over so there was more space between them, despite the fact that they now had the entire bench to themselves.

He followed his own logical advice not to read too much into that. His dick did not, thickening against his thigh as if he had all the control of a teenager sitting next to the hot chick in biology class.

"And this is totally normal for your family?" he asked, grateful in that moment that his voice didn't crack like it had when he *had* been in high school.

Hadley pivoted, her leg sliding against his. "When you're half an hour from your nearest neighbor, you learn to make your own fun. It was

Knox you have to thank for this one. He got a pair of toy cuffs for Christmas one year and hooked himself to PawPaw. Of course, the locking mechanism went haywire, and they made a game of working out how to pop the lock." She shrugged one shoulder. "Since then, PawPaw has provided the riddle and whoever is the designated duo has to solve it in three guesses or deal with the shame of not being able to figure it out."

As natural as breathing, he dipped his face and lowered his voice, making the circle that was them even smaller. "What, you have to wear an I'm-a-loser hat?"

She tilted her chin upward, the move bringing her lips within inches of him, one side of her mouth curled in a smile. He couldn't look away from that mouth of hers, just like he hadn't been able to last night.

He'd devoured her image in the mirror, committing it to a memory that not even a kick to the head with a steel-toed boot would remove. The fresh pink of her nipples. The curve of her hip. The roundness of her thighs. He'd remember it all, but it was her mouth that he'd kept returning to look at time and time again. Even as he fucked her, deep, hard, and with everything he had last night, he hadn't kissed her. Looking down at that mouth now, it was hard to imagine he'd been such an idiot to have missed the opportunity to kiss her again.

"No hat," she said before wetting her lips with the tip of her pink tongue. "But in this family, we don't play games for fun. We're here to win."

"I can get behind that." He turned a little more, the move bringing his leg under hers and moving her hand a little higher on his thigh.

"Good, because I am awful, and between this"—she lifted up her arm, which brought his into the air as well—"and a game of Donavan-Martinez Scrabble, we could be in cuffs all night long."

That gave him all sorts of ideas he should not be having, like he needed any help with that. For the past year, he'd either been thinking about fucking her or screwing her over—either way, the addition of handcuffs was going to add to that.

The hair toss, the light laugh, the hand that dropped back to his thigh, her fingertips grazing the inseam of his jeans. It was all part of her plan; it had to be. Otherwise... Well, he couldn't think about that.

"Okay, so what are your ideas?" she asked, her cheeks turning pink as her eyes widened. "For the riddle."

Riddle? It took his brain a second to regain blood flow enough to figure out what in the hell she was talking about.

"A stick of butter?" he asked. "That sizzles in the frying pan and can be long."

She bit her bottom lip, but a giggle escaped anyway. "I realize you're a city guy, but you do know that butter comes from a cow, not an egg, right?"

He should. He did. It didn't matter right then. "Guess I'll have to keep thinking up new ideas."

God knew he was having enough of them right

now. Every inappropriate can't-even-contemplate-it's-such-a-bad-choice was running through his head. All the warnings were getting muffled by being so close to her. A move of less than two inches and he'd be kissing her again, feeling her full lips open under his as she slid her hand higher on his thigh until—

The screen door slammed open and they both started, breaking apart. Hadley looked at him, wide-eyed with flushed cheeks, and pressed her fingertips against her lips as if he'd actually kissed her. Adrenaline and lust were raging through his body as if he had.

"Are you guys coming in?" PawPaw asked, taking a step out of the back door. "We drew Louise's team for Scrabble. It's her, Raider, and that Matt fella."

The mention of Hadley's ex, who was obviously ready to make a play, pierced the haze of attraction and anticipation that had him fisting his hands to keep from reaching out for her. Matt was staying, huh? Suddenly, winning game night got a little bit more crucial—not that losing was ever an option. He stood up and stepped over the bench seat, ready to send Matt packing.

"You explained the house rules to him?" PawPaw asked.

Hadley shook her head, her gaze a little fuzzy as she looked up at him and got up. Will reached out and helped her steady herself as she stepped over the bench seat and started toward the door.

PawPaw lifted a bushy gray eyebrow. "What have you two *not daters* been up to out here?"

Hadley cleared her throat and looked down at the patterned stone marks on the cement patio. "We've been working on the riddle."

"Uh-huh." PawPaw looked them both up and down before shaking his head. "So here's how it works. We're on a team of three. Instead of the usual seven tiles each, we get five. At the beginning of your turn, one of the members of your team will give you a tile from their pile without knowing what letters you have. Then you have to make a word playing off what's on the board plus using the tile your teammate gave you. Got it?"

Will nodded.

"Good," PawPaw said with a nod. "Now, hustle up. I have to get Louise a sun tea, and then we're starting."

Then the older man went back inside, letting the screen door slam shut behind him, which left Will and Hadley alone again.

"Is there a reason it's so complicated?" Will asked, looking at the handcuff around his wrist.

"Because when we were younger, everyone wanted to play. There were only so many pieces and Knox was too little to play by himself and be competitive, so we came up with the Donavan-Martinez house rules," Hadley said. "It all sort of grew from there."

He wasn't sure how to process that. It wasn't like he had any experience in his own family with something like that. For him and Web, being too young to participate meant that they didn't. Period. No exceptions. Yet here was Hadley's family willing to rewrite the rules so everyone could be a part of it. He didn't even have to guess at what kind of reaction that would have gotten from his grandmother. She would have taken one look at him or Web and would have told them that the world didn't make allowances and neither did she. There was no wiggle room for ability or age or just kindness—a person was either able to compete or not. He'd always thought that's how everyone's family was.

"That sounds—"

"Totally bananas?" Hadley asked with a wry chuckle.

"I was going to say kinda nice," he answered before he had time to think through his words, only realizing as they came out that it was exactly what he meant.

Hadley laughed, the sound light and musical—like the way she chuckled when Web told one of his jokes. "Don't tell me you're drinking the sun tea and thinking this"—she lifted their shackled wrists up again—"is normal behavior."

"I'm not sure there is a normal when it comes to you." At least not the way he would have described it before meeting her. Now? Well, things were starting to look different.

He held open the screen door for her and they made their way inside—a little more awkwardly than normal, since they were cuffed together—and that's when he spotted it. A pink-and-yellow-painted snake sculpture sitting by a trio of flowerpots.

"I sizzle like bacon and am made with an egg," PawPaw had said. *"I have a backbone but not a*

single good leg. When I peel like an onion, I still
manage to remain whole. And even though I can
be long like a flagpole, I can fit in a hole. What am
I?

A snake.

He opened his mouth, about to let the answer
out so they could tell PawPaw and get these damn
handcuffs off, but nothing came out.

"Think of something?" Hadley asked.

"Nope." He shook his head, not sure why he
didn't just come out with the answer but not
willing to examine it. Not yet anyway.

Then they walked inside to utter pandemoni-
um.

• • •

It took a while, but all the we're-gonna-kick-your-
butt family game night smack talk finally
simmered down enough that everyone was settled
around their particular board game in the family
room under the watchful painted eye of Miguel
Martinez, the original Martinez to own the
Hidden Creek Ranch.

The oil painting hanging over the fireplace of
Gabe's grandfather standing under the sign for
the ranch had been a gift from Hadley, Adalyn,
Weston, and Knox last Christmas. She'd found an
artist in Harbor City to paint it from a photo-
graph whose edges had started to curl that
Gabe's parents had kept on the fridge until
they'd retired and moved down to Arizona. Next
to the painting were graduation pics of each of

the kids, a photo from Gabe and her mom's wedding day, and a picture from the last family reunion that had been shot as a panorama to fit everyone in. A lot of the people in that photo were here, laughing, strategizing, and stuffing their faces with popcorn balls. In the middle of the room, Gabe and her mom were facing off against Knox and Weston in a cutthroat game of speed Monopoly.

They were all laughing and teasing one another, meanwhile PawPaw must be thinking that Hadley had banged her head on the overhead bins on the flight out here. He'd dropped the words "hiss" and "slither" and "rattle" on the Scrabble board, giving her a nudge with his elbow each time, as if she hadn't realized the answer was a snake. Yeah, riddles weren't really her thing, but he'd used this one before.

Meanwhile, all this mandatory fun family time was starting to overwhelm her, making her belly tight and her neck sore. She rolled her shoulders for the twentieth time since she sat down, trying to relieve some of the tension being surrounded by family always seemed to produce, but the uncomfortable, you-don't-belong unease didn't loosen its grip.

Across the table, Aunt Louise tried to come up with a word using whatever tile Matt had given her. Judging by the nasty look she'd sent Matt's way, it was probably a Q or a Z.

Will leaned closer, dipping his head so his lips almost brushed the shell of her ear as he whispered, "You feeling okay?"

"Just peachy." And now she'd add *inappropriately turned on* to all the other tension stringing her tight.

Grumbly? Her? Always around Will. He just brought it out in her. Hell, usually he did it on purpose. That she could handle, but this nicer side to Will? This version of him who'd check to make sure she wasn't having a panic attack in her parents' family room? Yeah, she had no idea how to deal with him, and that made her surly. And hot. And turned on. And—*dammit, pull yourself together, Hads.*

Determined to do just that, she kept her posture straight, her gaze focused on the game in front of them, and ignored completely the urge to tuck herself up against Will.

"Why?" she asked.

"Because you kinda look like me in the car," he said, scooting closer to her so there wasn't a single millimeter of light between them, as if he just understood that she needed that contact right now.

"Wow." She dug deep, trying to find her usual annoyance at being near him to keep from relaxing against his solid frame. "You really know how to flatter a woman."

He let out a low, rumbly chuckle. "I like to think that it's what else I can do with a woman that is more important."

Her breath caught as all the memories from last night rushed forward. The feel of him so gentle as he picked the flowers from her hair and undressed her. The hard length of him as he filled her, taking her right to the edge without even trying. The thrillingly harsh sound of his demand that she say his name. All of it slammed against her in a wave of want and need, nearly drowning her in desire, sending her jolting straight up out of her chair in panic.

She shot her cuffed wrist into the air, taking Will's with her. "Snake!"

Aunt Louise screamed and jumped up onto her chair while Matt, Raider, and everyone else in the room reacted by either screaming, climbing onto the furniture, or searching for a slithering intruder. Well, everyone but her, PawPaw, and Will.

Way to make it worse, Hads.

Using her fingers, she let out a loud whistle to get her family's attention. "That's the answer to the riddle."

"About damn time," PawPaw said as he unlocked the handcuffs while the rest of the family settled back into their chairs. "I was starting to wonder about you."

Aunt Louise shot Hadley a you-damn-fool look and laid down her tiles for the word "lovers." It wasn't until Will handed her a Q for the start of her turn and even that slight brush of his fingers against hers set off a sizzle of anticipation that realization hit. The only people who hadn't thought she was shouting a warning about a real snake were her, PawPaw...and Will. He must have known the answer all along, but he hadn't said a word. What did that mean? She had no clue, but it sure didn't do a damn thing to settle the butterflies running kamikaze flight patterns in her stomach.

She let out a shaky breath and tried to forget they'd be alone again tonight. In the cabin. She had to stay strong. He was Web's asshole brother. The evil twin. He thought she was a gold digger. Whatever this was between them, it wasn't a good thing, and the last thing she needed was to fall for her best friend's jerk of a brother.

And that's exactly why it wasn't going to happen.

• • •

The first thing Will heard when he opened the cabin's front door after walking from the house after their game night win was a low almost-growl that some caveman part of him instantly recognized as a warning. He jolted to a stop in the cabin's doorway and threw out his arm to keep Hadley from walking in.

She let out an *oof*. "What in the world?"

"There's something in here."

Blinking to let his eyes adjust to the dark inside, he searched out the source of the noise while moving to the left so his body blocked Hadley from whatever was inside. It would have to go through him to get to her, and that wasn't going to happen.

At least it wouldn't if she would stay still and completely behind him, something it seemed she was unable to do. Instead, she reached around him, moved her hand across the wall inside the door until she touched the light switch, and then flipped it on. Everything that had been pitch-black a second ago was bathed in light. If it was a bear, a lion, or the abominable snowman, it was pretty fucking good at hiding, because Will didn't see anything as he scanned the room, primed and ready to launch himself at whatever came at them.

Hadley, her hands on his waist, peeked around him and ewwed. "Oh, that's just nasty."

That's when he saw it or, more correctly, when he saw Lightning. The swift fox sitting on the one chair in the living room, munching away on what he'd carried in after the night's hunt.

"Lightning, this isn't your dining room." Hadley strutted into the room, assertive but not aggressive. "How did you get in here with that?"

The swift fox wasn't telling. Instead, he picked up the small rabbit / large rodent / whatever had not run away fast enough, leaped down from the chair, and darted out the front door. What he left behind on what was supposed to be Will's bed that night looked like the outtake from a vampire movie.

"Oh my God, that's so gross," Hadley said, gagging a little as she got closer. "You still want to move to the country?"

Yeah, living in his penthouse in Harbor City sounded pretty good—especially after he got a look at the carnage left behind on the chair. "We can't leave this in here."

Hadley agreed and held open the door while he carried the chair out the front door of their cabin and over to the stand-alone water faucet near one of the cabins that hadn't been renovated yet. He turned on the water full blast, and she aimed the hose at the chair and let loose, spraying it down and washing away what was left of Lightning's dinner.

He was a few steps away from the water faucet when she pivoted toward him. The water was still hitting the now clean chair, but—judging by the ornery grin on her face visible under the bright light of the full moon—it may not be for long. He measured the distance in a heartbeat. There was no way he could cut the water before she got him. What had he been thinking by letting her control the hose? He hadn't, that much was obvious.

"Hadley," he said in warning.

She gave him a cocky wink and then folded the hose, effectively cutting off the water. "Gotcha."

He hustled over to the faucet and turned the water off before she changed her mind. His grandmother may not have been the touchy-feely kind, but she hadn't raised any fools, either.

After getting the hose wound up, they started back to their cabin. He shortened his stride so they could walk next to each other, no doubt a holdover from spending the evening handcuffed together, not for any other reason.

Keep telling yourself that, Holt.

Yeah, he didn't even believe his own bullshit on that one, which was a problem—a big one. Hadley was a problem. She wasn't someone Web could depend on. When it came to that, he and his brother knew the only people they could depend on was each other. They'd learned that lesson time and time again—all before they'd turned eight and had been shipped off to boarding school for the first time.

Exhaling a deep breath to clear out the memories of that place, he glanced up at the night's sky and nearly tripped over his own feet in surprise.

The sky was huge, and the moon hung big and round in the middle, surrounded by a million bright, twinkling stars. IMAX had nothing on the real thing of being out here.

"Wow," he said, slowing to a stop and just staring upward, slack-jawed. "Look at that."

"It's the sky," she said, her boredom sounding a little too practiced to be genuine.

"No." He closed the short distance between them. Ending up so he was standing slightly behind her—close but not touching, no matter how much he wanted to, despite knowing better. "Stop and really look at it."

She did, tilting her chin upward. He should have looked back up at the stars, but he didn't. Instead, he watched as her usual smile softened into one that he'd never seen before, not even when she looked at Web. It wasn't that it was more genuine or easy so much as it was rare and a little bit sad.

A sudden, sharp jab of regret hit him square in the chest as he watched her, because the truth was he was at least partially responsible for that sadness because of all the shit he'd been giving her since day one. Yeah, he didn't want to trust her. Yeah, he'd been burned to a crisp by letting himself believe before. Yeah, he never made the wrong call, but that itchy something called doubt that he wasn't used to was scratching at the back of his brain.

"It's like a whole other world out here."

He let out a deep breath. Maybe that was it. It was the ranch and the stars that had gotten to him, not the woman beside him who he couldn't stop thinking about. "I can't disagree."

"A first for us," she said with a laugh. "Come on."

They walked back to the cabin under those endless stars, anticipation wrapped around them like a blanket. Once there, Hadley hurried up the steps to the front porch and started looking around the window, testing it to see if it was open. The light spilling out from it was enough that it outlined her, giving him a perfect view of her every curve. She was hot enough to make a drowning man thirsty, and he wasn't even close to going under the water.

"Checking to see if Lightning is lurking?" he asked, trying—and failing—not to notice the way her ass looked in her jeans.

She shook her head. "Trying to figure out how he got in."

"The door was closed." He'd opened it himself, and the latch had definitely been engaged.

"And the front window is shut tight." She twisted up her mouth and drummed her fingertips on the window frame. "I mean, they can get through even if it's only open a little, but that's not the case here."

Realization smacked him across both cheeks,

and he let out a groan. "Lightning could get in through a window?"

She turned, her eyes narrowing. "What did you do, Will?"

He gave her his most charming smile, the one that usually left women a little dazed. Hadley just lifted an eyebrow in a silent demand for the truth.

He braced himself. "I might have left the window in the bedroom open when I changed in there yesterday."

She let out a groan and hurried inside. Because there wasn't another choice, he followed behind and caught up to her just inside the bedroom. What had been slightly organized chaos was now a raging disaster. Boxes were overturned. Tools were scattered all over the floor. Claw marks were scratched into the wood. A can of paint balanced precariously on the edge of a workbench.

"Okay, I'm realizing now that I should have shut the window," he said, each word coming out as rusty as a person would expect, considering he rarely, if ever, admitted to fucking up or apologizing. "I'm sorry."

She looked so shocked at his admission of being wrong that for a second she just stared at him wide-eyed before coming back to herself. "Out here, if you leave the windows open, something will come wandering in."

He nodded. "Duly noted."

Some kind of weird truce being silently agreed to, they went back into the living room—all the more spacious now that the chair, also known as the extra bed, was gone. Shit. What in the hell

were they going to do now? Sleeping in the bed
with her was not an option. Last night had nearly
killed him. A man wasn't supposed to have a hard-
on for as long as he had, trying to fall asleep next
to her. At one point she'd rolled over and
snuggled up next to him, twisting one leg around
his. He'd almost come in his underwear. Going
through that again would be agony.

"I'll take the floor," he said, glancing down at
the hardwood that looked like it might put him in
traction.

She shook her head. "You don't have to do
that."

"Are you sure?" Did that sound hopeful? It
shouldn't. It couldn't. Aw fuck, he was so screwed.

"If you don't get any sleep and we end up
losing Monopoly tomorrow night, PawPaw will
kill me, so this is a better alternative." She took
off one of the couch cushions and set it down on
the floor where the chair had been as she began to
make up their bed. *Their* bed. "I'll try my best not
to disturb you with my snoring."

Yeah. Snoring. That was pretty much the least
of his worries when it came to sharing a bed with
Hadley.

• • •

Hadley stared up at the ceiling, more awake than
she'd been before she'd crawled under the blanket
and then tossed it off before she melted. Lying
down next to Will was like cuddling with a space
heater set on inferno, even though he was wearing

only a pair of low-hanging basketball shorts. She would have thought that it would help when he flung off the covers almost as soon as he'd gotten into bed, making a little blanket mountain between them.

It hadn't.

And the fact that there was just enough light from the full moon coming in through the window to give her a good view of almost every part of him she hadn't gotten to look her fill of last night—which was pretty much all of him—wasn't helping. Thank God her sense of self-preservation saved her from staring.

Instead, she pulled the blanket back over her and just baked under it with one foot uncovered and the rest of her roasting as she noticed *everything* about Will, from the steady cadence of his deep breaths to the way he was only inches from her, temptingly close. Not that she was thinking about it. "Obsessing" would be more correct, which was why she hadn't been able to close her eyes for longer than a few seconds.

If being ultra-aware of him while staring at the ceiling was bad, having her dirty mind fill in the blanks when she closed her eyes was even worse.

"Do you think that crack on the ceiling means it's going to fall in on us?" he asked, his voice a low rumble in the dark.

Her pulse picked up as her body, already way too attuned to him, buzzed with anticipation, and she took in a shaky breath. Okay, nothing to do now that she'd been busted but play it out. "Probably not but, if it did, we'd have a great view of the stars."

"They really are something." He rolled over—the move making the middle of the bed dip toward him—and propped his head up on his hand. "Don't you miss seeing them in Harbor City?"

Even if she wasn't doing everything she could at the moment to fight gravity and roll into him, she wouldn't have been sure how to answer that. When it came to home and family, things were always mixed-up and messy.

"Looking up at all those stars used to make me so frustrated," she said, turning to face him, mirroring his pose. "It was like I could see there was so much more than just this ranch, but it was so far away that I couldn't ever be a part of it."

That always-on-the-outside feeling lingered even all these years later, like a cold that she just couldn't quit. That's why she fought so hard to make her place in Harbor City, to prove she belonged there.

For the most part, it worked, but there were always exceptions, people who pointed out every single thing about her that still screamed *country* despite her attempts to hide them—one of whom was lying next to her in the dark.

"That's why I was so determined to move to Harbor City, but even there I'm still someone who's an outsider, different, other…and people aren't afraid to let me know."

Wow. She would not have put "confessing her biggest insecurities to her nemesis" on her bingo card for weird things that would happen during her sister's wedding week.

"I'm guessing I'm on that list," he said, giving her an apologetic smile that in this light looked genuine. "I admit it, I can be an asshole, but I have my reasons."

"Because of Mia." It wasn't a question. He'd covered it up well enough at dinner the other night, but an ex-fiancée would sting even for someone like Will Holt. "What happened?" The question popped out before she realized it was bubbling up inside her. "Wait!" She reached out, her hand brushing his chest before she pulled it away, fingers tingling. "You don't have to tell me. It's not like we're friends."

"Just two people in the foxhole together," he said with a wry chuckle.

"Yeah," she said. "Something like that."

Something like a whole lot of losing my mind.

She rolled onto her back, wondering if it was socially acceptable to pull the covers over her head and scream silently. Not only did she not need to be in his business, she didn't *want* to be in his business. She wasn't going to be fooled by fake cowboy Will, who she happened to have had sex with *in PawPaw's bathroom*! Oh God, she was never going to be able to use that bathroom again. Good thing she only visited a few times a year.

You. Are. So. Naive.

She had no clue how to break the awkward, heavy silence that enveloped them, punctuated only by the creepy coyote calls that sounded like babies crying for help, so she opted for staring at the ceiling. Maybe she'd get lucky and a chunk of plaster would come crumbling down and put her out of her misery.

"She refused to sign the prenup after telling me she was pregnant—which I found out later she most definitely was not," Will said, his voice an unexpected boom in the dark. "That wouldn't have been a big deal, but she let it slip that this was basically going to be an arranged marriage anyway, so she should get one thing out of it. Turns out our engagement was a scheme cooked up by her family and my grandmother as some kind of melding of two old-money Harbor City families—only one of whom still had cash—and all the relevant parties knew it for what it was except, of course, me." He grimaced and went quiet for a second, working his jaw back and forth as if he were chewing on the distasteful realization that he'd ever believed it. "I thought the whole thing was real."

"I'm sorry." Sliding her hand across the warm cotton sheet, she didn't stop until her fingers were intertwined with his. "That's awful."

"I lived. I learned. I know better now." The words came out cold and unyielding. "I should have known better then. Our grandmother has never been interested in anything but herself and her own interests. She's made it abundantly clear in nearly every interaction with us since she shipped Web and me off to boarding school a month after our parents died."

He locked eyes with Hadley and she shivered, the temperature in the room dropping to arctic levels.

"Her schedule didn't allow for children, let alone two who were grieving," he said, answering her question before she could have asked it.

"Will—"

"It is what it is," he cut her off and flopped back on the bed, his gaze turned toward the ceiling. "So trust me, being on the inside of Harbor City society isn't always so great." The words came out slowly, as if he'd never before put it into words. "Everything is so close, so in your face, that you can't see the stars at all and it's easy to still feel like you're the only one there."

"But you have Web," she said, giving his hand a squeeze.

"And you have an entire extended family who want you around so much, they'll handcuff you to keep you close. I don't think you realize how lucky you are for that." He let out a harsh breath and pulled his hand away. "If you think Web's money will give you that sense of belonging, I hate to break it to you, but it won't."

Hadley lay there, an angry white buzzing noise filling her ears, her cheeks burning with heat as if he'd smacked her across the face with his words. She didn't want anything from Web other than his friendship, and if Will couldn't see that, he could go jump in a lake because she wasn't about to justify his wrongheaded belief with a response.

She rolled onto her back and pulled the covers up to her chin. "Good night, Will."

She forced her eyes closed and timed her breaths with his long, steady ones. Miraculously, her thoughts got slower, the blanket got heavier, and before she realized it, she was being woken up by the not-so-gentle nudging of her brother Knox poking a stick against her shoulder.

"Wake up, sis," Knox said, keeping his volume low.

Hadley glanced over at Will. His eyes were still closed, his breathing even, and he had his hands tucked up under his chin. Before she could stop herself, she let out a mental *awwwww*.

Come on, Hads. Wolves probably look sweet when they sleep, too.

"What are you doing here?" she asked in a harsh whisper, giving him the bug-eyed, twisted-mouth, get-the-fuck-out-of-here face.

Forever the youngest brother, Knox ignored her silent leave-now message and lifted the two large sticks in his hands. "Time to go snipe hunting."

Oh, for the love of hazing the city slicker. "You cannot do that to him."

Knox shrugged and grinned. "It's a tradition."

"Since when?" Oh my God, the ridiculousness of this whole situation.

He looked down at his watch. "About five minutes ago."

"Knox," she whisper-shouted, reminding herself that her parents would be really pissed if she killed him. "I'm warning you—"

"I am awake, you know," Will said.

"Good," Knox said, dropping any attempt at whispering. "Let's get on out there. Best time of the day to catch snipes is right after dawn when they're tired after staying up all night. Not that you two would know anything about that."

"Shut up, Knox," she said.

"You've known me your whole life; you know that's not gonna happen." He headed toward the door. "Let's go, you two."

Sitting up, she tried to figure out how to explain that her brothers weren't wanting to make a fool out of him so much as bust his chops in a way that they'd no doubt document on video so the whole family could watch later. "There's something you need to know."

"Is it about your intentions toward my brother?" Will said, his voice rough with sleep.

He left the "and his bank account" unspoken, but it hung between them anyway. And here she was going to do Will a solid before he made a total fool of himself by explaining there was no such thing as a snipe. She should have known better. He was, after all, the evil twin incarnate.

"Good luck catching the snipe," she told him, covering her annoyance with a sickly sweet tone.

"You're not coming?" he asked.

She hadn't planned to, but after that comment? Oh yeah, she was going to be there to make sure they got all the angles of Will making a snipe-hunting fool of himself on video. "I wouldn't miss it for the world."

CHAPTER THIRTEEN

Will was turning into a sucker. That was the only explanation that made any sense to him as to why he was playing along with this snipe-hunt country hazing. There was no way in hell that banging two sticks together while whistling in three short bursts with exactly thirty-three seconds of silence between each trio was going to result in capturing anything, let alone a fake animal. Especially not while walking in the middle of a field where the cows were looking at Will like he was three bales short of…whatever hay bales added up to.

Not to mention the description of a snipe kept changing.

On the drive out to the cow pasture, he'd gotten about ten different descriptions, all varying just enough to make the whole thing completely ridiculous. He would have called them on it, too, but Hadley was walking ahead of him and he kept getting distracted by the view. She had her hair braided, the end coming out from underneath a baseball hat advertising Feed and Seed, and she was wearing a pair of jeans that just might give him a heart attack.

"What did you say these things looked like?"

he asked for the millionth time to see what kind of answer he'd get. Really, listening to their descriptions of the snipe put it somewhere between a feathered weasel and a rabid penguin.

"They're birds," Hadley said, twisting the end of her braid around her fingers as she slowed her pace so they were side by side. "But they don't fly very well."

"They consider cow patties a delicacy," Knox said. "So be sure to get as close to one as you can, then stand real still and whistle."

There was no way to take Hadley's youngest brother seriously. Knox had been cracking jokes the entire ride out here in his truck. They weren't even good jokes—they were dad jokes.

Will whacked his sticks together, which he'd been told earlier was the key to attracting a snipe's attention. "And why are you using your phone to video this?"

"It's part of the family game night Ironman." Knox grinned at him, not even trying to pretend any of this was real. "If you catch a snipe, you win the whole thing, no matter how many games you've lost."

He had two choices here. Call Knox and Hadley on their bullshit or keep playing along and use this opportunity to get more inside dirt on Hadley. Maybe if he could figure out what made her tick, he could find a way to convince her that her plans for Web's money weren't going to work out. He'd tried the direct route. It hadn't worked. He needed to go a more subtle route, which really was not his forte. He'd always been the bulldozer and Web had been the charmer.

"You ever think that you take this a little too seriously?" Will asked.

Knox, who was practically a Labrador in human form, happily shook his head as he started recording again. "Nope."

"So why aren't you hunting, Hadley?" Really, why should he be the only one going through this? "Wouldn't that increase our chances of catching a snipe?"

Turning, she stopped walking and stared him down. "I don't hunt."

"Oh, come on, Hads," Knox said, obviously thrilled at the idea of making fools of both of them. "It's not like you'd keep the little fella. This is a catch-and-release operation."

Will paused, resting the large sticks against his shoulder, and let his gaze travel from the rounded tips of her well-worn work boots to the frayed brim of her baseball cap. "I never took you for someone who backed down from a challenge."

"I don't know," Knox said, laying it on thick. "Maybe city life has made her go soft."

"Really?" She stood there, one hip cocked out, her arms crossed, and glared at them both. "That's what you're going with?"

Taking full advantage of the response he knew she'd give, he turned to Knox. "Don't suppose she was this stubborn growing up?"

"You have no idea." Knox pocketed his phone with a chuckle. "She walked away from dessert for a week rather than take one bite of butternut squash."

"And here I thought she'd never been in trouble a day in her life." Hard to be *in* trouble when you *were* trouble.

"Oh, that is so not the case. There was the time she got caught sneaking back in the house after—"

"Knox!" Hadley—her cheeks pink—hollered at her brother.

"Fine." Knox shrugged. "It's not like we're telling about the time you ate raw pie dough because you couldn't admit you'd made a mistake."

She closed her eyes and groaned. "You just did."

"Oops." Knox, a huge grin on his face, turned to Will. "So she insisted she didn't need any help making pie from scratch, but she forgot to prebake the crust—"

"That was not on the recipe card," Hadley interrupted.

"So when it came out of the oven and we all took a bite, the crust wasn't completely raw but it wasn't done, either. The rest of us took a polite bite, then said we were full. Meanwhile, Miss Always Right over there ate her entire piece, the whole time insisting the crust was supposed to be like that."

Okay, *that* Will could imagine without even trying. In the year he'd known her, he'd never seen her allude to things not being completely perfect or that she was ever wrong. He pivoted toward her, a comment about just that on his lips, when the look on her face stopped him. Her chin was tilted just a little too high, her smile a little too tight, and her posture a little too rigid. Knox may not have meant anything by his teasing, but it was clear as the blue sky above them that it had struck a nerve.

This is where you slide that knife home.

But he didn't. Instead, for reasons he didn't understand beyond the twist in his gut, he held up his sticks. "I'm not getting any traction here with the snipe. Can you show me how it's done?"

She shook her head. "No way."

"Come on," he cajoled, holding out the sticks to her. "I'm obviously fucking this up. Usually, you love to tell me all about how I should be doing things, so give me a lesson."

The corner of her mouth twitched upward as she took his sticks and started banging them together and whistling. He should have been taking that opportunity to gain more intel from her brother to figure out what vulnerabilities he could exploit to get her to back off Web—did he need to cut a check, offer her a job, buy her a condo in Boca?—but he got distracted by her ass again. He couldn't help it.

She'd ass-notized him.

• • •

Hadley was not laughing on the bumpy ride from the cow pasture a half hour after her brother had ratted her out for making the world's worst pie. She was not enjoying the fact that all the jostling meant she was sitting thigh to thigh with Will to maintain her balance. Also, she was not in the least bit bummed out about regaining her own personal bubble when Knox pulled the truck to a stop in front of the old barn where Adalyn's reception was going to be.

Peeling paint and all, the barn looked gorgeous set against the pasture behind it and the big blue sky above. Off to the west were a few out-of-commission work buildings and a small cabin like the one she was staying in with Will.

"The four-wheeler is around back," Knox said as she and Will climbed down from the truck's cab. "You can ride that back to the house."

Wait. What? Her pulse jacked up and she spun around. "You're not decorating?"

Knox shook his head. "I have other obligations, but I'll see you back at the house tonight for part two of game night. We have you guys in Pictionary."

Oh God. When that wasn't the worst bit of news she'd gotten in the past sixty seconds, that was saying something, because her artistic skill was so bad that stick figures were a reach. Since it wasn't an option to hold on to the open truck door and beg Knox not to leave her alone with Will because she didn't trust herself, she shut the passenger door and Knox drove off.

You can do this, Hads. You can ignore the way he looks in those jeans and the way his T-shirt fits with just the right amount of tightness across his shoulders. You will not fall for the packaging. Oh God. Package.

Her gaze dipped down to his jeans' zipper before she could stop herself.

Dammit, Hads. This is not part of the plan.

What was the plan? Hell if she could remember.

"Are you two coming in?" Adalyn called from the open barn door.

Shoulders lifting, Hadley let out a relieved sigh that evened out her janky blood pressure.

Thank you, baby Jesus.

Hadley was always thrilled to see her little sister, but seeing her now was like finding the oasis in the desert—a chance at survival. She rushed over and gave her sister a bear hug.

"You just saw me last night," her sister said, her voice muffled, since her face was squashed against Hadley's shoulder.

Taking a step back, because suffocating her sister was not on her to-do list, Hadley said, "I know, but you're gorgeous, your wedding is in a few days, and I'm so excited to help."

The doubtful expression on Adalyn's face and the knowing smirk on Will's all but confirmed that Hadley wasn't pulling it off, but she didn't care as long as they all just went with it. Mercifully they did—at least for the moment—and walked into the old barn.

For as long as she'd known about it, the building had been called "the old barn." It was one of those old-fashioned, curved-roofed red barns with a hayloft and horse stalls. Knox must have been out here with his renovation plans, though, because the musty, grimy, splintery, unused barn had been transformed. Most of the stalls at the back had been removed to create an open space big enough for a dance floor, long tables that went down both sides, and a raised dais for the wedding party to sit at. The remainder had been outfitted with booth seats that wrapped around the U-shaped half walls of the old stalls to offer a quieter space for guests to sit and chat.

The result was a unique reception area, pretty enough in its country charm to be Instagramable without even having to use a filter.

While she and Will took in the place like a couple of tourists, Adalyn stood in the middle of the barn with her arms wrapped around her waist, her hair up in a bedraggled ponytail, and dark circles under her eyes. Tension rolled off her in waves as she looked around at the etched mason jar vases on the tables and the strings of fairy lights hanging from the haylofts above them. Weddings were stressful, everyone knew that, but this wasn't the usual jitters and nerves. How could it be with her fiancé still a no-show? The urge to drive to Denver to smack that man upside the head was strong, but she stuffed it down. That wasn't what her sister needed at the moment.

"Wow, this looks amazing," Hadley said. "The reception is going to be almost as gorgeous as you."

Adalyn gave her a short, tight smile. "It took a while to talk Gabe and Mom into it, but then Weston, Knox, and I finally convinced them that rich people from the city who wanted something unique would pay big bucks for intimate destination weddings out here." She waved toward the open barn doors. "The plan is to use the cabins as guest cottages once Knox finishes those up. Pretty soon the bunkhouse will be outfitted with twenty junior suites, and we have a crew coming out to build a lodge house and additional cabins. Then we'll have everything to host weddings and corporate retreats during the off-season. With the way things are going, diversification is the name of the game."

"That's an ambitious plan." And one she could totally see her siblings carrying off.

Adalyn whirled around, turning away from Hadley and Will. "You aren't the only one with dreams, you know."

Hadley flinched. "I never said I was."

"Just because I stayed doesn't mean I resigned myself to dodging cow patties for the rest of my life or that I don't have plans for the future," she said, her voice trembling.

"Adalyn." She hurried over to her little sister's side, worry jabbing at her like splinters under her skin, and put an arm around her sister's shoulders. "What's wrong?"

"You have to ask that?" Adalyn shrugged off Hadley's touch and started pacing the wood dance floor. "I'm getting married in forty-eight hours; Derek still isn't here." Her voice got louder and more high-pitched with each word. "And I've spent more than I budgeted just to make this event fancy enough to impress my sister who thinks so badly of where she's from that she left and never comes home."

It only took a second for the shock of the declaration to transform into heavy, hot shame that clogged her throat. "That's not true."

"Really?" Adalyn started pacing again, her angry steps booming in the barn. "Then why do you only come home when you have to?"

Money? Her totally nonexistent free time? The fact that it's easier to maintain the fake-it-because-she-still-hasn't-made-it illusion by text than in person? "My life in Harbor City—"

Her sister threw her hands in the air. "Is perfect. We know. Your life is *always* perfect."

All the phone calls where she glossed over the hard parts of her life, the feeling of being lost in a sea of people, and the constant grind that never seemed to take a break all came back. She hadn't been honest. She'd been a photo filter in human form, smoothing out the cracks and adding a fake layer of soft light that turned everything rosy.

"Adalyn, that's not—"

"What you meant?" she interrupted. "I don't care. Not all of us are perfect all the time. Some of us work hard for things, pouring our hearts and souls into it, and never get the results we want." Adalyn's cheeks were mottled with emotion, and a frustrated anger burned in her eyes. "So yeah, maybe I went a little overboard to make everything extra to impress the woman who everything always does go right for. And what has it gotten me? A fucking clusterfuck of a wedding and a groom who can't seem to get here. I—" Adalyn's voice broke as the tears started rolling down her cheeks.

"Adalyn," Hadley said, her heart aching for her sister as she reached out to wrap her in a hug.

She avoided it with ease. "I gotta go." Then she rushed out of the barn, waving off Hadley's attempt to stop her.

Sinking down onto the cowhide-covered booth seat in a stall near the door and fighting to keep her own tears at bay, Hadley clenched her jaw tight enough to make her teeth ache. It was like all the lies she'd told her family about her life in Harbor City were piling up, one on top of the other, until they'd started tumbling down, landing not just on her but on those she loved, too. She hadn't meant for it to be this way.

Will sat down across from her and she braced herself for the sneer, the cut down, the call out. It was coming. It always did. If anyone saw straight through the bullshit she'd been slinging, it was him.

Nothing in her life had gone right since she'd kissed the wrong man in a coat closet. The very same wrong man sitting across from her right now. That was it—she was leaving. She got up and started out of the stall, but the feel of his finger curling around her pinkie for a second before slipping away stopped her.

"Speaking from siblings-being-pissed-at-you experience, it'll be okay," he said. "She just needs a minute."

Too shocked by his uncharacteristic kindness, she flopped back down into the seat, the words rushing out before she could stop them. "I never meant for things to turn out like this. I have fucked up everything."

He got up and crossed over to her side of the

wraparound booth seat and sat next to her before relaxing back against the seat as if he had nowhere to be anytime soon. "Vent away."

She shouldn't—especially not to him—and yet the words she'd never shared with anyone were bubbling up inside her, and she knew there was no stopping them.

"Adalyn was only five when our dad—" The rest of the words clogged her throat, fighting to stay silent, even now.

She bit the inside of her cheek and looked up at the ceiling, blinking fast. God, it wasn't supposed to still hurt this much. But she didn't even have to try to see the car in the closed garage, smell the fumes, feel the panic when she spotted her dad slumped over the steering wheel. Her mom had shoved her back into the kitchen, then rushed toward the car, yanking the door open as she cried.

She'd been faking it for so long that it didn't still hurt that she couldn't get any words out. It's where she'd first learned. Denial. Push it away. Don't talk about it. Make it look easy, better, perfect so her younger siblings wouldn't be scared, they wouldn't ask why Mom was crying all the time, and they'd stop asking when Daddy was coming home. *Never* didn't seem fathomable to them. It seemed kinder to just pretend everything was fine, and so she did.

And she'd never stopped.

Not since that day.

Not since that moment.

She was so lost in that memory that she could

still feel the wool thread of Weston's sweater bunched in her fist when she held him back before he could run after their mom. It was the soft cotton of Will's T-shirt against her cheek that pulled her back. How he'd made it around the semicircular booth and ended up with her in his arms, she had no clue. All she knew was that feeling the solid thump-thump of his heart against her cheek was exactly what she needed.

"Adalyn was too young to really remember what it had been like before our dad killed himself or what it was like after it happened and before our mom married Gabe," she said, remembering how small her sister had been, with her always lopsided ponytails and her gap-toothed smile.

Will tightened his hold on her and brushed his lips across the top of her head. "I'm sorry."

"It was a long time ago." The stock answer, the one that came out without her even thinking about it, following her motto to minimize, deflect, and move on before the pain became too real again.

"But it never goes away," he said, his voice as scratchy as Weston's wool sweater had been.

That's when it hit her. Here she was, talking to him as if he didn't know what it was like, but he was a double member of the dead parent club. The newspapers in Harbor City loved to bring up references to his parents' tragic car accident when the twins had still been in grade school.

She sat up so she could pivot enough to look him in the face as he sat next to her and confirm what she suspected. It only took a glance to spot it, that understanding look of having been there, too. He knew, and even though they'd still be enemies in an hour, right now they were both in the same shitty club that almost no one ever wanted to be a member of.

"No, it doesn't," she said, taking his hand in hers, entwining her fingers with his. "I used to pretend he was just out there, somewhere, and that he'd find his way back to us. Like he was lost or wandering the Black Hills or something." She shook her head and sighed as some of the pain eased in the telling, like a load made lighter because she wasn't carrying it by herself. "Even now, I'll catch myself going an extra block or two when I'm behind someone who has the same walk as he had or wears the same cologne. It never really goes away, that loss, the sense of betrayal, the wondering why when there really is no answer, and the guilt for still being mad and sad and everything in between. It just sits there, waiting, patient as a spider to trap me in its web whenever I least expect it. So I picture that image of me I want people to have and fake it until I make it true."

Will didn't say anything, didn't burst in with questions, didn't shush her like she had to herself. Growing up like he had, being under the tabloid microscope, must have given him more understanding of how invasive that could be. Instead, he squeezed her hand, turning enough so they were face-to-face, alone but together.

"My job was to keep Adalyn happy so she

wouldn't ask questions," Hadley went on, telling the man she'd always thought of as Evil Twin again what she'd never told anyone else. "No one gave me that job; I just assigned it to myself to make everything seem perfect so she wouldn't be sad—and it worked. So I guess I kept doing it, sharing only the shiny, happy parts and never the jagged, ugly parts." And the fact that everything in her life in Harbor City was starting to feel like a comb with most of its teeth broken into sharp spikes meant she really wasn't sharing anything. Instead she was a ghost with her own family, dodging their calls and texts, leaving her more isolated than she already was in the big city. "I guess I never stopped."

She let out the breath that she'd been holding since they'd found her dad and gathered herself up again, her gaze falling to her fingers intertwined with Will's. His hands were big, steady, as if he never worried about anything.

"We all have our coping mechanisms," he said, his voice soft. "The things that help us through a tough time. It's just that sometimes they stick with us past when we actually need them."

"You sound like you're speaking from experience."

For a minute, she didn't think he'd say anything. Tilting her head up so she could watch his face, she could practically see the war going on in his head by the way his jaw was clenched and the vein at his temple pulsed.

"Our parents died in a freak car accident," he said finally, after letting out a long sigh. "No other drivers, no dangerous conditions, no explanation really. All the reports state is that there were brake marks, but it obviously was too late. They slammed into a tree hard enough that we had to have a closed-caskets double funeral." He paused, looking past Hadley's shoulder as if he could see his parents behind her if he just stared hard enough. "Web and I woke up one morning, went down to eat breakfast, gave our parents hugs before they left for the day, and never saw them again. It was like they just disappeared—well, except for the news coverage. Even at nine, we couldn't avoid seeing all that."

She squeezed his hand. "That must have been awful."

"It was." He shrugged. "But you figure out ways of making things work."

His admission was like a light bulb going on in a dark room, it explained so much. "All the assumptions…"

"I like to think of it as thinking ahead. You can't be surprised if you're already prepped."

"Does it always have to be thinking that people's motives are bad?"

"It's not always like that—only when it involves someone or something that really matters," he said, his voice rough around the edges.

"Like Web," she said, glancing back down at her hand in his because she didn't want him to see the yearning in her eyes.

"And others."

He didn't say her name, and maybe it was some

wayward hope on her part that he meant her, but when she looked back up at him, something shifted. Her sadness that was always just under the surface gave way to a need to reconfirm that life wasn't just about hiding the broken parts or anticipating the worst of people. That there could be—was—more. That she could be happy just as she was without having to pretend at all.

It was almost guaranteed that she'd regret this later, but for right now, it was the only thing that mattered. She needed to blast away everything else and let that part take over. There was only one way she knew how to do that without faking it and only one person she wanted to do it with.

Without letting herself double- or triple-think it, she leaned in and kissed him, knowing she was only asking for trouble and she was more than okay with that.

CHAPTER FOURTEEN

Will froze. It wasn't because he wasn't burning for more—because he fucking was—but because Hadley needed to get away from the memories; the pain of the past wasn't for show. No one was that good of an actress, hundreds of millions on the line or not. She'd pull back in a second, the regret he'd seen in the coat closet clear on her face, and that would be it. And he'd still be here wanting the woman who meant to take his brother for everything she could. But as she moved her soft lips against his, the tip of her tongue teasing him, begging for more, it got harder and harder to hold on to that. Because knowing it was wrong didn't change the wanting.

He cupped the back of her head, threading his fingers through her brown hair and breaking the kiss. The move cut into him like an icy wind. "Hadley."

"We shouldn't," she said, her voice soft with an edge of need beneath it.

"No." Still he didn't move, the tension holding him in place, his fingers tangled in her hair, her body so close, he could feel the heat of her skin against him.

"But we want to." She looked up at him through her eyelashes. "At least I want to."

His cock thickened against his thigh as he white-knuckled his control even as it slipped through his grasp. "You are not alone in that."

"But we can't." Her hands on his chest, fingertips gliding their way over him and leaving nothing but unquenched fire in their wake.

He didn't mean to bring her closer, to glide his hands down to her hips and slide her over so she was on his lap. Her hands were on his shoulders, straddling him. Somehow, even though he knew exactly how perfectly her softness fit against his hardness, he managed to keep his hands light on her hips instead of pulling her down and grinding her against him.

This would kill him.

She would kill him.

God, he'd die happy.

"It'll complicate things," he managed to get out through clenched teeth as he fought against the lust burning him from the inside out.

Her cheeks flushed, desire swirling in her eyes, as she clutched his shirt as if she were as much on the edge as he was. "It already has."

Fuck. How did he argue with that? He couldn't. Not here, not now, with Hadley in his arms, her body pressed up against his in the tiny booth. The whole world collapsed in on this one place, the air heavy with promise and possibilities, as if they weren't just battling each other but that they were fighting the inevitable.

"One last time," he said, even though he wasn't

sure he'd ever get enough of her.

"Then we'll have each other out of our systems," she said, tugging at his shirt and pulling it free.

She worked it upward so slowly, it was more like torture than anything else, until the only thing against his chest was the cool of the fresh air and the heat of her gaze.

"Do you really think we can?" Because he didn't just doubt, he wanted to believe.

"Only one way to find out," she said, pushing his shirt up and off him in a fast, fluid motion that still took too damn long. "Please, Will."

She rocked against him in a slow rhythm that short-circuited his brain, but it was the sound of his name on her lips as she rubbed herself against his hard cock that snapped his last bit of self-control. There were better men out there who'd say, not wrongly, that this was the woman gold digging his brother—or more charitably, the woman fighting to forget old hurts—and, therefore, he should peel her off him, set her down, and walk away.

He wasn't that man.

Dropping his hands so they were flat on the smooth cowhide seat on either side of his thighs, his entire body hard and aching for her, he forced himself to hold on long enough to get out one last question. "Are you sure?"

She grabbed the hem of her T-shirt and pulled it off, dropping it so it landed on top of his on the seat. "Absolutely."

Thank. Fucking. God.

Her perfect tits were encased in paper-thin

purple lace, the pointed tips of her nipples jutting out, right at eye level. Later, he'd look his fill. Now, he needed more. He tugged down the lace cups and sucked her freed nipple into his mouth. Licked it. Teased it with his teeth. Swirled his tongue around its hard, sensitive peak as she moaned her pleasure, begging for more. The sounds she made, the way she let her head fall back as she rocked her hips, it ruined him.

"You're gonna be the end of me," he said.

Her hands tightened in his hair, a teasing tug as she let out a shaky breath. "That wasn't how I planned on taking you out, but a woman can dream."

"Such a smart mouth." So damn kissable. It was the kind of mouth that launched a thousand hard-ons since he'd first spotted her along the sidelines smiling at his damn brother.

"You wanna know a secret?" Hadley looked down at him from her perch on his lap, her tits brushing against him. "I think you like my smart mouth."

"For starters." Damn him, he liked so much about her, from the don't-even-try-your-usual-bullshit attitude to the way she cried out when she came.

"Oh yeah?" she asked, her voice husky. "What else do you like?"

"This bra, it's such a tease." He lowered his mouth, swirling his tongue over the stiff peaks straining against the lace. "And these nipples so hard and demanding." Skimming his palms from her ribs down over her waist, he took his time feeling his way down. "Fuck, these hips. You have no idea how many times I've jerked off thinking about these hips, that ass, all of you."

"Even my smart mouth?"

"Especially that."

For once, they wanted the exact same thing. Hands on her hips, he stood her up, hating losing the feel of her against him but needing to get her naked.

Now.

"Take them off."

"What?" she asked, skimming her hands down her soft belly to the button of her jeans. "These?" She unbuttoned her jeans. "Fair is fair—you too."

He would have responded if he could, but the second she started inching her zipper lower, he lost the ability, so he followed her orders, stripping free of the rest of his clothes before she'd even gotten her zipper down. The other night, everything had been filtered through the mirror, so it was like seeing her for the first time, the full curve of her tits, the pink tips of her hard nipples, the way her hips flared out—revealed inch by inch as she pushed her jeans and then her panties down.

"You are definitely gonna be the end of me," he said again as he got on his knees in front of her and then started to kiss his way lower down her soft belly.

"How about we find out just how far we can push it," she said, threading her fingers through his hair as he went lower.

So damn cocky. God, he loved it.

"Such." He kissed the freckle beside her belly button. "A." He kissed the spot above her barely there curls, trailing his thumb across them but just barely enough to tease and leave her wanting more. "Smart." He kissed a trail down the inside of her thighs, nudging them open and widening her stance as he guided her back down onto the edge of the seat. "Mouth."

He glided his hands up her thighs, his thumbs skimming across her inner thighs until he reached her slick, swollen folds. Her hold on his hair tightened as he stroked his thumb across her sensitive clit, slowly and steadily building the tension as she let out a shaky moan. Smoothing his fingertips over her, he teased her, following her nonsensical pleas and sighs of pleasure, getting her right to the edge of orgasm without letting her fall over. Not yet. He wanted to draw it out, make it last. Did that make him a jerk? He was okay with that, because when she did come, she'd remember this moment and she'd remember him.

Another moan escaped her lips when he slipped two fingers, crossed as if making a promise, inside her and slid them forward and back against her most sensitive spots, the whole time tasting her and using his tongue with the right amount of pressure to keep her strung tight and yearning.

"Will," she begged as he turned his fingers inside her, making sure they hit the tight bundle of nerves at her entrance.

God, he'd never get over hearing his name

her lips when she was on the verge.

"Please, Will." She lifted her hips, rocking against his mouth. "More."

In and out, this way and that, he couldn't deny her. He lapped at her clit, hard and fast, pushing her toward that line as her cries grew more frantic and demanding. The time for teasing her had passed. No soft, barely there touches. He filled her with his fingers, sliding in and out, as he worked his tongue on her clit, rolling and rotating around the bundle of nerves that had her moaning with pleasure each time he made contact. She was so wet, so ready for him, that he had to reach down and curl his hands around his cock, squeezing hard at the base to relieve some of the pressure. Her entire body contracted as she came hard, her body arching as she thrust her hips up and let out a cry of satisfaction as he slowed but didn't stop, riding the wave with her until she melted back, sated, against the seat.

Rocking back onto his heels, still tasting her sweetness on his mouth, he watched Hadley come down from her orgasm. God, it was so good, so right. It settled something in him, seeing her like this. Unguarded and relaxed, her eyes were half closed, her lips slightly parted, and her body slack. She let out a happy sigh and looked down at him, a teasing smile on her lips. He stopped breathing for a second because he knew in that moment that he'd been right—one last time would never be enough.

...

Still in some kind of post-orgasmic happy haze, Hadley watched as Will stood up, picked up his jeans from the floor, grabbed his wallet out of the back pocket, and pulled out a condom. She'd never been so glad to see latex in her entire life.

She got up and walked over to him as he tore it open because there was something she desperately wanted to do before he rolled it on. "Wait."

"You don't want to?" He nodded and moved to put the half-opened condom back in his wallet. "Okay. No problem."

"I never said that." She wrapped her fingers around his hard cock, stroking him as she got on her tiptoes and whispered in his ear. "You make a lot of assumptions about people. Maybe you should ask them what they plan to do."

His only answer was a sharp inhale of breath as she sank down to her knees. Watching him, she licked the tip of his hard cock, tasting the salty pre-cum pooled there.

"Do you want to know what I want to do?"

"I think I might have a clue."

"There you go assuming again." Grip firm, she stroked from the base of his thick length to the tip and then held out her free hand. "Condom."

"Aren't you going to say please?"

Oh, someone was getting cocky again. She liked it, found it hot as hell, and had a total preoccupation with wondering what would come out of his mouth next, but that didn't mean she was going to let him take control of this moment. Some protective part of her demanded that this not be her letting him fuck her but her fuck him. It was about agency, self-determination, and so much damn pleasure that her whole body was on the edge again, as if she hadn't just come so hard, she was surprised the barn doors were still on.

Keeping her gaze fixed on Will, she took him in her mouth, sucking him slow and deep, not stopping until the crown of his dick hit the back of her throat. His rumbled groan of pleasure was so growly, it made her toes curl and her core clench in anticipation.

"Did that count as *please*?"

His only answer was to hand her the condom. She finished tearing it open and rolled it on, her attention divided between staring at his gorgeous cock and watching the muscles in his jaw flex as he held on to the last bits of his control. Quite honestly, she was pretty impressed by his reserves. She hadn't thought he'd make it that long. But then again, Will had done nothing but surprise her this entire trip. Maybe he wasn't the only one making assumptions he shouldn't.

Having pity on him—hell, on them both—she stood up. "Will—"

That was as far as she got. He picked her up, sweeping her off her feet, and kissed her in one of those blast-your-hair-out-from-the-roots kind of a kiss.

"What was that?" Not that she was opposed, she just hadn't been expecting to go airborne.

He sat down on the booth seat, settling her so she straddled his hips. "You said my name."

"You like that?" she asked, trying to unwind

why that would be and why it made her pulse kick up to Mach four billion.

"I do when you're the one saying it." Cupping the back of her head, he brought her face down to his and kissed her deep and demanding, promising things she hadn't known she wanted until that very moment.

Then it morphed from being something she hadn't considered to all she could think about—if thinking was what she was doing. Really, it was more of reacting to him, recognizing on some level she didn't understand that this was right and good and as close to perfect as she would probably ever get. By the time she pulled back from that kiss—her lips swollen, her mind swirling—the questions didn't matter because she had the answer right in front of her.

Riding high on that kiss and the hot need coursing through her, she lowered herself down, slowly, a little bit at a time, keeping her gaze locked on Will's face. Taking in the crinkle around his eyes, the day-old beard that had felt so good against the inside of her thighs, and the hard, desperate lust in his eyes. He needed her as much as she needed him.

"So tight," he said, holding on to her and driving her up and down on his cock in time with her own undulations. "So beautiful."

Gripping the back of the seat tightly, she moved against him, up and down, over and over again until her thighs burned in the best possible way. His fingers bit into the fleshy part of her hips as she arched her back, changing the angle so that he went deeper, filling her completely as she rode him. Close, she was so damn close. All she needed was just a little more. Reaching between them, she dragged her fingertips across her clit, still so sensitive from before, and her core clenched in response.

"Fuck yes," he said, his voice strained. "Do that again."

She did, circling her swollen clit over and over again as she fucked him, the width of him stretching her and taking her higher with each thrust and twist as she came down on him again and again. The tingling started in her inner thighs, zipping down her legs and then ricocheting back up in an orgasm that stole her breath and sight.

"Let me taste you."

Without thinking, just responding to that demanding need in his voice, she held out her fingers to him. He sucked them into his mouth as he took over, lifting her and bringing her back down at a ferocious pace until he lifted his hips and drove into her one last time with a sound that was more a growl of satisfaction than anything else.

She collapsed against him and he loosened his hold but didn't let go, both of them breathing heavily as they came back down to earth and reality. Hadley let out a shaky breath.

There. That was it. We've had our one last time and now we're out of each other's systems. Nothing to see here, folks. Move along.

But she didn't want to keep moving, and that's when she knew she'd made a horrible mistake.

CHAPTER FIFTEEN

Will's hair was still damp when he and Hadley walked into the main house for dinner and game night. That got him a look and a hard glare from Hadley's brothers, no doubt because her long brown hair wasn't quite dry, either—and because of the barely-there-but-still-visible hickey at the base of her neck. He hadn't given anyone a hickey since he couldn't remember when.

However, sex in the barn had led to fucking in the shower, which led to a post-nap make-out session before a text from her mom had alerted them that they were late for dinner and to get a move on or miss out on chicken casserole with Bisquick biscuits. That was probably why everyone turned in their chairs and stared at them as they walked into the eat-in kitchen.

Hadley's family was gathered around several tables of different widths and lengths that were butted up against each other and stretched from the breakfast nook to the dining room. It was an oddball mix that still, somehow, managed to fit together. He tried to imagine the hodgepodge of furniture in his grandmother's dining room and not even in his most NyQuiled-up fever dreams could he. They didn't do that kind of thing. The Holts had one table. It was very long, very wide, sat twenty, and growing up, he and Web had sat at one end to eat while their grandmother sat at the other and sipped a never-empty glass of white wine.

He and Hadley sat down at the farthest end from her brothers—definitely not by accident—and across from the only other empty chair. A quick glance around confirmed that Adalyn wasn't there.

Hadley's eyes cast to the side as she gnawed her bottom lip. As they passed the biscuits, the glass bowl of green beans with slivered almonds, and the large casserole dish decorated with bright-yellow sunflowers, she kept looking back at the door as if waiting for Adalyn to walk in. When she didn't, Hadley pushed her food around her plate, listening to the conversation but not joining in as it whirled around them.

Needing in a way he couldn't quite explain to distract her from stewing about what had happened with her sister, he scooted his chair close and lowered his voice. "I've never had casserole."

Hadley turned toward him, her eyes wide. "They don't have that in your rich-kid boarding schools?"

"We only had the finest steaks, rarest seafood, and most expensive wines."

"You didn't get alcohol at school." She rolled her eyes.

"Didn't get steak, either." He couldn't even

imagine what that would have been like. The dean would have stood in traffic first. 'The Gravestone School believed in the old-school break-them-down tradition. It was all lukewarm showers, room-temperature meals, and a rigid devotion to social customs."

"That does not sound like fun," she said, her nose wrinkling in sympathy as she grimaced.

"It could have been worse." It could have been their grandmother's house. "Anyway, Web made it fun."

"Here, I gave you an extra helping." Stephanie handed him a plate loaded down with a creamy, cheesy chicken pasta with veggies mixture topped off with toasted bread crumbles and two large biscuits. "Put honey on the biscuit. You'll thank me later."

Once everyone was at the table, they bowed their heads and said grace, and then he took a bite of the casserole. It was warm and filling and settled in his stomach like a hug. After everyone had their delicious first bite, it was all smack talk about game night as they ate with everyone steering clear of any wedding discussions. Adalyn still hadn't come down for dinner, and while everyone was trying not to draw attention to it, her empty chair was a physical reminder.

"So," PawPaw said as he stood from the table and picked up his plate. "Are you ready for Pictionary?"

"Noooooooooo," Hadley said, groaning.

"There's no avoiding it." PawPaw shrugged. "Louise must have used weighted dice when we rolled for who got to pick the games."

"Stop accusing me of cheating, you old bugger," Aunt Louise hollered from over by the sink as she rinsed off her dishes and put them in the dishwasher. "I won fair and square."

"Pictionary sounds great."

Looking around at everyone—Louise grinning, Hadley groaning, and PawPaw glaring at his sister—Will was having a hard time trying to figure out what the fuss was about.

Thirty minutes into the family's version of the drawing game and he understood. Hadley was a detriment to any competitive person's sanity during the game. First of all, she was awful at drawing—even her stick people were a strange alignment of squiggly lines and circles. Then, there was her insistence on drawing the same pattern of shapes over and over as if on the twentieth try, he or PawPaw would understand that the arrow shooting out of the circle at the end of another line was a lightsaber, leading them to the correct answer of Star Wars. The real killer, though, was how she called out the most bizarre answers that made zero sense and the house rule that each team only got to throw out three answers. Invariably, at least two of those came from Hadley and were a full 180 degrees from the correct answer.

By the time it came down to the last phrase, PawPaw was stress pacing in the back of the room while Hadley read her clue and started for the giant dry-erase board up on an easel. Meanwhile, Will kept getting distracted by the way she chewed on her bottom lip while she drew squiggly vertical lines with what looked like lightning shooting out from the top in every direction and a rectangle that looked like maybe it was on fire. She put the cap on her marker with a snap and turned to him and PawPaw, a hopeful smile on her lips.

"Explosive farts," PawPaw said.

"Do you have to be so crude?" Aunt Louise said without even a hint of censure in her voice.

"Look at the picture!" Taking the bait, PawPaw's voice rose as he waved his hand at the dry-erase board. "What do you see?"

Will cocked his head to the side and squinted, trying like hell to see something besides a stick figure with an impressive amount of gas, but there was no hope. Once PawPaw put that image in his head, there was no seeing anything else.

"It could be interpreted in many ways," he said, grasping for something—*anything*—else that it could be.

The timer on Stephanie's phone rang out, and Aunt Louise gave a celebratory hoot. Hadley shot him and PawPaw a glare.

"It's *Jungle Book*. How did you not see the trees?" She pointed to the vertical lines and then the exploding rectangle. "And the book?"

Will took a billionth look at what she'd drawn on the dry-erase board, but even with her explanation, he couldn't see any of it.

"Well," PawPaw said, shaking his head. "That puts us in the consolation round."

Hadley took another look back at her drawing

and, judging by the way she cocked her head to the side, even she figured it was a lost cause. "Sorry, PawPaw."

Her grandpa got up and gave her a quick hug. "All you have to do to make up for it is beat Louise's team in the next round." He lowered his volume so only Hadley and Will would be able to hear. "There's no way I want to spend the next month getting snarky texts from her."

"Whatever it takes," Hadley said. "You got it, PawPaw."

"That's my girl." He turned to Will and leveled a do-not-fuck-this-up look at him. "I know you two will make that happen."

Aunt Louise picked that moment to interrupt their pep talk armed with the next game—Taboo—and with the announcement that since Adalyn wasn't there, one of them would have to sit out the final round.

"I'll be an observer," PawPaw said. "After all, you two really do make a great team."

Hadley's cheeks turned pink, but Will couldn't help but think the old man might be on to something there.

• • •

Will was sitting too close to Hadley and it was making her brain fry. Instead of being able to listen to him as he gave her clues about the secret word, she couldn't stop looking at his mouth and remembering exactly how he'd used it a few hours earlier.

A sudden, sweeping hot flush made her lungs tighten as she sucked in a quick breath. Holy hell, how had it gotten so hot in here? She grabbed the scorepad and started fanning herself.

"Tease," she said, blurting out the first word that came to mind that she could say in front of her family.

Will looked up from the Taboo game card at her and raised an eyebrow. "The clue was handbag."

Because of course it was. She closed her eyes for a second and took a bracing inhale. "Maybe I'm really into purses."

His grin told her he knew exactly what she was into—him. "Next clue is that it costs a lot."

Sure, she'd always known he had green eyes, but how had she missed the light amber flecks near the iris? Or the way they crinkled at the corners when he smiled? Or that his lashes were twenty-eight miles long?

"Earth to Hads," PawPaw said, cutting through her distraction.

Fuck. She'd done it again.

"Can you give me the clue again?" The question came out in a rush, as if that would cover the fact that she'd been making moon eyes at her nemesis.

And he was still that. Right? Hate fucking didn't change anything. *But is that what it was? Because it sure didn't feel like it.* Mentally telling that voice in her head to shove it, she tried to concentrate on the clues and not the man giving them. The one who had this thing he did with his fingers that—

"Oh for the love of Tom Osborne," PawPaw said with a tortured groan. "Stop your flirting. This is the last question. Get your heads in the game and win. After that, you two can go off and finish whatever this is because for the rest of us it's very awkward—and that's coming from me."

Cheeks burning, Hadley jerked her gaze away from Will and scanned the crowded living room where easily a dozen Donavans, Martinezes, and Donavan-Martinezes were watching them. Aaaaaaand there was nothing quite like being re-minded in such a public fashion that her entire family was there watching her forget how to play the one family game night game that she usually kicked ass in. Well, almost everyone. Adalyn was still a no-show. Guilt and regret did a you-suck-Hadley tango in her gut, stomping out all the distracting lusty thoughts that she'd selfishly let take over.

"Sorry, sir," Will said, looking anything but re-gretful. He turned back to Hadley and gave her a conspiratorial wink. "Well, now that I'm properly motivated—"

"We're still here, Holt," Weston said.

He and Knox stood by the fireplace, arms crossed, brotherly glares in place, and overprotec-tive attitudes on full display.

Will shrugged, seemingly not bothered in the least by the growly brothers. "Seems you're always around."

"Not quite enough, it seems." Knox tapped the side of his neck in the exact location where Hadley had tried to cover up her hickey with makeup.

"Clue," she all but hollered out, flustered by the weird testosterone-fueled drama, and slapped her hand down on Will's thigh a little harder than she meant. "Give me a clue."

"Michael Kors," he said.

"Designer."

He nodded, scooting forward so their knees touched as they sat across from each other. "More."

Somehow despite being suddenly and over-whelmingly aware of the erogenous zone formerly known as her kneecaps, the synapses in her brain continued to function. "Designer-brand clothes."

"Yes." Will shot up out of his chair, then picked her up, bringing her in close before spinning in a circle. "We win."

"That's right, Louise." PawPaw cheered, raising his arms in the air *Rocky* style. "I gotcha."

Aunt Louise rolled her eyes. "Only until next time."

It was the usual post-family-game-night smack talk, but Hadley barely noticed because Will was right there, his face so close to hers, as he held her up even though they'd stopped spinning. Instead, the room had spun away and it was just them. Awareness crackled between them, electric and enticing as he lowered his mouth—

"Hey, Holt," Weston said, his voice low.

The shock of her brother's voice was enough to make her jolt. Slowly, Will lowered her until her feet touched the floor, but he didn't step away from her.

"Winner has to clean up," her brother said, his

perma-glare around Will on full display before he turned and walked away.

Really, this was ridiculous. She was a grown woman. If she wanted to have a vacation fling or whatever, it was her decision. Not that she was having a fling with Will. It was just a strange mixing of circumstances and didn't mean anything and—

Still rationalizing, she caught movement in her peripheral vision. Adalyn, her smile wobbly and her nose bright red, stood in the doorway leading to the back stairs, angled so she was hidden from most of the family's view.

"I'll be right back," Hadley said, tilting her head toward the doorway.

Will squeezed her hand. "Go on—I got this."

Using the cover of the general rambunctiousness that followed a family game night, Hadley made her way over to the doorway and snuck into the hall. She wrapped her arms around her sister and pulled her in tight.

"Adalyn, I'm sorry. I—"

"No," her sister said, returning the hug. "I'm the one who should be apologizing. This wedding and everything with Derek just has me spinning. It was a stupid idea to try to impress you with the wedding. It all just sort of happened, and I guess I just never outgrew that eight-year-old girl always trying to impress her big sister."

Hadley stepped back, needing her sister to see her face and understand the truth of it all. "I'm your sister. I'm not judging you. Ever."

"Of course you'd say that." Her sister wiped

her cheek with the back of her hand. "Everything for you is perfect. You have the ideal big-city life."

A punch to the gut by Godzilla wouldn't have hurt as much as realizing how her inability to admit to failure had unintentionally hurt the people she loved most. "Is that what you think?"

Adalyn nodded. "It's what you tell us."

"Come on," she said, grabbing her sister's hand and leading her down the hall toward Gabe's office. "We need to talk."

CHAPTER SIXTEEN

Will watched Hadley disappear down the hall with her sister, and the foreign urge to go with her and offer her support had him taking a step forward before he realized what he was doing. However, Gabe's hand on his arm stopped him, making him look around at the fast emptying living room as all the family members said good night and went to their rooms.

"How about we go have a beer under the stars?" Gabe asked.

It might have been stated as a question, but Will knew better. "Sounds perfect."

Will followed Hadley's stepdad out the back door, expecting there to be more family on the patio because there were always people everywhere, it seemed, but they were alone. A rock settled in the bottom of his stomach as he took the beer that Gabe had pulled from the cooler by the picnic table. There was no way this was going to be a friendly little chat.

Gabe took a long pull from his beer and stared out at the land that seemed to go on forever and was held in only by star-filled sky. "My grandfather bought this ranch to give his family a safe place to call their own. Some people thought a guy like him wouldn't be able to pull it off. They figured he just wasn't the right shade of person to do that. He proved them wrong."

Small towns hadn't cornered the market on small thinking, but it had to be harder out here where a person's neighbors could be a lifeline or an anchor when things got tough.

Looking out into the dark, Will pictured the ranch as he'd seen it in the day and imagined building it from nothing. "It's quite a spread."

"That it is." Gabe nodded and took another drink, still looking out at all that great open space, shrouded in darkness that didn't seem to inhibit the man's ability to see it all. "Not everyone can appreciate its beauty and strength. It's easy to pass by this country and think there's nothing here but a moment's distraction. But for those who take the chance and open themselves up to the possibilities, well, it can change their life. I know it did mine."

"I can see how that could happen," Will said, trying to translate the undercurrents in the conversation that obviously was leading somewhere.

"It's a lot of work," Gabe continued, finally turning to look at Will. "Sometimes it feels like it's you against the world, but a place like this makes a man remember what's important and he vows to love it, help it realize its full potential, and do whatever is needed to protect it from those who would take advantage."

The man was about as subtle as a midtown bus during rush hour in Harbor City. "We aren't just talking about the ranch anymore, are we?"

Gabe cocked an eyebrow. "Were we ever?"

"No, sir. I guess we weren't."

The other man finished his beer, once again looking out at the ranch. "The girls are likely to be talking for a while, so you might as well head back to the cabin."

Message delivered and understood. "You'll let Hadley know where I've gone?"

"Of course." Gabe headed for the back door.

The man wasn't wrong. Like the ranch, there was more to Hadley than most people—himself included—saw at first glance. She had the natural beauty and strength that came from this place, even if she didn't call it home anymore. It would always be a part of her, and that was what he couldn't let go of, and he wasn't about to when they returned to Harbor City.

"I've never had a ranch like this before, but being here has definitely shown me that I've been missing out," he said to Gabe's retreating form. "If I'm lucky, I hope to have something like it someday soon. There's more to it than people realize."

Hadley's stepdad paused at the door, turning back to give him a look of approval. "That there is."

Then Gabe went into the house and Will made his way to the cabin, his thoughts swirling around in his head. Nothing about this trip had gone as planned—well, except for the look of absolute horror on Hadley's face when she'd spotted him at the airport. After that, everything had gone pear-shaped. He was supposed to be elbowing the gold digger after his brother's bank balance out of the picture. Instead, he was falling for the woman he just might have misjudged—*fine*, he'd totally misjudged her. What in the hell did he do now?

After he got to the cabin and did a quick check for uninvited swift foxes—luckily there was no sign of Lightning with or without a tasty dinner—Will pulled out his phone and called the one person he'd always been able to trust.

Web answered on the second ring. "Please tell me she hasn't killed you and this is your ghost calling."

Even though his twin couldn't see him rolling his eyes, Will still knew he'd sense it. "No one will ever mistake you for being the funny twin."

"That, my brother, is where you're wrong," Web said, his voice taking on that smug tone that meant he was up to something. "Everyone thinks I'm hilarious—especially when I tell them about your little setup."

Will stopped mid-step as he walked toward the pullout couch. "You aren't."

"Oh, come on. You don't think I could have kept something this good to myself, do you?" Web's gotcha-sucker chuckle left Will slack-jawed. "Big brother, you got punked, and I'm telling the world. I gotta tell you, though, your chicken was not great. Do not quit your day job."

But Web had been the one to warn him away from her. "You were the one who told me not to—"

"Fuck her?" Web finished.

Will's entire body tensed with an unfamiliar

overprotectiveness that he had no fucking clue how to process beyond a need to stop anyone, *anyone*, from thinking of Hadley as available. "Why, is that what you want to do?"

"Settle down there, cowboy. I set this up, remember?" Web mumbled something about blood relatives who were idiots. "Damn, I love it when a plan comes together." He paused. "But there is something I need to tell you about Hadley."

"Is it that you're interested in her?" Will's gut churned at the idea.

"As more than a friend?" Web let out an amused chuckle. "Not in the least—otherwise she'd already be mine. I am the more popular Holt twin. No, what I need to tell you is that she's softer than she seems. Be careful with her."

"I'm always careful." But it was too late. He was already in too deep, and there was only one way to figure out what that meant. He told his brother everything. "So what do I do now?"

Web let out a dismissive snort. "If you can't figure that out for yourself, then I can't help you."

Fuck, that hurt, but Web was right. "Thanks."

"For what?"

"Being just the kind of asshole brother to fake like he was puking his guts up so I'd finally pull my head out of my ass."

"Just have a good time." Web hung up without a goodbye.

Will tossed his phone on the pullout bed and stared at the wall until a very familiar four-legged swift fox came waltzing into the living room. How in the hell Lightning had gotten in, he had no idea, but seeing the fox did give him a brilliant idea for how to show Hadley that what was happening between them could be more than just a road-trip romance.

Now he just needed her to come back to him.

. . .

Guilt ate away at Hadley's gut, a constant gnawing that she felt all the way to her bones. Adalyn stood on the other side of Gabe's office, every square inch of which was covered with printouts, random pieces of ranch equipment, and no less than five sweat-stained baseball hats bearing the Nebraska Cornhuskers logo.

This room was the one place where all the kids had come for advice or just to hang out while Gabe did the work most folks didn't think about—the ordering, the accounting, the figuring out how to get through the lean years. It was the place where she and her siblings had all been given their horse nicknames when they first moved in and where they all informally took on the Martinez surname in a homemade ceremony devised by Adalyn right before Hadley had left for college. One family. One heart. One name, even if it wasn't court official.

And right now, Hadley realized just how much her inability to admit failure had betrayed that pledge they'd all made to be a family, in it together, always.

"I've been lying," she said.

Arms crossed, mascara smudged, Adalyn sniffed back her tears. "What are you talking about?"

Hadley took a deep breath, pushed back every ingrained instinct to cover up the ugly truth, and looked her sister dead in the eyes. "I'm a fraud."

Adalyn snorted. "That is so not true."

"It is." It was time. Really, it was way past time. The need to make everything seem perfect had been part of her DNA since she and her mom had opened the garage door and found her dad in the front seat, overcome by fumes. Today, she was going to rewrite her code. She was going to take control—disastrous warts and all—of who she was, inside and out.

"My job? Nonexistent since I got fired the week before I flew out here." She straightened her shoulders and let out a long breath. "My apartment? About the size of your walk-in closet, made to look bigger thanks to knowing the angles when I take pics. Plus, I share it, because there's no way I could afford it on my own. My boyfriend?" She glanced back at the half-closed door that, knowing her family, would soon be opened to admit the others. "Actually, Will isn't Web at all. He's Web's twin brother who pretty much hates my guts." She crossed over to her sister. "My clothes are second-hand. My credit cards are maxed. My patience is frayed. And my grasp on anything ever working out is tenuous on a good day, and those are getting fewer and farther between." She took her sister's hand in hers, amazed at how they were the same size. Just as she wasn't the girl she'd been at fourteen on that awful day, Adalyn wasn't eight and in need of shielding anymore. She was a grown-ass woman, and it was beyond time for Hadley to recognize that as well. "I failed at absolutely everything I set out to do when I left here, and I've been too scared to admit it to anyone."

"Too scared or too proud?"

Ow. That hit right in the feels. "Probably both."

Adalyn sat down on the couch, pulling Hadley with her, and let her head fall back against the afghan blanket draped across the back. "And all this time, I thought I had to put on this big wedding no matter what my gut was telling me because I wanted you to finally see me as someone who'd grown up and was worthy of your Instagram-filtered status and attention."

"Adalyn, you are so beyond worthy." She pivoted to face her sister, needing her to understand more than she needed oxygen at that point. "I'm so sorry for keeping my mouth shut."

"Why did you do it? Why didn't you trust us enough to tell us—tell me—the truth?"

The hurt in her little sister's voice grabbed Hadley and wouldn't let go. And when her mom, Gabe, Knox, and Weston filtered in, she realized that all she'd accomplished by pretending her life in Harbor City was perfect was to push away the very people she most loved—the last thing she wanted to do. They were overbearing, a little too involved, and knew exactly how to push every one of her buttons, but they were her family. She loved them more than anyone else in the world, just like they loved her. It was about time she acted accordingly.

"After Dad died..." No, it was time to use the words. "After he killed himself, well, it was easier to act as if everything was fine rather than to admit how sad and hurt I was." She'd gotten lost in the strangest things, like rearranging the fridge to accommodate all the casserole dishes people dropped off or playing round after round of Rummy with Knox. "I loved Dad, and it felt like the worst kind of betrayal to be mad at him. I was old enough to know he'd been very sad for a very long time even if he tried to cover it with jokes and pranks and surprise trips for ice cream. Showing how damn angry I was didn't seem like an option, so I didn't." She'd become perpetually peppy and positive. Everything would work out because of the sheer force of her will alone. "After that, it just got to be a habit. I didn't want Mom to worry when I went to Harbor City, so I spiffed up the truth." She glanced over at her mom and offered up an apologetic look. "I took on this fake-it-until-you-make-it philosophy about everything—even when it came to my family. I lied to all of you."

Weston sat down on the corner of Gabe's desk. "So the nonprofit consulting job?"

"I had that," she said. "I just happened to be at the very bottom rung of the ladder, and then I got fired."

"And you don't have an apartment?" her mom asked.

"I do, but it's tiny, and I have a roommate."

"And the guy out there who looks at you like

he can't wait to carry you off and do things I won't mention in front of Mom, Gabe, and the boys, he's pretend?" Adalyn asked.

"No." She glared at her sister, whose expression had changed to one of smug I'm-right-and-you're-wrong that only a sibling could give. "He's real. He just hates me."

Gabe lifted a dark eyebrow. "Huh."

"Sounds to me like yes, you've been lying to us, but the bigger issue is that you've been telling a helluva lotta lies to yourself," Knox said as he looked at her like she was the world's biggest dumbass.

What in the hell was going on? She'd fucked up, but it wasn't because she was being willfully obtuse. She'd been protecting them.

Hadley looked from one member of her family to the next. "What are you talking about?"

"We don't care how fancy you are in the big city or if the guy you are obviously head over heels about is fake," Adalyn said. "We just want you to be happy. Are you?"

Swallowing the urge to spill even more feelings onto the floor in Gabe's office—what was it about this room that always seemed to encourage confessions?—she ignored her sister's question. "I didn't come back here to deep dive into my brain but to apologize for making you feel like you had to throw this big wedding to impress me."

"So you're good with me holding a bouquet of wildflowers out on the prairie with Gabe singing Elvis?"

Hadley laughed. The mental image was too

funny not to. "I'd recommend against the Elvis part, but if that makes you happy, then yes, do that."

Adalyn's smile faltered and then disappeared. "What if I'm not sure what makes me happy?"

"Does Derek?" her mom asked as she sat down on the couch with her daughters.

"When we're together, yes." Adalyn let out a heavy breath before her chin went all trembly. "But when it's like some kind of missed connections personal ad for the guy who is my fiancé? Not as much. It's probably just wedding nerves."

Her strained chuckle did nothing to lessen the impact of her words.

"Are you sure?" Hadley asked.

Adalyn shrugged. "Maybe."

"You know we'll support you no matter what," Knox said. "It's the Donavan-Martinez code."

Gabe nodded. "That it is."

After a group hug during which she may or may not have cracked a rib—Weston still acted like he was the younger brother from hell sometimes—her brothers left with Adalyn to raid the fridge and inhale the leftover casserole. Judging by the stay-right-here-a-minute look her mom sent her way, Hadley was not invited to join in on the gluttony.

"So what are you going to do now?" her mom asked.

"I don't know." Hadley sank back against the couch and let her head drop to her mom's shoulder. She hadn't sat like this in forever and had forgotten just how nice it was to let down her guard around her family. "Fiona—who, surprise, isn't just my friend but also my roommate—says it's a sign that I should finally start my own company, but I don't know."

"You don't think you're ready?" Gabe asked as he took Weston's spot, sitting on the corner of the desk.

"I am." Okay, so she hadn't said those words out loud before, but it was true. She was ready for this. Mentally, at least. "It's just, there are a lot of logistical and financial hurdles."

"Adalyn does have an accounting degree, you know. She can help with your books," her mom said. "And Knox's business degree doesn't just apply to running a ranch."

"And we can lend you some seed money," Gabe added.

For a second, there was nothing in Hadley's head but white noise, blocking out everything as she tried to wrap her brain around what they were saying. Money. Expertise. Support. All of it had been right there all along, if she'd only looked past her own pride and seen the people she loved for who they were. Instead, she'd spent too long projecting her version of an interfering family because that's what she'd needed to believe because of how she was treating them. God, she'd been so dense.

"And I don't want to hear a word about you thinking you're taking advantage of us," Gabe said, his voice low and hard. "If anyone in your family needed help, would you step up?"

She didn't need to think about her answer. "Yeah."

"Well, it isn't any different if it's us helping you," her mom said.

Hadley mashed her lips together and blinked really fast to keep the tears at bay. All this time she'd wasted because she was afraid and, yes, too full of herself to be vulnerable and honest with the people she cared about.

"I don't know what to say," she said once she finally could say something.

"Say you're done pretending the world isn't hard on you." Gabe pulled her up from the couch and into a huge bear hug. "It is. It's hard on all of us, but together is how we make it through. We're your family and we love you just the way you are."

"I love you, too," she said, her voice muffled by Gabe's shoulder.

Her mom stood up and joined in their hug, and they all stood there for a second cementing what had been there the whole time. Strength. Support. Love.

"Okay," her mom said as the hug broke up. "We better get into that kitchen before we miss out on all the leftovers."

"If Will isn't with them already, you should invite him back to the house," Gabe said. "I'm pretty sure you're wrong about how he feels about you."

Hearing his name was like having someone turn on a light in a dark room. Suddenly, she saw things differently. If she'd been so wrong about her family, could she have been wrong about him, too? What if everything that had been happening between them wasn't just because of them having to team up to survive a trip to the sticks? What if they'd both been fighting something bigger and it was past time to hang up the gloves?

"I gotta go."

She gave her parents another quick hug, then hustled out of the house and all but sprinted back to the cabin.

CHAPTER SEVENTEEN

Will was well on his way to memorizing every single knot in the ceiling beams when he heard Hadley's footsteps on the front porch. How did he know they were hers? The same way he'd always known when she was on the sidelines at a rugby game or just around the corner at a charity event. His heart beat faster, his muscles tensed with anticipation, and a certain sense that the fun was about to start had him grinning.

The lone light in the cabin was the single beam coming from the half-closed bathroom door. It was more than enough, though, to watch her as she walked in—whatever of her that he couldn't see in the dim light, his imagination filled in. He didn't even have to work at it; he'd been memorizing her every curve since the moment he'd first laid eyes on her. Damn, for being someone who was thought of as a killer when it came to business smarts, he sure was an idiot when it came to Hadley Donovan.

"Did you and Adalyn work everything out?"

Hadley gasped, slapped her palm to her chest, and did a quick turn so she was facing the pullout bed where he was lying. "I thought you were asleep." She let out a long breath that ended in a giggle. "You owe me about five years back on my life span."

He sat up slowly, looking her up and down as he planned out every spot he would kiss, every curve he'd caress, and every inch of her he'd worship. "I think I know how I can make it up to you."

"Really?" She flicked open the button of her jeans, lowered the zipper, and shimmied out of the denim. "I have some ideas, too."

"Glad we're both thinking the same thing." Thank God.

He rolled off the bed and reached behind his head, grabbing his shirt before pulling it off and flinging it across the room. By the time he had his jeans and boxers off, Hadley stood on the opposite side of the bed wearing nothing but a plain white bra, cotton panties, and his black cowboy hat. He'd never seen anyone look as good or wanted someone more.

Having enough of there being a bed between them, he started toward her. "You look good in my hat."

"You're not so bad yourself." She nodded toward the floor. "And your boots look pretty damn fine under my bed."

"Your bed?" He rounded the end of the mattress. "It's been ours since we got here."

Hadley shrugged one shoulder as she wound a strand of dark hair around her fingertip, not moving, no doubt knowing she didn't have to. Wherever she went, he'd be there. "I've made many sacrifices."

"I'll be forever grateful." For her. For this trip. For all of it.

His entire body humming with anticipation, he finally got close enough to touch her, wrapping an arm around her waist and pulling her against him.

Then he fell backward, taking Hadley with him so she landed on top of him, loving the feel of every inch of her pressed against him.

With her long legs straddling him as she pressed a palm to his chest and lifted herself up, she said, "That was quite a ride."

"You haven't seen anything yet, darlin'."

She tipped the brim of his hat as she undulated against him. "Yeehaw."

It was ridiculous and hokey but still the hottest situation he'd ever been in. No doubt being with a nearly naked Hadley had something—*every-thing*—to do with it.

She leaned down and kissed him, her full, soft lips demanding against his. Lifting his hips, he gripped her waist and held her to him as he kissed her back just as hard and hot as she was giving. God, she was wet, so much so that he could feel her damp heat through her panties as she rocked against his cock. When she sat up and laid her palms on his chest, changing the angle as she ground her core against him, he let out a harsh hiss of breath. This woman. She was going to kill him. He couldn't care less. Reaching up, he cupped the back of her head, tugging her down so he could kiss her again.

The feel of her, the taste of her kisses, the way

she had him on edge with just a look, all of it meant that if she kept doing that, he was going to lose it, flip her over, and sink inside her, and he didn't want that yet.

Breaking the kiss, he lifted her hips up off him. "Be sure to hold on."

He glided his hands down so he cupped her ass and then pulled her north until her sweet panties-covered pussy was right above his mouth. Heaven didn't even begin to describe it. And just as soon as he thought it couldn't get any better, she stood up, balancing on the bed as she took off her panties, tossed his hat across the room, and slipped off her bra. Always one step ahead of him, she gave him a sassy *gotcha* wink and then lowered herself to her knees above his face. It was close, so fucking close, but it wasn't enough for either of them.

Barely breathing, hard as a fence post, and desperate for her, he glided his palms up the outside of her legs, rounded the curve of her hips, and pulled her down so he could taste her. The moment his tongue lapped at her clit, her thighs tensed on either side of his head before she started rocking against him in tandem with him as he licked and sucked and teased her. Listening to her breathing catch as she edged closer and closer to coming was better than any other sound. This was what he wanted, needed—to take her higher, to show her that what was between them was more than just two people stuck together for a week pretending to be who they weren't. This could be them. It should be them. Here. In Harbor

City. Anywhere. They belonged together.

Her ass, overflowing his hands in the absolute best way possible, tightened as she bit down on her bottom lip and increased the pace of her rocking, telling him without words what she wanted from him. She didn't have to worry. He'd always give her exactly what she needed. Pulling her more firmly against him, he closed his eyes and got lost in the slick sweetness of her swollen folds. He swept his tongue over her clit again and again, harder and faster with each pass, until her orgasm pulled her body taut above him and she cried out.

Holding her, steadying her, she came down from that high and collapsed onto the bed next to him. If there were words to explain everything he wanted to tell Hadley at that moment, he didn't know them. It was all too big, too new, and too important. Then he rolled onto his side so they were face-to-face and the sight of her, flush and satisfied, took even the possibility of forming words out of the realm of possibility.

"I'm done pretending," she said and kissed him as if she'd been waiting her entire life to do it.

Will knew the feeling because that was exactly how he kissed her back.

•••

It was like Hadley was high—when Will touched her, it was more intense, more pleasurable, more perfect. Something had changed tonight when she'd come clean with her family. It was as if the oppressive fog that kept her from seeing anything clearly had finally lifted and the world was practically glowing with possibilities. And the man in her bed? He wasn't just a possibility, he was a promise, and she was done lying to herself about how she felt about him. How she'd always felt. All that denial was a footnote in the history of her life because starting tonight, it was all about tomorrows.

Breaking the kiss, she trailed her lips over the barely there stubble along his jaw, down the column of his throat, over his quickly beating pulse point, and across his muscular chest to lap at the flat nub of his nipple. Of course, it wasn't just her mouth staying busy; she was exploring with her hands, too. What could she say, women were natural born multitaskers. The second she wrapped her hand around the hard length of him, his entire body moved with his groan of appreciation.

Keeping a firm grip, she stroked her hand up and down. "You like that?"

"I like it any time you touch me," he said, each word coming out deep and growly.

She glanced up at him, putting on as much of an air of innocence as possible when they were both naked and she had her fingers curled around his cock. "Only when I touch you?"

He grabbed her wrist, pulling her hand away from him, and rolled them both so she was on her back and now he was above her, a nearly feral, possessive gleam in his eyes.

"I like it when you walk in a room. When you walk out of one." He trailed his fingers across her sensitive skin. "When you look at me." He rolled her nipple between his fingers with expert ease. "When you smile. When you shoot me that little smirk telling me you know you've one-upped me again. The absolute best, though…" Dipping his head down, he delivered a string of soft kisses across the upper swells of her breasts. "Is your snore."

It took her brain a second to override the delicious sensations he was delivering with his mouth, but once it did, his words had her spluttering. Planting her palm in the middle of his chest, she pushed him up so he loomed above her without touching. "Are you kidding me?"

"Nope." Will grinned down at her. "Because whenever I hear it, I'm going to remember our first night together and how it was the beginning of everything changing."

If she hadn't already been lying back on the bed, she would have collapsed from the shock of it. Will "The Evil Twin" Holt had a gooey, soft, everyday-hero kind of center. "You're such a sentimental softie underneath all your assholery."

His smile faded, replaced by a look of raw honesty. "Only when it comes to you."

Her breath hitched and her heart sped up as she bit down on the inside of her cheek to keep the sudden onslaught of emotion at bay. Looking past his shoulder at the ceiling, she inhaled a deep breath and blinked about a million times before she could speak.

"You're the worst, Will Holt." How often had she said that in her head or out loud? A million? Two? But this time, she could finally admit that she had never really meant it. "How dare you make me tear up while we're both naked?"

Here's where she would have expected another teasing remark, a smart comment, or something else to lessen the emotion of the moment. Instead, he leaned down and kissed her, his strong lips demanding and gentle at the same time, pushing her toward the edge of losing-her-mind need. She reached up and cupped the back of his head, intertwining her fingers in his hair, matching him move for move as the kiss deepened and he rolled them so she was on top again.

His hands were everywhere on her, skimming down her sides and then coming back up to her breasts. Touching and teasing, he whipped up every sensation from damn-that-feels-good to oh-my-take-me-now. By the time he added his hot mouth to the mix, letting his tongue lap at her nipple in a slow, torturous motion before grazing his teeth over the hard bud was almost too much to take and yet she still wanted more. She wanted all of it—all of him.

Pulling back, she slid her body down his, kissing her way from his shoulders, over the hard lines of his abs, and following the light-brown line of hair to his hard cock. Watching his face, she traced her tongue around the swollen head and then took him deep inside her mouth as he fisted the bedsheets in his large hands.

"Hadley," he called out, his voice strained.

She stilled her movements but kept her fingers wrapped around his girth. "Did you want me to stop?"

His jaw squared. "Fuck no."

"Glad to see we can actually agree on a lot of things." She kissed the tip. "Like that." She sucked him in, taking him in until he hit the back of her throat again and again and again. "And that."

He was so hard in her hand, smooth, warm iron, as she stroked up and down. God, it felt good to see him like this, his eyes closed from the pleasure of it all, the fight he was obviously waging not to come in her hand as she kissed and licked and sucked him. There was a sense of power in it all and a special joy from giving this kind of pleasure to someone she loved.

The realization hit hard right there in that moment, and she pulled back, jolted by the shock of it.

"Are you okay?" Will asked, concern thick in his voice. "We can stop."

That was the last thing she wanted. What she needed was for this to go on forever. All of it. Him. Her. Them together.

She was so wet and aching for him that even a second more of this was going to drive her over the edge into insanity. "I need you inside me."

He tensed. "I don't have any more condoms."

"I'm on the pill." No condom wasn't usually something she did, but with Will, things were different.

"Are you sure?" he asked, his tone carefully neutral.

As if either of them could deny how much they both wanted this right now. "Have you been tested lately?"

"Yeah." He nodded. "I'm clear."

"Me too."

He kissed her, rolling them over so she was underneath him again and then pulled back, looking down at her as if he were seeing her for the very first time. "What is it about you that makes this so fucking perfect?"

"The fact that I'm not." The words that she would have fought to her last breath to never utter out loud came freely, and it was like the last of that weight she'd been carrying since her dad's suicide melted away.

Will dipped his head and gave her another kiss. "Neither am I." He slid into her, filling her completely. "Damn, Hadley. I just—"

Whatever he was going to say next was lost to his sharp intake of breath when he started to move. That was okay; it wasn't like her brain was processing anything but the feel of him as he withdrew and thrust forward, each stroke taking her higher. Later, they'd have all the time in the world to talk. Tonight was for showing herself that everything had changed—she'd changed—and there was no going back.

• • •

Will had to hold himself perfectly still. He couldn't breathe. He couldn't think. He'd be shocked if his heart was still beating. He was lost in Hadley and had never felt more found. Then she moved her hips, the world came back into focus, he sucked in a needy breath, and his pulse beat in his ears. That certainty, though? It didn't go away, just became stronger with each stroke.

"You feel so good," he said, reaching down and cupping her ass so he could lift her and change the angle, driving deeper. "Fuck."

"Oh my God, do that again."

She only had to ask. Whatever she wanted, he'd give. Withdrawing almost fully, he waited a beat before pushing forward, his hard length sliding into her, rubbing against all the sensitive nerves bundled just inside her opening. Again and again, he thrust deep into her hot, tight core. His eyes rolled back with pleasure as pressure began building in his spine. Her hips met his every move, her words made incoherent by lust.

"Hadley." Her name came out in a strangled groan.

He couldn't hold on much longer. Settling back so he was on his knees, the hard coils of the pullout couch's mattress bending under his weight, he lifted her up so only her shoulders were on the bed. Holding her hips, he fucked her, watching as her tits bounced with each thrust and mesmerized by each lusty moan and desperate demand for more coming from her. Fuck. He was so close, dancing on the edge, but he couldn't come yet.

"Don't stop," she said as she reached down and slid her fingers between her swollen, glistening folds, circling her clit.

Like there was any chance of that. Her fingers moved so quickly, her core getting tighter and tighter around his cock until her whole body tensed as she came around his dick with a cry. His balls tightened and he buried himself to the hilt and came so hard, he wasn't sure if he'd ever come down from the high.

Chest heaving, he rolled onto his back, wrapped a hand around Hadley's waist, and pulled her close. He was fucking floating right here with her on a pullout couch in a half-renovated cabin in the middle of nowhere. At absolutely no time in his life had he ever felt more at home.

"I'll be right back." She slipped off the mattress and headed toward the bathroom.

As he lay there watching his future walk down the hallway, he had never been so relieved that his usually 100-percent-correct instincts about someone's ulterior motives had been completely off when it came to Hadley Donavan.

CHAPTER EIGHTEEN

Hadley woke up the next morning with a smile on her face and a note on the pillow where Will's head should have been.

Hated to leave you when you were still snoring, but I had to go take care of some cowboy things. Counting down until I can see you at the barn later.

XOXO,

W

Okay, if someone had laid a cool billion in front of her and asked her all she had to do to keep it was say whether Will Holt was an Xs and Os kind of guy, she wouldn't have hesitated. The "no" would have been out on the next breath. The reality—again—was far different from what she'd always figured. Damn, had she been wrong about that man.

Just how wrong was pretty much all she thought about in the shower as she got ready for the day's pre-wedding family togetherness. Okay, she had about a million personal mental viewings of everything that had happened last night, too. What could she say, when everything finally started to fall into place with the hottest guy she'd ever counted as her worst nemesis, it was pretty impossible not to bask in it.

By the time she walked into the old barn fully decorated for the wedding reception the next day, her cheeks had started to hurt from smiling so much. Luckily, everyone in the barn was grinning, too—weddings had a way of doing that to people. Everyone was gathered up by the dais where the bride and groom would sit along with the bridal party during the reception. There were old-fashioned soft-glow light bulbs hanging from the rafters; delicate hand-folded paper birds sat on all the place settings, each one a unique piece of art; and then there were the bright prairie wildflowers already in mason jars etched with the date in the center of each table. It really was an Instagramable scene: the old and the new wedded together into something that was all about new beginnings.

Or maybe it was just that Hadley was still on a post-coital high, but she doubted it. Everything was just about as close to perfect as possible—including the fact that the guy with hair that was aggressively slicked back into a nearly impossibly short ponytail had to be Adalyn's fiancé, Derek. Breathing a sigh of relief for her sister—and still feeling more than a little floaty—Hadley joined everyone.

"It looks amazing," she said, giving her sister a hug and then turning to Derek and holding out her hand. "It's so nice to finally meet you. I'm Hadley."

His hand was damp as he shook hers. "Yeah, work's been crazy."

Before she could ask him what he did or how excited he was for the wedding, his cell rang. He held up a finger and backed away as he answered it.

Okay, that was...something, to put it nicely. What in the hell was going on with Adalyn's fiancé? That, of course, was not a question she could ask out loud. So instead, she turned to her sister and gave her another hug as she searched for the right words to say.

"He seems..."

"Busy," Adalyn finished, her tone flat.

"Well, yeah," Hadley rushed on, wanting to smooth the awkwardness for her sister—some habits died hard. "But I guess he's getting everything sorted so that after tomorrow, there won't be any interruptions."

"No, we have to delay the honeymoon for this work conference thing he has." Adalyn didn't sound very broken up about it, but there was a tension drawing her shoulders tight. "And honestly, I've been doing a lot of thinking since last night about my life, priorities, and what I really want."

"And that is?"

Her sister smiled at her, looking anything but weirded-out by Derek's behavior, the wedding tomorrow, or anything else. "I'm still trying to figure that out."

She pulled her sister into another tight hug. "Well, no matter what it is, you know we'll be there for you."

Adalyn squeezed her back and then abruptly

let go. "Oh my God."

"What?" Hadley turned around to see what her sister was staring at.

Will stood in the open barn doors, the light shining around him like a movie spotlight, but this time he didn't look like someone from a cowboy-of-the-week movie. This time he looked like the real thing, from the Wranglers that clung to his muscular thighs to the soft but obviously worn long-sleeve shirt to the scuffed-up cowboy boots to that black hat she was going to forever associate with hotness for the rest of her life. This was where she normally would have been ultra-concerned about appearances—about not seeming too eager or too interested or too anything that actually meant something and hung back. Not anymore. She strutted over to where Will stood with Aunt Louise.

She let out a low, appreciative whistle. "What happened to you?"

"Aunt Louise gave me a makeover," he said as he reached for her hand and then intertwined their fingers.

Looking every bit as smug as she did when her team won family game night, Aunt Louise said, "Had some of Harold's old things in the back of the closet and they fit perfectly. Knew there was a reason why I liked your fella from the get-go."

Okay, Hadley was going to skip right on over the part where Will reminded Aunt Louise of Uncle Jim. That was just too ew.

"You look amazing," she said, going up on her tiptoes to give him a quick kiss. "I gotta admit, those jeans look good on you."

He leaned down and whispered in her ear. "Don't suppose we can ditch the group dance lesson and head back to the cabin?"

His words made her skin sizzle, a teasing little brush of anticipation dancing across her nerve endings. "Believe me, I wish we could, but Adalyn has her heart set on this bridal party dance. She's been talking about it to me for weeks."

And before she lost the battle and agreed to go back to the cabin, she slipped her arm into the crook of his elbow and they walked across the barn to the area that had been set up as the dance floor. For the next hour, they laughed and moved as Knox and Adalyn taught everyone the moves to what was a mix of line dancing and two-stepping to this old country song about finding love where it was least expected. While Derek remained standing in the corner on his phone the entire time, Will fit right in, twirling Aunt Louise, making jokes with Weston, and pulling Hadley in close for a few extra whirls around the dance floor. Life wouldn't be like this back in Harbor City—after all, it wasn't like people in his income bracket were known for having barn dances. Still, Will could carry it off.

"I think you won the bet," Hadley said as the music stopped. "You're practically a cowboy."

He tipped his hat at her. "Thank ya, darlin'."

Then he dipped his head down and kissed her. For a second, the rest of the world disappeared and it was just the two of them again, fitting together like they were made for each other. By the time they stepped apart, her heart was going a million miles an hour.

"Your sister called you."

Hadley blinked several times, trying to come back down to reality. "She did?"

"Yep." He lowered his mouth to her ear. "But don't worry, we'll be finishing that later."

As tempting as it was to make later right now, Hadley knew their time was coming. Right now, she was actually looking forward to getting in on some family time with her mom and sister doing God knows what beyond a whole lot of together-ness.

· · ·

Will took a glass of sun tea, the condensation on the outside of the glass cool on his fingers, and stood off to the side watching Hadley talk with her mom and Adalyn. He was already thinking about taking her to his favorite diner in Harbor City, the one with these phenomenal shakes and a dog that very much was not allowed to hang out in the booths but did anyway. Then there would be the dates they'd have in the Holt Enterprises suite at Ice Knights Arena.

Considering how much she hollered during his just-for-fun rugby matches, there was no way she'd be calm during a hockey game. He couldn't wait to see her get all riled up. Of course, he'd take her to the Black Hearts Gallery to check out the new artists that the gallery owner Everly always managed to find. He'd want Hadley's opinion because she'd be looking at the art every day when she moved into his penthouse, and he really wanted her to love it.

Was he getting ahead of himself? Definitely, but he was a man who always had a vision and a gut feeling about things. That whole Hadley-is-a-gold-digger thing? That was just the exception that proved the rule.

For the first time in about as long as he could remember, that always-there edginess that acted as an early warning signal for the bad shit about to come seemed too quiet. He wasn't that kid he'd been when his parents died and left him and Web in the care of their no-time-for-kids grandmother. Nor was he the guy who had been so distracted by the empty space in his life that he'd let Mia fill it before he realized that she was really only there for his money. He knew Hadley was different. How? The alarm bells in his head had finally quieted. If anyone had told him a week ago that he'd feel like this, he would have laughed his ass off. Now, he'd never been more glad to be wrong, even if it was unsettling as hell.

As he was contemplating how weird life was turning out to be, Weston came over and poured himself a glass of sun tea.

He glanced between Will and Hadley. "Stare any harder and people are going to think you two are actually a thing."

Of course her brother picked just the moment Will had taken a drink to lay it down that he and Hadley had been faking everyone out—right up until they weren't. Shock made his throat malfunction and the tea go down the wrong pipe. He ended up spluttering for breath while Hadley's mountain of a brother smacked him hard between the shoulder blades.

Weston chuckled. "There's no reason to freak out; she spilled the beans last night."

"She failed to mention that to me."

Hadley's brother took a long drink of iced tea. "Must have slipped her mind when she told you about how she's finally starting up her own consulting business."

Something scratched against the back of Will's brain, that you're-about-to-get-fucked-over alert. When he'd explained his "assumptions" to Hadley, she'd acted as if she'd understood that always-on-edge feeling that a person just couldn't shake and what it meant when he said it wasn't there with her.

But what if what she'd really picked up on was a vulnerability that he hadn't meant to admit to—one that a smart hustler like Hadley could exploit? It's what he'd do in the boardroom. He'd discover the weakness and find a way to use it to get what he wanted. Of course, he was doing it to improve the company and the lives of those who worked there. She was doing it to fatten her bottom line.

The iced tea sloshed in his gut and his shoulders tensed until he could feel the pinch all through his body. He wanted to hurl.

"Now that she's finally got the money to set up shop," Weston went on, "there's nothing that will stop her. Hadley's always been determined and ambitious like that. She deserves to be happy in all parts of her life, don't you think?"

All Will could hear beyond the white noise blaring in his ears was Hadley saying last night that she was done pretending.

Is this what she meant? Had she finally gotten the cash from Web without having to secure a wedding ring first? And was she really on the pill? Mia had thrown a fake pregnancy at him—and he'd told Hadley. Was she one-upping that and going for the real thing? Why go through all the trouble of faking falling in love, waiting for a wedding, and then having to deal with the person long enough to get the good alimony payout when a surprise baby would accomplish the same thing?

Web had said there was something he needed to tell Will about Hadley—was it a warning? He'd told Will to have a good time. He'd never said Will should fall in love.

An icy certainty chilled him from the inside out and his body—making him feel a bit like it belonged to someone else—started to loosen up. He had to hand it to Hadley, it was a helluva plan. He'd never seen it coming. Too bad for her that he did now.

Finishing off his sun tea, Will eyed the woman who'd gotten past all his defenses and slid the shiv right between his ribs without him ever seeing it coming.

"She definitely deserves something," he told Weston as he set his empty glass on the table and headed for Hadley.

Keeping the smile on his face was work, but he

managed as he strolled across the room to where Hadley stood with her mom and sister. Hooking his arm around her waist and pulling her in close, he looked down at her as if she wasn't due an acting award.

"Do you guys mind if I steal Hadley for a little bit?" he asked.

"We're done here," Stephanie said. "Go ahead, she's all yours."

Yeah, a few minutes ago, he'd been a big enough fool to think that she was. What a fucking moron he'd been.

• • •

Something was very off. Will had been all smiles and soft touches inside the barn, but as soon as they walked out in the hot summer sunshine, his jaw had squared with tension and he'd let go of her hand. They marched in silence down the path to the cabin as the breeze that was always blowing across the prairies and twirling her hair around her face, smacked it against her cheeks and got strands of it stuck in her lip gloss.

"Is everything okay?" she asked as she tugged the strand away and tucked it behind her ear.

He held open the cabin door. "Let's talk about it inside."

The bed was still a mess of tangled sheets, and her bra from last night was still on the floor where it had fallen last night. The vibe inside now, though, was completely different. Edgy. Cold. Harsh. Rubbing her palms up and down her arms, she went through every possible scenario for what could have happened. The worst-possible scenario landed like a punch to the gut.

Whirling around to face him, fist pressed to her belly, she asked, "Did something happen with Web?"

Will's left eye twitched, but that was all the reaction he had. "Web's fine. When were you going to tell me about your business?"

The words were innocuous, but that didn't stop the icy dread slithering through her veins. Something was wrong, really wrong. She stood there in the middle of the cabin with the man she'd fallen in love with, and it was all she could do not to cry and she didn't even know why.

"Come on, Hadley, don't hold out on me now." Each word came out hard and cold, completely erasing the Will she thought she knew. "The gig is up—we both know you've been working on this little plan of yours for months."

She had no idea what was going on. How he'd found out about the loan from her parents or why he was so mad about it. "Will—"

"And last night, that was for insurance obviously." His lips curled upward, but it wasn't any kind of thing that could be called a smile. "A nice touch. I mean, some people might say it was a step too far, but the Holt fortune is pretty big."

Getting trampled by the bull in the north pasture couldn't have hurt more than that accusation thrown out so casually that the cruelty was doubled. It sent her two steps back and reaching out for the wall to keep her balance.

"That is bullshit," she finally got out, her voice hoarse.

Will let loose with a harsh chuckle. "Come on, you said it yourself: it was time to stop pretending."

What. A. Bastard. Heat rushed up from somewhere deep inside her, a reservoir of fury she didn't realize she possessed. "That's what you think I was talking about? My nonexistent gold-digging scheme that you're obsessed with?"

"Vigilant, not obsessed," he snapped back. "Really, I think you should be proud of yourself, of just how you were almost able to pull it off."

"The level of assholery here is epic." Not to mention the case of emotional whiplash she had now—it had been what, a few hours since he signed his note with Xs and Os? Wow. He must have really meant everything he said.

"I agree." He stalked forward, not getting anywhere near her but still moving around the room like a caged animal. "You really should have picked a brother and stuck with it."

"You need to get your head out of your ass and stop assuming that everyone out there is just waiting to fuck you over. Grow up and learn that not everyone in the world is waiting to fuck you over, but with your shit attitude you sure do make it tempting."

"I'm sure you'd like me to think that this was just my imagination."

"Seriously, what is wrong with you?" She clamped her jaw shut so tight, her molars would have winced if they could to keep the angry tears building up from falling down her cheeks. For someone who'd spent most of her life faking that everything was perfect, she sure had been fucked over by someone who put her skills to shame. Fuck her, she'd believed him. She'd believed in them. She was an unrivaled moron. "I thought I'd been wrong about you, that I could just be me, that's what I meant about not pretending. I thought we had something real."

He scoffed. "The most dangerous lies are the ones we tell ourselves, darling. Then again, I bet that just makes you a more convincing gold digger."

"Get out."

"What, you don't want to try to convince me of your down-home country truthfulness?" he asked, smirking as if this was all just a game.

Each word was salt getting ground into all the jagged wounds in her heart and at some point in time, a woman had to know when she'd reached her limit. *Fuck this.* She may not be perfect, but she was a better woman than he deserved.

"I'm done wasting my time with you." She tossed him the keys to the rental. "Just go. Follow the gravel road to the highway and then your phone GPS will start working well enough to get you back to the airport."

He paused inside the open door, keys in hand and a smug look on his handsome face. "What? No goodbye kiss for the road?"

"You really are the worst, Will Holt," she said, truly meaning every single word of it for the very first time ever.

The bastard just took off his black cowboy hat and sent it sailing onto the bed. It landed with a soft *thump* in the middle of all the twisted-up sheets, a final fuck-you to what she'd been foolish enough to think meant something. Then he walked out the door and drove off in the rental.

Hadley kept it together until the dust cloud kicked up by the car's tires disappeared. Then, with a silent cry, she let the tears flow.

CHAPTER NINETEEN

Still seething and his gut a block of ice, Will boarded the plane back to Harbor City. The entire drive back to the airport, he'd spent mentally reviewing every single second of the trip, looking for what he'd missed, that telltale sign of Hadley's true plan. Like some kind of masochistic fool, though, instead of finding the answers he wanted, he kept remembering the softness of her hair, the way she smiled when she didn't think anyone was looking, and her absolutely hilariously awful drawing attempts during Pictionary.

He pulled his phone out of his pocket before sitting down in seat 3A and called the number he'd found a million reasons to avoid until he couldn't anymore. Web picked up on the second ring, his hello too happy for what was about to come next, but Will didn't have a choice.

"Cancel the check to Hadley," he said without returning his brother's greeting.

"What check?"

Will's grip on his phone tightened. Sometimes his brother's literal-mindedness was enough to send him over the edge, and he didn't need any help today. "Fine, don't make the money transfer."

"Did you get kicked in the head by a horse? Because you are not making sense."

Of course his brother would think that. He was the fun Holt twin, the funny one, the nice one. It had been that way since they were kids. Why? Because Will cleaned up the ugly so Web didn't have to see it. This time the only way to make that happen was to pull back the curtain.

"Dammit, Web," Will said, his frustration peaking and making his voice louder than he meant in the plane's crowded interior, gaining him some curious looks from the other passengers. Letting out a deep breath, Will lowered his volume. "She's just in it for the money. Whatever she told you about loving you and whatever she promised, it was a lie. She's a damn gold digger."

"Hadley Donavan?" his brother said, disbelief and amusement still thick in his tone even if he wasn't outright laughing. "One of my best friends, Hadley?"

Will gritted his teeth, willing himself not to yell again. "Yes."

"One, she's not a gold digger and two, I didn't give her any money," Web said.

"Thank God." The tight pain in his chest remained, but some of the agony twisting his gut relented a bit. "If it's just a promise, she doesn't have a legal leg to stand on."

"You know who you sound like right now?"

"The brother who just saved you from a gold digger?" The words left a foul taste in his mouth.

"Our grandmother."

Of all the things Web could have said to him,

nothing would have hit home as hard as that comparison. "Bullshit."

Web scoffed. "You're obsessed with two things right now: our family money and being right. That sure sounds like Grandma to me. Of course, you're obsessed with Hadley, too."

"I was watching out for you." The roiling in his gut rushed back, worse than before, making his palms sweaty and his chest ache. It was as if his body were revolting, calling him out for being so far off the mark—but he wasn't. "She's good. She almost fooled me."

"No, the asshole who fooled you was you," Web said. "Hadley and I are friends, just friends. I've tried loaning Hadley money so she could leave that job where they treated her like shit and finally start her company. She turned me down every time. My guess is that if she has the money now, it's because it came from her family. Did you even bother to ask her where it came from, or did you just make an assumption?"

The mental image of Hadley in the cabin flashed in his mind. The way her eyes had gone wide as she flinched back as if his words had struck her. He'd taken it as a sign of guilt, the shock of being caught. What if…

Ignoring the doubt creeping in like Lightning through an open window, Will refused to consider any alternative. "She would have told me."

"Why? Did you give her the chance, or did you walk in assuming you were right?"

Before he could answer, the flight attendant's voice came over the plane's speakers. "We have closed the cabin door. All cell phones must be turned off or put in airplane mode."

"I gotta go," he said, glad for once to be flying commercial so he couldn't continue to use his phone.

"We'll finish this when you land."

Yeah, that wasn't going to happen. He knew the truth. He'd known it since the first time he'd seen Hadley; he'd just let himself get distracted. Will hung up and watched out the window as the plane taxied away from the gate.

He was right. Hadley was a gold digger—just like Mia. She was just subtler, so much so that if he hadn't known what signs to watch out for, he would have missed them.

Or maybe you were just looking too hard.

Will shoved the errant thought out of his head. No. He was right. He was always right. Hadley was only after the money, no matter how well she'd hid it with denials and smiles and sweet sighs.

You know what assuming does, Mr. Right? It makes an ass out of you and me.

No. Not in this case. Not with Hadley. He'd— *Oh, fuck it.*

He dialed her number when the flight attendant stopped by his seat. "Sir, please put your phone away."

"It'll be quick." He just needed to hear her voice one last time to quiet the doubts that were starting to scream in his ear.

The phone didn't even ring a full time before going straight to voicemail. As Hadley's voice told him to leave a message, he put the pieces together. She'd blocked him.

"Sir," the flight attendant glared at him. "Do not make me ask the pilot to turn the plane around so law enforcement can have a chat with you."

"Sorry," he mumbled and put away his phone.

Well, that took care of that. He had to be right about Hadley's motives. If he wasn't, then he'd just ruined the best thing ever to have happened to him, and he was too smart to have ever done that.

. . .

Hadley's first instinct once she'd woken up the next morning was to crawl under the bed and hide until she could come up with a decent cover story about why her eyes were puffy enough from crying to use as a pool float. That wasn't happening, though, for two reasons. One, she was done lying to her family to keep up her perfect image. Two, and more importantly, it was Adalyn's wedding day and she was due at the main house now to help her sister with her hair and makeup.

Every part of her ached, right down to the scar in the middle of her foot where she'd gotten six stitches when she was twelve, but still she rolled out of the bed that smelled like broken dreams and Will's soap. What a total fool she'd been. After living the fake-it-until-she-made-it lifestyle for so long, she'd obviously lost her ability not to lie to herself. She'd wanted to believe Will actually cared, maybe was falling for her the way she'd already fallen for him.

Hads, you are an idiot.

But she didn't feel like a fool. Everything ached too much for this to be about pride. Blowing her nose, stuffed from hours of teary misery, she straightened her shoulders, lifted her chin, and did her best to be bent but not broken. It was her sister's wedding day. She could pull it together for Adalyn.

After a quick shower, she was back at the main house walking into the bedroom she and Adalyn had shared until Hadley had left for college. Her sister sat on the queen bed that had replaced their two twins on opposite walls. She was still in her PJs, hadn't showered judging by her wicked bedhead, and was smiling from ear to ear while their mom and Aunt Louise stood there, jaws open and eyes wide with shock.

"What happened?" Hadley asked, hurrying in as all thoughts that didn't center around Adalyn got shoved into a deep, dark hole. "Is it Derek? Do I need to grab one of Gabe's shotguns and track his sorry ass down?"

Her sister giggled and shook her head. "Nope, I sent him on his way this morning. I woke up, realized that the life I wanted for me didn't have him in it."

Of all the things Hadley had been expecting to come from her sister's mouth, that was pretty much the last. Looking over at her mom and aunt, she sent out the silent question of *what the fuck?* Both women just nodded.

Hadley plopped down onto the chair opposite Adalyn's bed, her brain playing catch-up with what must have been a helluva night. "Are you sure?"

"I've never been more positive about anything in my life." Even though it didn't seem possible, Adalyn's smile got even bigger. "I realized somewhere in my second pint of panic ice cream last night that I love the person Derek could be. That's just not fair to him or to me. Everyone deserves to be loved for who they are, not who they might be in the future."

And to think she'd been acting as if Adalyn was still the eight-year-old who needed to be protected. "You just might be the smartest person I know."

"It's been an enlightening week." Her sister grabbed a still-steaming mug of coffee. "So the plan is to go ahead with the reception—well, party now—so that the photographers can shoot it for the wedding venue brochure. It seems a real waste to have everyone home and with all our dresses and tuxes available and not turn this into a win for the business Knox and Weston want to launch."

"What about you?" Aunt Louise asked.

"I'm twenty-six, newly single, and, according to my sister, the smartest person in the world—"

Hadley interrupted with a chuckle. "That wasn't exactly what I said."

"Close enough." Adalyn grinned at her. "So the opportunities are endless. Who knows, maybe I can get a job as the chief financial officer for this up-and-coming charity consulting company I've heard about."

"That would be amazing." And Hadley meant every single word of it.

Adalyn hopped up from her bed at the same time that Hadley bounded up from the chair, and they met in the middle of the room and hugged in one of those mind-meld events that only sisters could have when you said about a million things without uttering a single word. By the time they broke it up, they were both happy crying and, looking around at their mom and Aunt Louise, they weren't the only ones.

"The photographer is going to be here in a couple of hours," Adalyn said, wiping away a tear. "Go get dolled up in your bridesmaid dress. We have a party to kick off. Be sure to tell Will that we wear cowboy hats with tuxes around here."

Every single champagne bubble of happiness filling her chest popped at once and Hadley flinched. Looking at the hopeful faces and smiles, she almost gave in to that little voice that told her to make up some excuse as to where Will was, to keep the perfect image intact. However, those days were gone.

Releasing a deep breath, she let the truth out. "Will's gone."

"Where did he go?" Aunt Louise asked.

"Back to Harbor City."

"What happened?" her mom asked.

Bringing her family up to speed wasn't fun, but it was so much better than feeding them a bunch of excuses. By the time she told them about tossing the rental car keys to Will and telling him to get lost, there was no doubt from the grim expression on the other women's faces that they were most definitely in agreement that she did the right thing.

Of course, the only problem was that she still hurt as if there was a gaping hole in her chest where Will used to be. For the past year, he'd been a constant—driving her nuts, teasing her, turning her on, making her laugh, surprising her, and yes, showing her the man she'd finally fallen for so hard that she'd never even realized it was happening until it was too late.

"Well, I sure called that one wrong," her mom said once the true story was all out in the open. Then she pulled Hadley into a hug. "I'm sorry. I thought he really cared about you."

"Me too. I mean, not at first, but with everything that happened and—" Emotions clogged her throat, making it next to impossible to talk and the tears that in the past she would have held in to keep her family from seeing the real her fell free.

"So it's an independence party tonight," Adalyn said, joining in on the group hug.

Aunt Louise wrapped her arms around as much of the trio as possible. "Yee-fucking-haw."

Their mom gasped. "Language, Aunt Louise."

"Some days call for water and some call for vodka, Stephanie." Aunt Louise squeezed harder. "This is a vodka kinda day."

Their mom squeezed her girls a little harder, too. "Yee-fucking-haw."

The shock of hearing their mom cuss—let

alone drop the F bomb—was enough to make everyone burst out in laughter. And by the time Hadley was headed back to the cabin to change into her bridesmaid dress, her steps were lighter, if still dogged by heartbreak. It wasn't until she walked inside and saw Will's black cowboy hat on the floor that it hit her like a Mack truck and she forgot how to breathe again. Then the absurdity of the situation came to her in a whoosh of hot fury. She hadn't done anything wrong beyond falling in love with the wrong man. She'd learned her lesson. She wouldn't ever let that happen again.

Fuck him. He's an asshole.

Will fucking Holt really was the evil twin and the absolute worst. She swept the cowboy hat up off the floor. That was coming with her tonight. No doubt there'd be a bonfire, and this was going to go right in the middle of the flames.

By the time she was done up in full makeup, her hair pulled back in an updo, and wearing her bridesmaid dress, the tears had stopped but the pissed-off remained. She swiped the hat off the bed and walked out the door, ready to have the time of her life with her family because that's what the Donavans, the Martinezes, and the Donavan-Martinezes did—whatever it took to support one another because they were family and that was pretty much the most awesome thing there was.

• • •

Three days later, Hadley was back in Harbor City and once more sharing a bedroom with her sister. Last night, Fiona had welcomed Adalyn into their cramped apartment with a hug and a beer.

"I come from a family of seven kids," she said as she helped haul one of Adalyn's five suitcases up the four flights of stairs to their place. "Three people in one home is nothing. Trust me."

This morning, the two of them had taken off for a tour of the neighborhood—aka Bloody Marys at Medusa's Grill and Adalyn's first trip ever to a bodega—while Hadley stayed behind and tried to figure out how in the world she was going to take her charity consulting firm from a box of business cards under her bed to a real live business.

She needed two things: a plan and clients.

Harbor City had more billionaires per capita than any other place in the world, so there were definitely people with money who wanted to do good, or at least get a write-off on their taxes and some positive PR. She preferred to work with the first group, but the money from the second still helped fund the food kitchens, children's cancer wings, and adult education efforts throughout the city, so she wasn't about to be a snob about it.

Staring at her open document on her laptop, she exhaled a deep breath and started typing.

Possible Clients

Then she sat back. The only billionaires she knew were both verboten. Brokenhearted and now without a best friend, since she wasn't going to force Web to make the awkward pick between her and his brother, she allowed herself a moment of self-pitying sniffles. Each day was a little bit easier when it came to getting out of bed in the morning, but the nights were still long, sleepless, and too full of memories and hopes of what could have been if Will Holt hadn't turned out to be such a dick.

The knock on the door pulled her from staring blankly at the computer screen while trying not to remember the past week. Figuring her sister and Fiona were back early, she walked over to the door, pulled it open, and then her heart stopped beating.

Will stood in the hall wearing jeans, a T-shirt, and a smile, as if the past week had never happened. Her breath came back in a whoosh and she was ready to shut the door in his face when she noticed the mole. The person waiting on the other side of the front door wasn't the last person she expected to see, but he was next in line.

"Web," she said, not sure what else she could say at the moment as her adrenaline rush began to slow.

"So since you're not answering my texts, I had no other choice but to bring brunch to you." He lifted a large bag with the Medusa's logo on it. "While there, I spotted your roommate, who glared at me and then flipped me off. Did I do something to piss Fiona off or did she think I was Will?"

"Will."

He shrugged. "Yeah, that happens more than you'd imagine."

"Web, you don't have to." She waved at the bag, unable to come up with the words. "He's your brother. You have to stand by him. I understand."

"You understand that I'm not my brother or that I'm just as annoyed with him as you are?" He took a closer look at her puffy eyes and probably still red nose. "Okay, maybe not as much, but I have sustenance—including a carafe of Bloody Marys that I had to promise never to tell anyone I got them to let me take off the premises."

As if the Harbor City cops were going to arrest a Holt. "You own the restaurant."

"True, but liquor laws are liquor laws." He walked in and headed straight toward the bistro table in the tiny kitchen and started to unpack the bag.

"Why are you here, Web?" Quite frankly, she couldn't take another breakup from a Holt.

If Web was aware they were about to have a friendship breakup, he didn't act like it. "To feed you and ply you with spicy liquor until you agree to do me a huge favor."

"I'm not talking to Will."

"Me either." He grabbed two clean glasses from the drying rack next to the sink and poured the Bloody Marys. "No, this is for the Holt Foundation. I have a last-minute job, and I know you probably have other clients already lined up, but I'm desperate. We have an event on Friday to raise funds for the Best Buds organization and need someone to talk to potential donors about why it's such a great opportunity."

"That was the charity I recommended we work

with before I got fired." It paired shelter animals with kids newly adopted from foster care who helped to take care of them, the end result being that they bonded and it made the transition easier for both kids and animals.

The people at her old job felt the charity was too "downtown" and had opted to stay with their current projects of building hospital cardiac wings and adding libraries to university campuses.

"It was? Imagine that." Web took a long drink of his Bloody Mary, looking anything but surprised. "Anyway, we're not working with your last employer anymore and could use an innovative consultant to make sure we're doing the most with our donations and the funds we raise at events."

Damn. The tears were back. Sucking in a deep breath, Hadley stared extra hard at the kitchen cabinets to the left of Web. She didn't want to turn down the chance to help Best Buds, but there was no way she could work with the Holt Foundation, not after what Will had said. Then she would just be using him, maybe not as a gold digger, but it was close.

"Web, you don't have to—"

"But I do." He took her by the shoulders, looking her straight in the face, his green eyes so similar to Will's but not the same. "We only work with the best at the Holt Foundation, and that's you. Please. I'm asking as a friend. I need your help."

The sincerity in his words hit her right in the feels. Damn it. Why was it so hard to do the right thing when it came to the Holt brothers? "I don't know what to say."

"Tell me you'll do it so we can toast with these Bloody Marys and then trash talk my idiot brother."

"Yes." The agreement came out before she had a chance to stop it.

Web, knowing he'd won, handed her a glass and clinked hers in a toast before they both took a big drink to seal the deal.

"He misses you, you know," Web said a few minutes later. "I just wanted you to be aware that he knows he was an asshole. I wouldn't be surprised if he showed up on your doorstep. Of course, I'm not going to interfere in what happens with you two next. I'm not that type of guy. I let people take care of their own lives, and I stay out of it."

Even with the extra-strong Bloody Mary starting to hit her system, Hadley knew bullshit when it was flung her way. "Web, what are you up to?"

"Absolutely nothing." He pushed a to-go container of food and a set of plastic utensils across the table to her. "Come on, these eggs Benedict aren't going to eat themselves."

Hadley wasn't fooled, not even a little, by Web's protests, but the food from Medusa's smelled too good to argue about it—at least at the moment. It could wait, because no matter how much she still thought about him, she was done with Will Holt. Period.

There was absolutely nothing that would change her mind.

. . .

Will hadn't slept more than two hours at a time since he left the ranch, because every time he closed his eyes, he saw Hadley. It was like his subconscious was determined to make him relive every moment with her until he lost his fucking mind. Well, he was damn close. So much so that he was actually beginning to consider he might— *might*—have been wrong about her motives.

Pacing the length of his sixtieth-floor office, the high-rise-dotted skyline of Harbor City outside of the floor-to-ceiling windows, the unfamiliar sense of uncertainty crept up his spine like ants he couldn't flick away. Had he been wrong? Had she been telling the truth the entire time? He'd spent his life imagining the worst, prepping for disaster, knowing before anyone else in the room what was going to happen next. It was the only way to protect himself and Web from a chaotic world where no one answered why. Bad shit just happened, end of story. He couldn't have gotten it wrong. Not this time. Not when it mattered this much.

Then why can't you sleep at night, dumbass?

"Damn, you look like shit," Web said as he walked into Will's office like he hadn't been ignoring his twin for the past week.

"What, you're talking to me again?" Will asked.

Web shrugged and plopped down in one of the two leather chairs in front of Will's desk. "I figured you've had enough time to sit and marinate

in your own idiocy and were ready to go grovel to
Hadley."

Grovel? Why in the hell would he do that?

Because you were a class-A dick.

"And to think people consider you the nice
one," he said.

"There's more to me than a pretty face and my
naturally charming personality."

As if he wasn't well-aware of that. While the
rest of the world saw this one-dimensional nice-
guy version of Web, he knew his brother too well
for that. Their parents' death and how their grandmother raised them had left their marks on Web,
too—he was just better about hiding them. Will,
however, knew his twin's control-freak, manipu-
lating ways all too well.

"You know, one of these days, your natural
inclination to be way too interested in things that
are not your business is going to get you in
trouble."

"Maybe, but not today," Web shot back.
"Hadley is my best friend. You're my brother. And
I know where she's going to be tonight."

All week, it had taken everything Will had not
to go to Hadley's apartment—yeah, he'd done a
Google search—drop in to check on her, get
another look at that smile...or more likely hear
her curse him out. He'd even gone so far as to
have a cab drive him down her street. Pathetic?
Fuck yes, but he wasn't himself without her, and
that was the real truth of it.

"I'm not interested in that information."
Desperate for it was more likely.

Web threw back his head and let out a big, full-throated, oh-my-God-you're-a-jackass laugh. "You're full of shit," he said once he finally stopped being so loudly amused.

"Fine." Will ground out the word, admitting if not in so many words that lying to his twin was impossible but he had to try anyway. "Let's pretend I don't know my own mind, that she hasn't blocked me, and that for once you're right—where is she going to be?"

"A Holt Foundation fundraiser. One of us has to be the smart Holt brother and that sure as shit hasn't been you lately, so I hired her because she's good people and fucking fantastic at her job."

All the hot air and desperate denial making Will spin his wheels instead of go after the woman he loved whooshed out of him. "You think I was wrong about Hadley."

"I know you were and so do you." Smug didn't begin to describe the look on Web's face. "That's the magic of twin-o-vision."

Because pride was a helluva drug, Will was about to tell his brother that he had no fucking clue what he was talking about when a sharp knock sounded on his office door. "Come in."

His assistant, Barry, walked in carrying a box. "The delivery instructions said you were waiting on this, and I was supposed to deliver it right away."

"I don't—" Will took the box, looked down at the return address, and made a quick verbal left turn. "Thanks, Barry."

He carried the box over to his desk and

opened it using a combination of poking a pen through the shipping tape and sheer determination. A note sat on top. Will picked it up and flipped it over to the side with the block letters printed on it.

TIME TO COWBOY UP.
PAWPAW

A bit of black was visible underneath the balled-up copies of the Sandhills Senior Living Village weekly newspaper. Will reached in and pulled out his black cowboy hat. It still smelled of wide-open spaces and what could have been. Just seeing the black brim had him picturing Hadley when she'd teased him by trying on the hat. It had looked so damn good on her. Hell, everything did.

Holding the Stetson instead of her was a punch in the gut. It made him want. It made him need. It made him realize that of all the things in the world that he could buy with his money and power, Hadley's love wasn't one of them.

For a man who'd been so cluelessly wrong about her being a gold digger, he'd never wished so hard that he'd been right. Then she'd be his. Now, she never would be.

He started toward his office door, a little weary from a lack of sleep and deficit of food, his days-old beard starting to itch and his tie feeling more like a noose than anything else. "I gotta get out of here."

Web fell into line beside him, harder to get rid of than a matchmaking socialite's mom. "I know exactly where you need to go."

"I know where the best bottle of scotch in

town is, too." At his penthouse. It was outrageously expensive and impossibly rare. He was going to drink the whole damn bottle as fast as possible so he could forget about Hadley and pass out so his dreams wouldn't be haunted by her.

Continuing to bulldog his steps, his brother followed him into the executive elevator and glared at him. "You're not going to find Hadley?"

"It's too late for that." It had been too late the moment he'd seen her at the rugby game. He'd fallen and he'd fought it anyway, made every excuse to push her away until he finally did—at least physically. It was too late to really get her out of his head, though. She was a part of him, just like the ranch was a part of her. They could fight it all they wanted, but it wouldn't change. They were who they were supposed to be, even though it didn't feel like he was whole without her.

Web yanked Will to a stop as soon as they walked off the elevator and out into the bustling lobby. "You're a giant chickenshit. You have to go fight for her."

If only it were that easy. It was too late. "Fuck off, Web."

Will didn't wait for a response; he just walked out of the lobby. He didn't turn right to go out the door where his driver would be waiting. He turned left and went out the Sixth Avenue entrance. The best bottle of scotch might be in his penthouse, but there was no way he could stand to be there right now. The views felt too crowded, the kitchen too quiet, and the bed too big since he got back. So instead he walked into the first door with a neon beer sign and bellied up to the bar.

The bartender gave him a slow up-and-down, pausing to stare at Will's hat as if he'd never seen one in real life before. "What'll it be, cowboy?"

Fuck the scotch. He needed something more like bare-knuckle boxing than golf on the highlands. "The biggest, highest-proof shot you've got."

The bartender didn't ask twice; he just reached for a bottle of clear liquid on the bottom shelf and poured a double. "Woman or family?" he asked as he set the shot down in front of Will.

"Both," he said before downing the liquor. It left a burning trail of fire from his tongue to his gut, and he couldn't wait to have another.

"Well, don't look now," the bartender said. "But I'm guessing the family just walked in."

Will looked over his shoulder and there was Web. His brother must have followed him, and he was in too much of a fog to notice. Web sauntered over and sat down on the stool next to him.

"I'll have what he's having." Then Web turned to Will. "So you really fucked this up, huh?"

Will lifted his empty glass in the universal sign for one more. "You really have to ask?"

"Not judging by how shitty you look." Web sniffed the single shot the bartender put down in front of him and then downed it.

"Is that your new thing, telling me how crappy I look? You do realize we look exactly the same."

"Maybe, but at least I'm wearing shoes that match, and I look like I slept sometime in the past twenty years."

The bartender didn't say anything, but the look he slung at Will when he dropped off another shot—a single this time—pretty much yelled *he's right*. Will scoffed and slammed back the liquor. Whatever was in his glass tasted like radioactive poison, but that was fine. It's what he deserved.

"Why don't you go home," he snarled at his brother. "Just leave me alone."

Web laughed as if he were having the time of his life. "I can't."

"Sure you can. You just take a cab and bam, you're there."

"You aren't going to figure out how to fix this on your own. You're fucking it up even more than you already have by wimping out."

Fury and whatever he'd been drinking had him up off the stool on the inhale, then grabbing his brother by the shirt collar and hauling him up on the exhale. "Don't tell me what I'm doing. I know what I'm doing. I'm walking away because she doesn't want me."

Web didn't flinch. "Or is it because you just can't stand to admit you were wrong about her, about how you feel, and about what's really important?"

Important? Will had always known what was important. He'd been protecting his brother practically since he was born. That's what older brothers did. They watched over the younger ones. They protected the family fortune. They made sure that they always won, they were always right, that nothing bad ever happened. Like their parents dying. Like going to boarding school when they were so young. Like falling in love with the woman he'd thought was out for his brother's money and then accusing her of being a gold digger to cover up his feelings.

Fuck.

He let go of Web and slumped back onto his stool, realization like a million-pound weight on his shoulders.

"I failed at everything. I'm sorry."

"My God, you're an idiot. You're one of the most successful people I know, but you can't control everything. Anyway, you're my favorite brother."

"I'm your only brother."

"What can I say, I have low standards."

But Hadley didn't. "How do I make this up to her? Diamonds? That's what our grandmother always wanted."

Web grimaced. "Oh yeah, nothing shows affection and esteem like sparkly things."

"That was about as close to a nursery rhyme as she ever told us," Will said, covering the shot glass with his hand when the bartender held up the mystery bottle again.

He'd spent his entire life thinking that buying someone's affection was normal, and then he met Hadley. Seeing her with her family was like stepping into another dimension. For them, it wasn't the money that mattered but time and togetherness. Even with all his money, he couldn't buy that. Hell, even if Hadley had his money, she'd probably spend it on helping her family's new business, charities, and getting out to see them more often.

Something settled in his chest, a certainty that he knew what he needed to do next.

"I gotta get to that fundraiser," he said. "I have to get Hadley back."

"Finally." Web held up his car keys and jingled them. "Let's go."

The Porsche logo on the key fob caught the light and on the next heartbeat, Will knew exactly what he needed to do to show Hadley he understood exactly how wrong he'd been about her. The chances of it working might be slim, but as a space cowboy once said, never tell him the odds.

Fuck the odds. He had to believe this would work.

CHAPTER TWENTY

Toes pinched from the shoes she'd borrowed from Fiona and wearing a cocktail dress tailored via safety pins, Hadley kept her chin high and her steps steady as she walked by the coat closet—yes, *the* coat closet—at the hotel ballroom. Of course, up until that moment, she refused to notice the coat closet. She'd barely even glanced in that direction. Certainly, she hadn't found an excuse to walk by it multiple times while working the floor at her very first fundraising event run by her fledgling company.

Nope.

She'd stayed clear.

And that whisper of "maybe he'll show here, since he never appeared on your doorstep," could just shut up already. Will was out of her life and good riddance to him. It wasn't like she missed him or thought about him or dreamed about him every single night.

She didn't.

Not.

At.

All.

He'd left. She'd blocked his number. Life went on.

Still, she searched the crowd in the ballroom, looking for the absolute worst man who she still loved because emotions were a bitch. If she could, she'd have hers surgically removed. Scientists really needed to get to work on that one. Maybe that could be her next charity funding recommendation.

Shoving all thoughts of Will into a deep, dark hole where they belonged, Hadley worked the room, talking with donors and influencers about the Holt Foundation Fund and the work it was doing to support Harbor City's charities. Then the band started playing the first notes of a song that stopped her in her tracks. It was the song from Adalyn's reception dance that they'd listened to repeatedly until she and Will had the steps down.

In half a breath, she could feel his arms around her again and could practically smell the musky scent of his cologne. Unable to stop herself, she whirled around to face the stage as her heart hammered in her chest, expecting to see Will standing up there. Her disappointed breath came out in a whoosh. It was just the band.

"May I have this dance?" Will asked, appearing all of a sudden on her other side.

Fighting a battle within herself, she took in the sight of him. The bastard didn't just look good. He looked amazing. He wore a custom-made suit without a tie and the black cowboy hat she'd had every intention of burning before it had disappeared during the family festivities.

"Where did you get the hat?" *Because that should really be the first thing you say to him. Way to go, Hads.*

He tipped the brim and gave her a wink. "PawPaw sent it."

"I should have known." *Was there anything her family didn't lovingly involve themselves in? No, thank God.*

Will held out his elbow to her. "Dance?"

There really wasn't a way to get out of it without drawing attention, so she nodded in agreement, slipped her hand into the crook of his arm, and made her way onto the dance floor.

The second he placed his palm on the small of her back and took her other hand in his so they could two-step, she gave in to the tide of rightness that followed. For a second, she allowed her eyes to close and let that sense of everything falling into place fill her. Did that make her weak? Maybe, but that was the thing with love. Even when it was inconvenient or wrong or perfect, it was there. A person couldn't stop that. So she gave herself that moment to remember what could have been and pretend it still could be before opening her eyes to the reality of the situation.

Will was looking down at her, the depth of feeling in his eyes the best and worst thing to see at that moment when it was taking everything she had not to fall prey to that old fake-it-until-you-make-it feeling.

"Hadley, I'm sorry," he said as they moved along to the music, each step bringing their bodies closer together until they were aligned, fitting together like two puzzle pieces. "I was wrong. I know that."

She managed not to flinch, years of covering her true feelings coming in handy, but that didn't mean his words didn't hurt. They were all she'd wanted to hear, but how could she trust them after everything that had happened?

"I should have known all along what an idiot I was, but it turns out that defense mechanisms are a helluva thing to realize you're using," he went on. "It took Web telling me that I was acting like our grandmother for me to really open my eyes to what I was doing. Please, say you'll give us another chance."

The music stopped, but they stayed there on the dance floor, his palm warm against the small of her back. On the ranch, it would have felt like the first moment of the rest of her life. Now it just seemed like a cruel tease of what could have been. She wanted to believe him, really she did, but she wasn't sure she had it in her anymore to believe. She had her family. She had herself. Could she really think that she could have Will Holt, too? Damn it, she wanted to believe. She really did, and that was the one thing that scared her enough to push every knee-jerk fear of what happened when things stopped being perfect to the forefront, making her whole body ache. No one knew better than she did that perfection was only an illusion; the only thing that was real was love — and he'd made no mention of that.

"So when all the perfect newness wears off you can wonder again if I was just a gold digger?" she asked, her voice barely above a whisper. "We can't help who we're drawn to, but we can help what we do about it." And she knew what she had to do, because God help her, she loved him. She stepped back, her palm pressed to his chest just above his heart. "Goodbye, Will."

Chin held high even if it was trembling, she turned and started to walk away. She got two steps before his voice stopped her.

"I was wrong. My assumptions most definitely made an ass out of me. But you? I want to make you the sole beneficiary of the Donavan Trust. You'll be one of the richest women in Harbor City."

Shock poured over her like ice water and she whipped around to face him. "What are you talking about?"

"I want to transfer everything into a trust for you," he said as the upper crust of Harbor City gawked, taking in every syllable. "I want to make it yours. All of it."

It took Hadley a second to process the meaning of his words. All of it? Hers? And by the time she did, the entire room was buzzing and cell phone cameras were aimed right at her.

"I don't care about the damn money, Will," she said, fury filling her like the bonfire she should have burned that damn cowboy hat in. "I wanted your love, not your money, but you never understood that. I'm not sure you can."

Frustrated tears beating at the back of her eyes, she turned and rushed away before they had a chance to fall, going through the first door she passed.

• • •

What in the hell had he done?

He'd made it so no one could ever call Hadley a gold digger again, not when she was one of the richest women in the city. It all made perfect sense. How could she not see that, especially when he did it because he lo—

Realization rolled over him like the midtown bus rolling over an empty beer can.

Oh, fuck.

He was the dumbest human being alive.

Eyes wide and mouths agape, the Harbor City elite in tuxes and ballgowns split like an ocean parting as he made his way to the coat closet. Without a doubt, the news would be on the front pages of tomorrow's paper. His grandmother would be on her way back to Harbor City from Paris on the family jet as soon as someone texted her the news so she could try to bully him in person. This was about to land him exactly where he hated to be—in the middle of the public eye— and he didn't give two shits about the money or the exposure or anything else. All he cared about was Hadley, and he'd been an asshole to her.

Exhaling a deep breath, he turned the doorknob and walked inside. Hadley had her back to him as she stood at the back of the tiny room filled with jackets. The light from the single bulb above them gave him just enough light to see how her shoulders were shaking as she cried silently.

"Hadley. I fucked all of this up. Again," he said,

staying where he was so he wouldn't crowd her or make her feel trapped. "The thing is, I love you. I've always loved you. It just took me a long time to realize it because, quite frankly, all the private schools I attended and my Ivy League MBA didn't prepare me for you. Hell, I don't think anything could. You are a force of nature."

She didn't turn, but he could tell from the way her body stilled that she'd stopped crying and the tilt of her head told him she was listening. Christ, this was hard. Feelings. Who in the hell had invented those? They were swarming him, making him hot and cold at the same time while his heart was going fast enough to make him worry he'd keel over before he could get the words out, but he'd be damned if he'd let that stop him.

"Here's the thing: I should have realized I loved you the first time I saw you standing along the sidelines of that rugby game. Your nose was red with cold, you were white-knuckling that dripping coffee travel mug, and when I offered you my coat, you turned me down because you didn't need a damn thing from me."

Hadley turned around. Her cheeks were wet with tears, but she nailed him to the wall with a glare anyway. "I didn't *want* anything from you. Not then. Not now."

"I know." Knowing there was no way it was a good idea but unable to stop himself, he stepped forward, just enough to be within touching distance if she reached out. He wanted to always be there for her, whenever she needed him—all she had to do was reach out. "The money, it was a gesture—a stupid one, I'm realizing—to show you that you never had to worry that I truly knew how wrong I'd been about you. I love you, Hadley Donavan, and I don't ever want to stop loving you."

She let out a shaky breath but didn't move away. "Hate to be the one to have to break it to you, but you don't always get what you want."

"I know that." If there was anything he'd learned from falling for Hadley, it was that.

"Oh really," she scoffed. "What in the world have you ever wanted that you didn't get?"

"You." It was true, more so than he'd ever known until the words were out. "You're all that matters. You're everything to me."

"Don't." She put her hand to his chest as if to push him away, but she didn't; instead she fisted his jacket, holding him tight. "This isn't some game. I'm not someone to slot into your win column."

"No." He brushed back the long brown hair that had come loose, tucking it behind her ear, wiping away some of the wetness from her cheek with his thumb. "You're more than that. I love the way you fight for the people you care about. I love that you're willing to do whatever it takes to make your dreams come true. I love that you are absolutely cutthroat at Scrabble but will give up your bed for the night for a three-legged fox. And I love you."

"You don't even know me." It sounded more like a croak than English, but it was still gorgeous to him.

"That's where you're wrong." He cupped her face so she could see the sincerity in his face as he said what he should have said back on the ranch. "I've spent the last year learning everything about you, watching how you interact with people, and fighting to see you as an enemy when all I wanted was to be with you. I've never loved anyone more."

She took a step back. "You thought I was a gold digger."

He'd spend his life making that up to her, and he wouldn't regret having the opportunity to do so. Hell, he'd be the luckiest man on earth. But first he needed to say the one thing he'd been avoiding since he met her.

"I was wrong. No, I wasn't just wrong—I was lying to myself. It was easier to think you were after my brother for his money than to think you were in love with him. Pushing you out of his life was acceptable as long as it was because I was protecting him and not because I was in love with you myself."

• • •

Hadley just stared at him. She'd been less shocked when he'd walked off the airplane in Denver than she was now. Really, besides Lightning showing up with his fourth leg, she had no idea what would throw her more than Will Holt standing in front of her in one brown shoe and one black, wearing his TV movie cowboy hat, and telling her he loved her.

Discombobulating. Flabbergasting. Confusing as hell. It was all of that—but that wasn't all. That little bubble of hope had her feeling lighter as she listened. She wanted to believe him, like, really wanted, but how could she trust that he really got it this time? That he understood?

"Why are you telling me this now?" The question came out as a whisper, as she knew on an instinctual level that all of this could disappear again in a moment, and there was nothing in the world she wanted more than to have this moment last forever.

He took off the cowboy hat, holding on to it with such a tight grip that it was as if it was a talisman. "Because I'm a wreck without you. I can't sleep. I can't eat. I can't stop thinking about you."

Heart pounding, hope expanding, she could barely stand to look at him, but looking away was an impossibility. Not now. Not ever. Will Holt was the man she loved, and he loved her.

"You are…" The words died on his lips as he looked at her with a kind of vulnerable hope that echoed what she felt. "You're my everything. Please give me another chance. I love you. I know I can be the worst, but—"

Unable to stop herself, she cut him off there by closing the distance between them.

"Will Holt," she said, lifting herself up on her tiptoes and bringing her mouth within millimeters of his. "You are the best man, the absolute best."

"Only because of you. I love you, Hadley."

"I love you, too."

Dipping his head down and meeting her halfway, Will kissed Hadley. She put everything in it that she felt, promising the world and meaning every bit of it.

By the time they walked back out into the ballroom, her dress was a bit askew, his cowboy hat sat cockeyed on his head, and both of them had that half-dazed, kissed-out-of-my-mind look on their faces.

The Harbor City elite staring at them as they emerged from the coat closet were buzzing with gossipy glee as well. Not giving a shit and grinning like a man in love, which she now knew he was, Will picked Hadley up and carried her out of the ballroom, past the huge mural of a sunset that took up an entire wall, and into the rest of their lives together.

EPILOGUE

One Year Later...

Will was wearing his black cowboy hat again, and Hadley was so beyond the point of denying that seeing him in it and his worn-in Wranglers was hot as hell. And the fact that they were back on the ranch to celebrate Adalyn's decision to move to Harbor City and become an equal partner in Hadley's charitable consulting firm, of course, meant only one thing: family game night.

She and Will had barely survived the first round of charades after dinner, which was what must have him so nervous. The bench at the outdoor picnic table they were sharing was practically vibrating from the speed of his knee bouncing up and down, and he hadn't stopped shoveling Puppy Chow into his mouth since her mom had put it down in front of him with a wink.

She leaned in close to him, lowering her voice. "You okay?"

"Fine," he said through clenched teeth. "Everything's fine."

"Weird" didn't begin to cover this. After a year of spending nearly every non-working moment with him, she'd pretty much pegged all his moods.

This one, though, was totally new.

"If you want to concede, we can totally do that." She gave his thigh a comforting squeeze, then glided her hands up about as high as possible, considering her entire family was out on the patio with them. "That would mean we could sneak off to the cabin sooner."

"No," he said, the single word coming out sharp as a firecracker. "Sorry. I just really love Scrabble."

Okay then, nothing to see here at all. Just her boyfriend passing on hot cabin sex for a game involving wooden square tiles. Letting out a sigh, she turned back to the board, her shoulders slumped with disappointment. So much for that whole honeymoon, can't-get-enough-of-each-other period.

PawPaw laid down the first word. Marry.

"Really? You couldn't have gone for more points than that? You wasted an M on a square that didn't even have double points?" Aunt Louise rolled her eyes. "I should have partnered with the dog."

"Oh yeah?" PawPaw shot back, his question sounding oddly practiced. Of course, after decades of the siblings needling each other, how could it not? "What do you have that's so amazing?"

Aunt Louise's cheeks turned red. "You have no idea how painful this is for me."

Then she laid down a single E beneath the M.

"A whole two points." PawPaw let out a low whistle. "That's really going to win us the game."

"And this is why you two aren't allowed to

partner up during family game night," Adalyn said
as she stood at the end of the table messing with
her phone. "Great-Grandma always said you have
been bickering like this since you were kids."

"We know how to work together when it matters," PawPaw grumbled.

His knee still going a million miles an hour,
Will laid down an O and a U going down from the
end of the word "marry."

For someone who loved Scrabble more than
orgasms, it was a really disappointing point total.
Judging by the way his jaw was clenched tight, he
was none too happy about it.

"Don't worry," Hadley said, injecting an extra
dose of chipper into her tone. "I've had those kind
of tile choices before, too. We'll catch up."

Surveying her tiles, she was trying to work out
how to use the W so it would land on a multiple-
point square when Will snagged her tiles.

"I got this."

What the hell? Slack-jawed, she stared at him
as he laid down the tiles, usurping her turn as if
she wasn't sitting there.

"That's not legal," she said, looking to PawPaw
and Aunt Louise for backup. "You can't just play
my tiles for me." She glanced down at the board
and realized that he hadn't even connected his
four-letter word to the others already played.
"And you can't have a disconnected word."
Turning back to Will, she sucked in a breath.
There was a sheen of sweat on his brow and his
jiggling knee was going fast enough to launch
them into hyper speed. Something was definitely

wrong. "Are you sure you're okay?"

He nodded toward the board. "Read it."

She glanced down at the sorry excuse for a Scrabble board. The whole thing—even if the last word counted—couldn't add up to more than twenty points.

"Marry. Me. You," she said, going in the order that they were played. "Your word doesn't count."

"It really does," he said, sounding more like his usual cocky self.

"That goes against the rules and—" Her brain finally caught up with what was going on, and she lost the ability to talk as her heart double-timed it in her chest.

Will stood up, pulled a ring box out of his pocket, and then got down on one knee. "Hadley Donavan…" He opened the box, revealing an antique ring made up of square-cut diamonds surrounded by rubies that screamed out "old money" the same way his scuffed-up Justin boots said "ranch ready." "Will you marry me?"

It took all of her effort to put together a three-letter word from the jumble of ecstatic emotions making her feel like she'd swallowed every bubble in a champagne bottle. "Yes."

Everyone cheered loud enough that it set off an answering howl from Lightning out there somewhere in the dusk. Out of the corner of her eye, she spotted Adalyn no longer trying to disguise the fact that she was recording the whole proposal on her phone. Hadley's attention, though, was focused on the man who'd driven her crazy before stealing her heart.

"Thank God you said yes." He slipped the ring on her finger and gave her a sly wink. "Otherwise the rest of this game was going to be extremely awkward."

"We're finishing the game?" The question slipped out before she remembered all of this was being recorded and, knowing her siblings, it would be played at the wedding reception.

One side of Will's mouth lifted in a grin that did stupid things to Hadley's knees. "I'm sure your family will understand if we don't."

"We concede, PawPaw and Louise," she hollered, not even bothering to look back at the picnic table because there was no looking away from the man she loved.

"Because we already won." He picked her up in his arms. "At least I know I did."

"Believe me," she said, wrapping her arms around his neck. "We both did."

He dipped his head down and kissed her, a quick brush of his lips that promised a forever of mores and carried her off to their cabin so that forever could start immediately.

ACKNOWLEDGMENTS

First of all, I have to thank the readers who've generously decided to spend their precious free time with me. Thank you! None of this would be possible without you. Also, I couldn't have ever gotten this book from idea to completion without the help of the good people at Entangled. The fact that they haven't poisoned my coffee by now always amazes me. Thank you, Liz, Jessica, Bree, Elizabeth, Curtis, Stacy, and everyone else who went above and beyond. Y'all are the absolute best. As always, a huge thank-you to my family (those in Nebraska and on the East Coast) for putting up with me when I'm on deadline and hangry. I promise next time, I'll remember to eat lunch.
Xoxo, Avery

Turn the page to start reading the hilarious and sexy new rom-com

her
aussie
holiday

USA TODAY BESTSELLING AUTHOR

STEFANIE
LONDON

CHAPTER ONE

Cora Cabot knew three important things about Australia:

1. The men were hotter Down Under (Chris Hemsworth, Hugh Jackman, the other Hemsworth...)

2. It was hot. Period.

3. Pretty much every animal could kill you.

Okay, so maybe not *every* animal could kill you. But a country that prided itself on having the deadliest snakes in the world was not a country to be trifled with. Add to that spiders—of the hairy and poisonous variety—sharks, stingrays (RIP Steve Irwin), all kinds of creepy crawlies, and Cora knew she would have to be on high alert at all times.

But standing outside a slightly run-down yet utterly charming house surrounded by huge, swaying trees whose leaves rustled in the dry, sea-salted air made Cora instantly understand why Aussies put up with their infamous critters. It was truly beautiful here.

She walked up the unfinished driveway, careful to avoid the dozens of small, podlike things littering the ground. Her suitcase bumped behind her, wheels rattling and lock jangling with each step.

So what *was* a dyed-in-the-wool city girl—a New Yorker, no less—doing thousands of miles from the nearest Saks?

Healing…escaping.

It sounded a little melodramatic, sure. But Cora wasn't exactly opposed to a little melodrama. After all, one did not grow up with a mother famous for her daytime television relationship therapy segments without developing a passing interest in the theatrical and over the top. But right now, Cora needed to get as *far* away from that stuff as possible. A whole hemisphere away, in fact.

Pausing at the front door, she sucked in a breath. Finally, after what felt like an eternity of airports and immigration lines and endless road, she was here. Alone. The sound of nature enveloped her—birds and leaves and wind and the ocean creating a soothing cacophony that melted into her bones.

This was *exactly* what she needed.

Cora slipped a carefully folded piece of paper out of her bag and flipped it open.

Dear Cora,

I am so excited for our house swap! Seriously, thank you. You've saved my butt. I had no idea how I was going to afford to rent a place in Manhattan for a month without going totally broke. Anyway, my little place isn't anywhere near as fancy or glamorous as yours, but I hope you find it comfortable. A few things:

1. *The bathroom pipes rattle terribly. Give them a second to run and the noise will eventually stop. If they're too annoying, let me know and I'll have my brother come by to work on them.*

2. *There's a cockatoo (noisy white bird with a gold crest) who likes to pop in. I call him Joe and keep some bird feed by the back door. He's very friendly!*

3. *Print this email out because reception is terrible, and you'll need the access code to get the key. There's a little box under a red pot. The code is: 2513.*

Now get to work on your novel! When you become a famous author, I'm going to rent this place out as a tourist attraction and charge people a fortune to visit the creative retreat of the great Cora Cabot, literary genius.

Love, Liv.

Cora cringed. Why had she even told Liv she was working on a novel?

Maybe it was a moment of giddy excitement at typing those fabled words: The End. But clearly she should have curbed her enthusiasm long enough for her literary agent father to cut down any delusions of grandeur. He'd called her book *unpublishable*, her lead character *unsympathetic*.

And then he'd declined to represent her.

Of course the feedback wasn't intended to hurt her feelings—she knew that. Her father had a black belt in tough love, and his criticism was meant to help her grow and improve. To make her a better writer. And she absolutely intended to rise to that challenge.

But right now, she had more pressing concerns…like liberating the front door key from its hiding place.

"Please, please, *please* don't be hiding anything more than a key," she said as she crouched down, reaching for the pot described in Liv's email.

Cora felt like Dorothy in *The Wizard of Oz*. Only instead of lions, and tigers, and bears, *oh my!* it was more like snakes, and bugs, and poisonous, hairy, eight-legged freaks of nature waiting to suck your blood like B-movie vampires.

Too squeamish to pick up the pot, she nudged it over and hoped nothing would scuttle or slither out. Thankfully, the only thing underneath was a plastic box containing the key. The simple gold thing didn't look secure enough to protect much. Cora's New York apartment had a twenty-four-seven doorman, a concierge, swipe key, and two physical keys to get inside.

But maybe around these parts, people trusted one another. What a thought.

Cora unlocked the front door and dragged her suitcase inside. The house was in the middle of renovations, as Liv had previously warned. On one side there was a kitchen, gleaming and modern with white subway tiles and a soft-white granite countertop with pretty silver and charcoal veining. The family room, on the other hand, was older-looking and well-loved with a heaving bookshelf and big couch in faded blue.

There was a section of floral wallpaper. It looked vintage, but not in a good way. More like in a "grandma was a pack-a-day smoker" kind of way.

But her friend Liv had thrown her own *joie de vivre* onto the weary canvas, with a collection of colorful mismatched cushions on the couch, quirky wall hangings and photos of her family dotting several surfaces. This was a house with love embedded in the walls and floors and shining in through the windows.

A *real* home.

Liv had been worried it might not be up to Cora's standards, but frankly, luxury furniture and expensive art handpicked by New York's best interior designer hadn't made her happy. And it had become painfully obvious that the fancy handbags and red-soled shoes her mother had taught her to covet were a poor substitute for the things that actually mattered in life. Cora would trade it all in for the real deal: a loving husband, a family who supported one another, a career that made her soul sing.

"Oh, bloody hell!"

Cora jumped and whirled around, pressing her palm to her heart. "Who's there?"

"Bugger off!"

The noise was coming from the kitchen, where a window facing the back of the property was totally open. Gee, they *really* didn't worry about security here. A white bird sat on the windowsill, staring at her. Its golden crest fanned out above its head, demanding her attention.

"You must be Joe," Cora said, narrowing her eyes. So much for friendly. She was pretty sure being told to *bugger off* wasn't a nice thing in this country. But she also understood that it was easy to say something you didn't mean if you were "hangry." It happened to her all the time. "You want something to eat, little guy?"

The bird squawked, as if offended at being called little. But then he bobbed his head in this strange boppy dance, and Cora couldn't help but laugh.

"I'll take that as a yes."

It took her a few minutes to locate a sack of bird seed, which had a note taped to it: *1 x small handful. He'll eat from your hand, or scatter into the backyard.*

Cora looked at the bird's curved, pointed-tipped talons—the damn things looked sharp enough to carve a Thanksgiving turkey. So that was a hard pass on the hand feeding. Joe chattered away, clicking and chirping and making all kinds of funny noises while he waited for his lunch.

"All right, mate! Who's a pretty boy?"

In spite of her trepidation and emotional exhaustion, Cora found herself feeling lighter than she had in weeks. Hell, maybe in months.

Don't fool yourself—it's been years. You don't get this messed up without a solid foundation of BS from way back.

Her snarky inner voice was cut off when Joe whistled at her in a way that sounded a whole lot like a catcall. Now *who* had taught him to do that?

"Sorry, little guy, this vacation does *not* include

a fling. I've only got eyes for fictional men right now. Book boyfriends all the way."

She tossed the seed through the window, and it scattered across the grassy area behind the house. Joe immediately flapped his wings, swooping down to collect the bounty and trying to intimidate a couple of smaller birds looking to join the meal. He puffed his chest out and stomped around, claiming the territory.

"You guys are all the same, only after a free lunch," she said, shaking her head.

Being wealthy wasn't uncommon in Manhattan, not by a long stretch. Coming from a famous family wasn't, either. But that didn't stop the opportunists and users from piling up.

Warning: Traffic conditions in Cora Cabot's life are dire. A collision containing one ex-fiancé and one narcissistic mother have created untenable conditions in New York City. Watch out for the ego spill on Fifth Avenue. Get out while you can.

For the next month, Cora would forget all about her fame-hungry mother, her string of failed relationships, and her unfulfilling job. She was going to enjoy being away from the drama and having a beautiful location to work on achieving her dream: producing a novel worthy of publication.

Right now, that was the only thing that mattered.

Cora's nose wrinkled at the smell of something unappealing and, with horror, figured out it was *her*. Looked like her grand life reset would have to wait until after a very long, very hot shower.

• • •

Trent Walters's ute navigated the winding, overgrown road to his sister's house. Although calling it a road seemed a little generous. More like a root-infested, teeth-rattling, wild, life-dodging driving "experience." Why his adorable, social butterfly baby sister had chosen to purchase a home so secluded was beyond him.

But Liv had her own house and he didn't, so who was he to judge? Being a builder by trade and a general handyman by hobby, Trent wanted the perfect house with the perfect view. Unfortunately, despite securing the ideal block of land upon which to build his dream home some time ago, he'd yet to make a start. Too many other commitments kept getting in the way.

To make matters worse, his best mate had decided to move his girlfriend into their shared house, and the nightly squeaking bedsprings and cries of "yes baby, do it harder" had finally become too much.

All of that was to say, Trent's living situation was…fluid. For now, he would camp at his sister's place while she was away. It was the perfect opportunity to get some extra work done on her renovations without her standing over his shoulder. First up: fix the shitty plumbing. The old pipes rattled like that angry, chained-up ghost in *The Muppet Christmas Carol*. It was like the Ghost of Bad DIYs Past. How Liv put up with the sound, he'd never know.

So he'd taken the plumbing apart earlier that morning in the hopes that he'd get it all fixed up by lunchtime tomorrow. Then he could *finally* have a shower without the walls moaning and groaning.

Never mind that Liv had told him to pause the work while she was away—*that* was an advantage. The less she suspected, the more impact the surprise would have. He was already picturing the big smile on her face when he did the "grand reveal" like he was on some home improvement reality show.

Trent eased the ute around the sharp corner to where his sister's house was nestled among the bushland. Warm, salty air washed over him as he pushed the door open and hopped out onto the ground. He was covered in grime from spending the morning on a construction site for a new home overlooking the Patterson's Bluff shoreline. It had an *amazing* view. They could see the smooth, calm waters of Port Phillip Bay and on a good day, the view would stretch endlessly, as if they could see all the way to the edge of the world.

Trent's heavy steel-capped boots crunched over the path, crushing gum nuts and twigs as he headed toward the house. From the outside, it didn't look like much, but by the time he was done with the inside…well, it would be an oasis for his little sister.

He kicked off his boots before heading inside. It was hot and stuffy in that typical late-summer way, with the kind of heat that could feel oppressive if you hadn't grown up with it. Especially if you were inside with no air conditioning. Feeling sticky already, Trent pulled his T-shirt and socks off and dropped them into the hamper by the laundry. A funny feeling settled into his gut as he padded barefoot into the kitchen.

Something was off.

For starters, the kitchen window was closed. *That* would explain why the house felt so warm. The new air-con unit wasn't due to arrive until later that week, so leaving the windows open was the only way to keep the place cool. He'd planned to fit the flyscreen after work so he could leave it open overnight without getting eaten alive by mozzies.

Maybe he'd accidentally closed the window without thinking. Shaking his head, he wrapped his hand around the refrigerator door. But something froze him in place. A sound. More specifically, a sound he should *not* be hearing.

Running water.

"What the…?" Trent abandoned his plans for a cold beer and headed toward the master bedroom.

Liv's tiny en suite bathroom had the worst pipes Trent had ever seen. Whichever bozo had built this house originally had no idea what he was doing, Trent was sure of it. Not only were many elements *not* up to current—or former—building codes, the finishings had a DIY feel…and not in a creative, handmade, one-of-a-kind way, either. More in the "I have no idea what the hell I'm doing" kind of way.

"Liv?" Trent poked his head into the bedroom. His sister had flown out yesterday, texting the

family's WhatsApp group earlier to say she'd
landed safely at JFK Airport.

Now that he looked closer, he saw a suitcase
sitting by the bed. It wasn't the one his sister
used—which had been a hand-me-down from
their mother, tied with a ratty red polka dot
ribbon at the handle to distinguish it from the
thousands of other beat-up black wheeled boxes
that graced the airport's luggage carousel.

This suitcase looked expensive.

But Trent's concerns about figuring out who
was showering in his sister's house were suddenly
overtaken by a much larger concern.

"Oh shit!"

Without giving a moment's thought to what he
might see in the bathroom, he rushed toward the
door and yanked it back. Just as he thought, the
place was entirely flooded.

CHAPTER TWO

Cora held her hands over the open pipe, attempting to stem the aggressive flow of water into the bathroom. But she was failing miserably. And moistly.

"No, no, *no*!"

The water kept coming, like a tsunami of bad luck manifested. What *else* could possibly go wrong? She was soaked from head to toe, her hair dripping and hanging like a heavy sheet around her shoulders. Strands stuck to her arms and her cheeks as the water pounded her in the face.

Cora coughed and turned her face away, but the stream sprayed her ear and she winced. How the hell had she missed the gaping hole in the wall where the sink should have been? What else did she need, a giant flashing sign?

She'd been drawn zombie-like to the deep bathtub and the promise of feeling clean after her long flight. Nothing like being stuck in a flying tuna can for fourteen hours to make you crave running water and a bar of soap. That's what she got for not stopping to freshen up at the airline's lounge before the two-hour drive from the airport to Patterson's Bluff.

Are you feeling fresh now?

"Stop already!" She squeezed her eyes shut as more water came, pushing past her fingertips and spilling onto the floor. It rose up to where her knees pressed into a soggy bathmat. Her dress would be ruined.

Everything would be ruined.

Cora hadn't even stripped out of her clothing before disaster hit. She'd been here all of five freaking minutes and she'd ruined her friend's house.

How can you be this much of a disaster with even the simplest thing?

The water kept coming, and now she had so much in her eyes that she couldn't even open them to look around. She hadn't been able to figure out how to make it stop, and no amount of twisting the bathtub's taps had worked.

This was the end. She was going to flood the entire house, have nowhere to stay, and her only real friend was going to hate her forever.

RIP, Cora Cabot. She didn't live long, but she owned a lot of pretty shoes.

"What the hell are you doing?" An angry voice boomed over the sound of rushing water, and Cora squeaked, surprise causing her to yank her hands back from the open pipe. Mistake! The water gushed out harder, and she immediately tried to cover it again.

"What are *you* doing?" she shouted, her voice shaking. Great, now, on top of being a complete hot mess, she was going to get murdered by some stranger while she looked like a drowned rat and smelled like a dead one. "Who are you?"

"Who are *you*?"

Cora could barely keep her eyes open long enough to see who was shouting at her because water droplets kept finding their way in. Should she run? How far would she get on this slippery floor? And where would she even run to? This place was in the middle of nowhere.

"You stay there—I'm going to shut the water main off." The sound of footsteps sloshing through water faded.

Minutes later, as sheer helplessness almost overwhelmed her, the water mercifully stopped. She withdrew her hands and used her forearm to push her hair out of her face so she could survey the damage. The entire bathroom was soaked. Totally and thoroughly soaked. The fuzzy pink mat made a squelching sound as she stood, her feet sinking into the sodden material. Her suede ballet flats lay ruined next to where the door opened up into the bedroom, and beyond that, the powder-blue carpet had a huge dark patch stretching all the way to the foot of the bed.

For a moment, Cora stood still as a tree, her heart pounding in her ears. The place was silent except for the drip, drip, drip of water sliding from her fingertips and her hair. Catching sight of herself in the mirror, she cringed.

She looked like that freaky little girl from *The Ring*.

As she stepped onto the carpet, water pooled around her feet. A cute pink cardboard box sitting on the floor next to Liv's chest of drawers was ruined. The cardboard had warped, softening and losing shape so that the box leaned precariously to one side. Biting down on her lip, Cora peeked inside and sighed with a heavy heart.

It contained a scrapbook that said "Happy 40th Wedding Anniversary" on the front with a picture of a man and woman who looked a *lot* like Liv. On top of ruining her friend's carpet and her bathroom, she'd also ruined a handmade gift. Cora swallowed against the sadness tinged with green-eyed envy climbing up the back of her throat. It was clear her friend had put a lot of time and thought into it. And even more than that, it was clear she had the kind of family where such a thing would be appreciated. Where a gift of time was worth more than a swinging price tag containing as many zeros as possible.

Pressing the heels of her palms to her eyes, Cora let out a strangled noise of frustration. This was her life at the moment, one ridiculous problem after the next.

"You'd better tell me who the hell you are and what you're doing in my sister's house." The angry voice was back, booming through the quiet room.

The man was barefoot and shirtless and bronzed, with water dotting his skin like glimmering freckles. His hair flopped over his forehead and he raked it back, biceps flexing with the movement. There were muscles...everywhere. Like his muscles had muscles in some kind of mind-bending hot guy trick. For a moment, Cora was convinced she'd actually drowned, and this was some weird earth-to-heaven transitory phase.

Sexy limbo.

Crap. This was Liv's older brother? He looked pissed. Apparently, her day *could* get worse.

She pressed a hand to her chest in the hopes of slowing her thundering heart. Though only part of the accelerated beat was due to getting pummeled in the face with water. "Don't you know it's rude to sneak up on a person like that? What if I'd been holding a weapon? I could have hurt you."

"Explain to me how you would have been holding a weapon while you were occupied with a flooding pipe?" He came closer. Now she could see his eyes were blue—a perfect sky-at-noon blue. Almost too vibrant to be real. "And what was your plan, anyway? To hold your hands over the pipe until the world ran out of water?"

Shame flushed through Cora's face, heating her cheeks until she was certain she resembled a tomato. Okay, sure, she wasn't the handiest person around. She didn't know how to do things like fixing leaks or sanding wood or…hammering nails or whatever other handy things people did to their houses.

"I was taking a moment to think," she said, folding her arms over her chest. A water droplet ran down her forehead, racing along the line of her nose and then clinging to the tip. But she refused to wipe it away, because on some silly level, that felt like showing weakness.

Yeah, like pretending not to be a drowned rat is going to make a difference.

Drip.

"How was that going for you, huh?" The man

shoved his hands into his pockets, and the action drew Cora's eyes down to where denim stretched across his crotch. Snapping her eyes back up to his, she caught the tail end of a fleeting smirk. If she'd thought her cheeks were hot before, they were twin blazing suns now.

Could you maybe not *ogle his man bits for five seconds and figure out what's going on here?*

"It's going...poorly," she admitted.

"So, question number one is who are you?" He came closer still, sauntering toward her like some silver-screen cowboy but with the most delicious accent she'd ever heard. The vowels were broad and lazy, like a scorching summer day.

"Cora Cabot," she replied, swallowing back the strange fluttering feeling wreaking havoc inside her. "I...I'm friends with Liv."

Judging by the raised brow, Mr. Bronzed and Shirtless had not been expecting anyone at the house. All Cora knew about Liv's family was that she was the youngest of five, with four rough-and-tumble older brothers, each one more protective than the last. From the tidbits she'd shared and the anecdotal evidence of the scrapbook, Liv's family seemed close-knit. Loving. Like how Cora had always hoped her family might be.

"You're friends with Liv," he repeated, looking confused. "She's not in the country at the moment."

"I know that. She's in Manhattan, staying in *my* apartment," Cora said. "When she told me about her internship, we agreed to a house swap. She didn't mention it?"

• • •

Trent scanned his memory for information of a friend staying at Liv's house, but nothing sprang to mind. Although, to be fair, his sister liked to blow up the family group chat with long messages that made Trent's head spin. He was more of a two-word-response kinda guy. The occasional emoji. Precise. To the point.

Liv liked to recreate *War and Peace* every time she got on her phone.

"If she did, I don't remember," Trent said.

"I have an email from your sister." The woman picked up a small bag perched on top of his sister's bed that had a long gold chain attached and a fancy-looking clasp made out of two Cs. "She sent me some instructions and the code to get into the house."

She thrust the piece of paper in his direction, her wet hands blurring the ink in places. But there was his sister's email address, clear as day at the top, *and* the pin code for the spare key.

Cora stood, her hands knotted in front of her. Her long hair was soaked through, and it stuck to her shoulders and arms. She wore a fitted black dress, which, now that it was wet, clung to her body like a second skin. He could see every contour, every mouth-watering line, from her shapely legs to the subtle dip at her waist to the enticing flare of her hips. He could even see the texture of a lacy bra covering her perky breasts. Her blue eyes were icy pale, and they stared at him unwaveringly.

"You're here for a month?" He scrubbed a hand over his face, wondering how in the hell Liv hadn't thought to *tell* him about her house swap. She knew he never checked his emails and group messages. Who had time for that? "That might pose a problem."

"You mean aside from the flood damage?" She attempted a smile that was so sweet, a little part of him softened.

"Didn't it occur to you that there was a reason pieces of pipe were lying all over the ground?" He'd have a hell of a mess to clean up now, not to mention that in the height of summer, they had to keep an eye on water usage. Australia was abundant in many things, but rain was not one of them. "You've made my job a whole lot harder now."

"I can't believe I did that," she said with a sigh. "I honestly was so tired from the flight, and all I wanted was a soak in the tub. I didn't even notice there was anything off. It was like I had blinders on. I'm so sorry."

It would have been easy to rule Cora out as an oblivious princess with her designer luggage and fancy handbag and a dress that looked more suited to a cocktail party than an international flight. But she looked genuinely distressed.

"Oh…" She bit down on her lip and scrunched up her face. "There's one more problem."

"What else?" Trent tipped his head back and looked at the ceiling, as if he might find strength there.

"This." Cora reached into a sad-looking box that had lost all structural integrity due to extensive water damage and pulled out a book covered with silver and gold material. The edges of the pages were crinkled with moisture, and the thick black letters spelling out "Happy 40th Wedding Anniversary" had bled ink everywhere.

"Oh no." Trent's shoulders sagged. "Liv is going to be devastated."

His sister had been working on the scrapbook for *months*, collecting old photos and writing out fond memories and even interviewing people who had known their parents when they were first dating. Trent held his hands out, and Cora handed over the sodden mess. The pages had soaked up water like greedy plants after a drought. When he flipped open the cover, a picture of him and his siblings from when they were kids stared up at him. He counted five sets of baby blues and gap-toothed smiles. Five lots of gangly limbs and sun-streaked hair. Five hands sticky with half-melted ice creams.

A perfect memory captured forever.

The paper disintegrated under his touch, a piece of it tearing right off and splitting Trent away from his siblings. Thank god Liv hadn't used all originals. They were photocopies that could be replaced, but hours of flipping through albums, photocopying and cutting and pasting and drawing decorations, were now for nothing.

"Do you think we can save it?" Cora asked hopefully.

"If by *save* you mean start the whole thing

completely from scratch, then yeah." He tossed the ruined gift onto the ground, and it landed with a moist *splat*. "But my more immediate concern is where you're going to sleep tonight. We need to get the water sucked out of this carpet and bring the dehumidifiers in. You can't breathe this damp air all night. It's not safe. *And* we've got to prevent mold from growing. My brother and his wife run a bed and breakfast—"

"I'm staying here to help," Cora said, folding her arms over her chest, a determined set to her jaw. "I made this mess, and I'm going to clean it up."

Trent raised a brow. Cora didn't look like the kind of person who'd done manual labor a day in her life. "This is a job for the professionals, I'm afraid. I'll need to call my crew in."

"Then I'll make coffee and snacks. I can go through the scrapbook and make a list of everything in there so we can start putting it back together."

He laughed. "We?"

"The only reason water came out of the pipes was because you didn't turn off the main before you took the bathroom apart," she pointed out.

Well, *touché*. Maybe Little Miss City Slicker wasn't so clueless after all. "I didn't anticipate having a stranger in the house who'd mess up all my plans."

"And yet, here we are." She looked him dead in the eye, and Trent had to admire the woman's resolve. She was stubborn; he'd give her that. It wasn't a quality that had a good reputation, but

Trent liked stubborn people. People who stuck to their guns and followed through on their promises. People whose words meant something.

"You'd better be willing to put your money where your mouth is," he said, shaking his head. "You really want to help?"

Her pale gaze held him captive, unwavering and daring him to challenge her. "I really do."

"Then I hope you know how to use a glue gun."

her
aussie
holiday

USA TODAY **BESTSELLING AUTHOR**

STEFANIE
LONDON

Available wherever books are sold!

always a
bridesmaid

Violet Abrams may have been a bridesmaid no less than seven times, but her wedding day was near—she could feel it. Until her longtime boyfriend left her for someone else. That's just fine—she has her photography and a new project redesigning her sister's bakery to keep her happy and fulfilled. Fast-forward to the day of his wedding, though, when Violet might have accidentally, totally not on purpose, started a fire. And... Officially the worst day ever.

Firefighter Ford Maguire thought he'd seen it all. Until he's called out because someone tried to set the local bakery on fire…with a wedding magazine? The little arsonist might be the cutest woman he's ever seen, but he's too career-focused to consider something serious. Still, Violet seems like a great person to help him navigate his upcoming "man of honor" duties in his best friend's wedding.

Pretty soon, not only is Violet giving him lessons on all things weddings, she's helping him train his latest rescue-dog recruit puppies and weaving her way seamlessly into his lone-wolf lifestyle. But forever is the last thing on Ford's mind, and if there's one thing a perpetual bridesmaid knows, it's the importance of a happily ever after.

*Smoke jumpers and a steamy romance
collide in this new romantic comedy series
from* USA TODAY *bestselling
author Tawna Fenske.*

the
two-
date
rule

Willa Frank has one simple rule: never go on a date
with anyone more than twice. Now that her business
is providing the stability she's always needed, she
can't afford distractions. Her two-date rule will
protect her just fine…until she meets smokejumper
Grady Billman.

After one date—one amazing, unforgettable date—
Grady isn't ready to call it quits, despite his own no-
attachments policy, and he's found a sneaky way
around both their rules.

Throwing gutter balls with pitchers of beer? Not a
real date. Everyone knows bowling doesn't count.

Watching a band play at a local show? They just
happen to have the same great taste in music.
Definitely not a date.

Hiking? Nope. How can exercise be considered a date?

With every "non-date" Grady suggests, his
reasoning gets more ridiculous, and Willa must admit
she's having fun playing along. But when their time
together costs Willa two critical clients, it's clear she
needs to focus on the only thing that matters—her
future. And really, he should do the same.

But what is she supposed to do with a future that
looks gray without Grady in it?

Look for New York Times *bestselling author Katee Robert's 3-in-1 mass market paperback full of sexy cowboys and the women who tame them.*

WILD
COWBOY
NIGHTS

FOOLPROOF LOVE

Jules Rodrigez isn't interested in the role of town spinster. Being seen with a hell-raiser like bull rider Adam Meyer is the perfect way to scandalize the residents, make her ex jealous, and prove she's a sexy, desirable woman. And if their plan includes ridiculously hot sex—all the better.

FOOL ME ONCE

Aubry Kaiser's in a bind. She needs a plus-one for a convention, and when annoyingly sexy cowboy Quinn Baldwyn offers to go along in exchange for her being his fake date to a wedding, it looks like the perfect solution. Heck, they already fight like an old married couple. If only their fighting wasn't starting to feel a whole lot like foreplay...

A FOOL FOR YOU

It's been years since Hope Moore left Devil's Falls, land of sexy cowboys and bad memories. Back for the weekend, she has no intention of seeing Daniel Rodrigez, the man she never got over...or the two of them getting down and dirty. It's just a belated goodbye, right? No harm, no foul. Until six weeks later, when her pregnancy test comes back positive.